ORANGE COUNTY NOIR

ORANGE COUNTY NOIR

EDITED BY GARY PHILLIPS

Published by Akashic Books
©2010 Akashic Books

Series concept by Tim McLoughlin and Johnny Temple
Orange County map by Sohrab Habibion

ISBN-13: 978-1-936070-03-9
Library of Congress Control Number: 2009939085

First printing

Akashic Books
PO Box 1456
New York, NY 10009
info@akashicbooks.com
www.akashicbooks.com
Printed in Canada

ALSO IN THE AKASHIC NOIR SERIES:

FORTHCOMING:

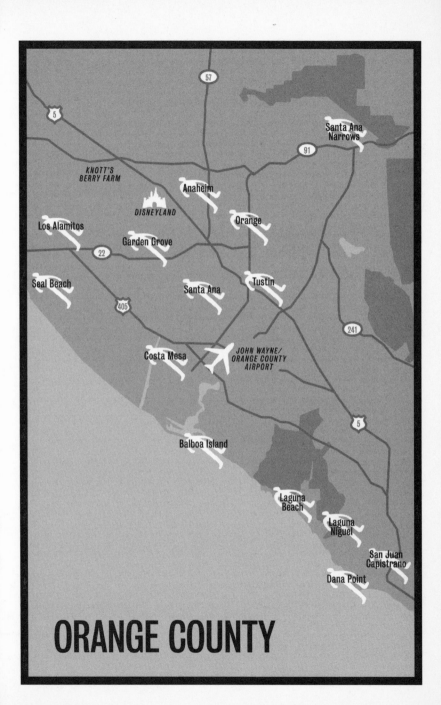

ORANGE COUNTY

TABLE OF CONTENTS

PART III: LUSH LIFE

FOREWORD
BY T. JEFFERSON PARKER

H istory seems slow in the making until we stop for a second and look back on things. Then the past hits the present like a bullet and we all dive for cover.

I first set foot in Orange County half a century ago. Our new Tustin tract home cost $21,000. The dads wore showing-scalp flattops and skinny neckties. The moms sported hardened coifs and dorky glasses. There were orange groves falling fast and Santa Ana winds blowing hard and station wagons called the Country Squire and the Kingswood Estate rolling, kid-filled, down the suburban streets.

Now look at it. How that Orange County became the one we see today is a tale of migration and war and race and economics and even climate. In ways that are not difficult to see, the changes of Orange County have been the changes of the nation. We are all Orange County and it is us.

Like a beautiful woman, Orange County is easy to label but hard to understand. Gone are the orange-packing houses and the white Republican demographics and the four half-gallons of bottled milk left cold on your porch early in the morning. Gone is the John Birch Society. Gone too are Leary and the Brotherhood of Eternal Love.

But it is often easier to list what is gone than to truly see what is now here. How do we define these 3.1 million souls? *Who* gets to define them?

Sometimes it's good to let our artists and writers be our

eyes and ears. That's part of their job. Sometimes they really get it right. Sometimes they can see around the corners. You can read Kem Nunn's *Tapping the Source*. You can watch *Orange County*, or listen to Richard Stekol or No Doubt.

And you can read the book you are now holding in your hands.

Here are fourteen stories about this intriguing and somehow ineffable locale. Orange County through *noir* eyes? Why not? There's a dark side to most places and certainly the names Ramirez and Kraft and Famalaro haven't slipped your mind. Noir writers are bent toward the darkness, so don't expect the Orange County in these pages to be quite as sunny as it thinks it is.

But noir writing has its own brand of humor too, and I can foresee a grin or two as you read about a deranged security guard at Disneyland (where else?), or a thirty-something woman who trades in her penniless but hot boy-toy for a paunchy Orange County Republican who can provide her with the good life in east Costa Mesa.

You'll see some of Orange County's wonderful diversity on display in these tales. You'll see an Orange County that looks very little like it did a few short decades ago. You'll meet insiders and outsiders, power brokers and wannabes, rich and poor, the sacred and the profane.

They're all out there, whatever *there* really is. That's up to you to decide.

Enjoy the black orange.

INTRODUCTION
BEHIND THE ORANGE CURTAIN

C oincidence that I was born the same year Disneyland opened and Charlie "Bird" Parker died. A lot of things begin and a lot of people die in any given year. But those two events have stayed with me—given the accident of occurring in that particular year—and they provide a hint as to how we arrive at this collection of all-new, tough, unblinking stories in *Orange County Noir*.

As everybody probably knows, Disneyland is located in Orange County, the city of Anaheim specifically. When I was a kid growing up in South Central Los Angeles, what I knew of life behind the Orange Curtain—beyond bugging my dad to take me to the theme park—was nil. None of my relatives lived there, nor did my folks have friends in the area. Except for going to Walt's Adventureland or Knott's Berry Farm in Buena Park, all I knew was that getting to Orange County was too long a trip on the freeway for a nine-year-old anticipating the thrill of riding the Matterhorn roller coaster and realizing the birthright of Southern Californians of driving a car—at least for a few minutes solo on the Autopia.

Now, I'd heard of the Beach Boys and associated their songs of the endless summer with the surfers I'd seen on TV piloting those majestic waves down in Orange County (even though it turned out those guys grew up in the South Bay area of Los Angeles). By the time I was a teen, I finally understood the chuckles my dad and his friends had over beers when they joked about not letting the sun go down on them in Orange

County, "where all them Birchers are." Referring, I'd find out, to the ultraconservative, anti–civil rights John Birch Society.

Time and the social evolution of the Southland have brought change even to vast Orange County with its forty-some miles of coastline. I was recently told by a resident of Newport Beach, one of the tonier enclaves of the county, that her district, which launched ex–pro quarterback Jack Kemp to office, went for Barack Obama in the 2008 presidential race.

Because and beyond being a GOP stronghold, Orange County brings to mind McMansion housing tracts; massive shopping centers with their own zip codes where Pilates classes are run like boot camp and real-estate values are discussed at your weekly colonic; and ice-cream parlors on Main Street, U.S.A., side by side with pho shops and taquerías. Los Angeles has been and continues to be explored as the place where noir, if it wasn't spawned there, sure as hell flowered. But what about its neighbor to the south? What secrets do Orange County's denizens have to tell . . . or hide?

This volume, like coming in from a sudden storm and then being gripped by a heavy riff from Bird's horn, takes you on a hard-boiled tour behind the Orange Curtain. Among those you'll meet are a reclusive rock star who has lived way too long in his twisted head, a crooked judge who uses the court for illicit means, a cab driver prowling the streets with more than the ticking meter on his mind. In *Orange County Noir*, cultures clash, housewives want more than the perfect grout cleaner, and nobody is exactly who they seem to be.

Enjoy.

Gary Phillips
Los Angeles, CA
January 2010

PART I

ONLY THE LONELY

BEE CANYON

BY SUSAN STRAIGHT

Santa Ana Narrows

S ee, right now, if the phantom was roaming around like he did back in 1977, haunting the freeway and busting up people's cars, stealing food—damn, he even stabbed a deputy in the neck!—somebody would shoot him. No hesitation. Blow him away. A cop. Hell, a driver. Everybody's got guns in their cars. The freeway's a battlezone. People follow each other off the ramps and pull out automatic weapons. People lean out the window and shoot a nine like *Grand Theft Auto*. People die every day just for cutting each other off or throwing up a finger.

I almost shot the phantom thirty years ago, when he came out of that hole. His hair all dusty and his shirt in rags. I had my gun out. I thought I would have to kill him, but I waited to see if he remembered. If he'd look at my face and shout it out, what he'd seen me do. If he said it out loud, my life was over.

I saw him just before the rock hit my windshield. It was twilight. Strange word. My father always called it *ocaso*. In school they told us twilight, dusk, evening. Before night.

That's the only time the phantom ever appeared. A shadow lifted up and twisted for a second, in the center divider of the freeway. I was heading west, toward Santa Ana, and on my left this movement—like when you have a nightmare as a kid and you can't see the guy's face, the guy chasing you.

He was small. Compact throw. The rock flew into the glass and the windshield exploded like music. A crazy instrument. Most people panicked and that's why they crashed. I felt the splinters on the side of my face and neck like wasps stinging me but I kept driving until I could get out of the fast lane and off to the side.

The blood dripped into my right eye. Thick. It stung. The salt. I had an extra T-shirt in the backseat and I held it to my temple. I pulled down the visor. One sliver of glass was stuck in my neck like Frankenstein's screw. Not by my jugular—higher up, just under my jaw. I pulled it out and not as much blood came out as from my temple. I held the T-shirt to both for a long time before I headed to the call box.

It was darker now, red-smog sunset hanging west, where I was headed to work. But even though I was California Highway Patrol, I had to call this in, stay here, just like all the other people he'd thrown rocks at. People driving out of Riverside and the desert, heading to Orange County.

I'd gone to Riverside to visit my friend Manny, who used to live at Bryant Ranch with me. He and his father gave up picking oranges and went to work in the packing house near Casa Blanca. I'd passed the Prado Dam in Corona, where the big flag they painted for the 1976 bicentennial was getting dusty after a year.

"Where are you?" the dispatcher said.

I'd gone about a mile and a half trying to get over, off the freeway. It was a Sunday. He threw rocks at twilight, and usually near Featherly Park.

I squinted at the hills on the north rim of the Santa Ana Canyon. I knew them better than anyone but him—the phantom. "Bee Canyon," I said.

"What?" she said. "Bee Canyon?"

Nobody would know that name. I told her the mile marker. Then I hung up. Bee Canyon was already black in the fading light. Like someone had poured tar down the side of the hills. We'd called in a fire there last year.

But I'd been up there just before the fire, when I watched what happened to that girl.

I stood on the side of the freeway, where I'd stood a hundred times before taking reports or writing tickets or hearing about flat tires, and looked back at the center divider. But the headlights went straight into my eyes. Between that blinding and the blood, I couldn't see anything.

I don't remember why they called it Bee Canyon. All those little canyons along the Santa Ana Canyon, and the Riverside Freeway winding along the edge. At City College, when I was taking general ed before law enforcement, I had a professor who showed us how all the world was just a big irrigation system. The water fell, the water moved, the water shaped the earth. Bryant Ranch took up a lot of the hills and the canyon because it had water. The perfect place for citrus and cattle. I grew up walking all the arroyos and canyons, since I was born on the ranch. After that college class, I realized it was the everyday water that wore down the dirt.

My dad was born in Red Camp, and my mom in La Jolla Camp. They met at a dance in Sycamore Flats, near Bryant Ranch, and they got married and had me in 1954. All I ever knew growing up was the ranch, the river, the railroad tracks along the foothills, and the canyons.

People think Southern California is a desert, that it never rains here, cause of that stupid song, but in winter rainfall pours down all those gullies and makes them canyons too. When I was a kid, I wondered how they picked names: Gypsum Canyon, Coal Canyon, Brush Canyon, Bee Canyon.

Somebody must have kept bees up there once. Had I seen the white boxes, the ones that always looked like random dumping until you heard the hum swell up like the air was infected all around you?

Bee Canyon was where he was buried. The guy. I thought of his long brown hair. Gone now. He was a skeleton. The girl woke up and tried to stumble away, and he punched her in the face, and he kept coming toward me. Taunting me. "You a wetback? You just come up outta that river, Frito Bandito? You swum all the way here from Tijuana?"

The phantom had seen it all. I heard the noise he made. He'd been living in the canyons for a long time by then. He knocked down some loose granite while I was digging. But then I waited for a long time, when I was done, and it seemed like he couldn't help himself. He looked out of his shelter, a wall of creosote and rabbitbrush, and I saw his face.

He was darker than me. Small. His hair was wavy and black, but covered with dust, and one eucalyptus leaf dangled like a feather near his ear.

I was off-duty. I knew CHP and Orange County Sheriff's Department and Riverside County had been searching him out for a long time. The freeway phantom. But I couldn't tell anyone I'd seen him, because then they'd see the grave in Bee Canyon.

"He got you, huh?" the Riverside CHP said. Fredow. They pulled over about ten minutes after I called. "Goddamn. That's thirty or forty this year. He's gonna kill somebody."

"That one guy he hit lost his eye," his partner said. Anderson.

"And you're CHP? That's what the radio said."

"Yeah," I replied. I pulled the shirt away from my face—my white Hanes looked like one of those tests they make you stare at. The blots. I'd say flowers if they asked what it looked like. Flowers that came out of my skin. My mother's favorite hibiscus, before she died. How did the blood thicken up so fast? "Heading in for night shift."

"November 6, 1977. Jerry Frias? F-r-i-a-s? How long you been with O.C.?" Anderson asked.

"Two years."

"Just past rookie," he said. Then, "You born here?" and I knew what he meant.

"Right there on Bryant Ranch." I pointed to the hills. Not Mexico.

"Is that right? I was born in Indianapolis."

"Wow—the Indy 500." I tried to be polite. I felt the crusting over on my neck.

"What did he look like? This fucking phantom?" Fredow asked, writing the report.

"I wouldn't call him that. Makes him sound like a comic book, and this ain't funny," Anderson said. "I call him a goddamn idiot. I don't care if he's a Vietnam vet. I did a tour in Nam and I ain't throwin rocks at people in cars. If he chucks one at me, I'll shoot him."

Fredow frowned at him. He said to me, "No description?"

I shrugged. "It's so damn fast," I answered, and it was true. "You're doing sixty and he's just there like a shadow. You know. You turn your head and then you're past him."

Twilight. *The Twilight Zone*—me and Manny's favorite show when we were kids. This phantom was like something Rod Serling would talk about—*He glides through a river of speeding cars as if not afraid, and in his hands, he holds the possibility of death.*

"You didn't want to pull over on the divider?"

"Remember what happened in May? The off-duty saw him in the divider and pulled over, chased him around, and then the guy stabbed him in the neck with the homemade knife?"

"Damn." Anderson looked at the freeway beside us.

"The deputy he stabbed said he's a short black guy. Named James," I said.

"But we got other descriptions too."

I knew it was him. And I'd seen the reports over the last year—six-two, five-nine, white, Chicano, long-haired, short-haired, huge, thin.

I shrugged again. "A guy with a rock." I bent over and got it out of the passenger seat. The windshield glass was piled up like some broken mirror in a fairy tale. "A rock the size of an orange."

Then their radio crackled, and Anderson leaned in to take it. "He just got somebody else. A lady."

When I got to work in Santa Ana, someone had already told Chuck George about it. He'd been special assigned to the phantom for months.

In the locker room, I felt the bandages over my neck and temple. I had a cut on my right hand that I hadn't noticed until the tow truck came for my Nova.

Somebody in the locker room said, "Who the hell runs through traffic on the Riverside Freeway?"

"How does he do it over and over and not get plastered, man?"

"Hey, he hit somebody else after he got Frias. Broke five bones in her face and she's got deep cuts. He's gonna kill somebody tomorrow."

"George has the tracker," I said, over the lockers. "The

one from Oklahoma. He wants to talk to me. He says they're going out Thursday night."

But all night, driving my route, winding along the 91 and the 55 and the 22 and the 57, back up the 91, the way the engine chugged under me when I went after an idiot speeding near Imperial Highway, the way the exhaust smelled when I was writing the ticket—the tumbleweeds were green and big by November, like explosions all along the frontage road right there, and the guy's arm dangling in his white cuffed shirt, the burgundy Buick Regal and how he was so pissed—I thought about how long the phantom had already been living in the Santa Ana Canyon, how smart he was, how he slid down the pick he had to have made himself.

"Hijo, what happened to your face?"

I went to see my father almost every day before work. I got my own apartment a year ago, but all I had in there was a TV, a couch, two chairs, and one of those coffee tables made from a burl of wood. The apartment was in Corona, because it was cheap, so I would leave a couple hours early and stop at the ranch to see if he needed me to carry anything for him. He was only fifty-seven, but his shoulders were wrecked, full of loose cartilage. One day he said, "Stand here," and he moved his shoulders, and the popping was loud. "Sounds like that cereal you always wanted."

Rice Krispies. We'd had tortillas for breakfast, lunch, and dinner. Same as my mother and father had grown up eating.

My cuts were scabbing over, two days later, and they itched like hell.

"The phantom," I said. "He busted my windshield."

"Yours?"

"He doesn't know who's driving." I leaned against the

tractor. He had it set up to disc weeds. "The tracker's going out tomorrow with a search party. Tell everybody we'll be up in Brush Canyon. He thinks the guy is holed up there."

"We?"

"He told me to come along because I know the area. He and George have been talking to people in the canyon."

People who lived on the ranches had caught glimpses for more than a year. He'd thrown a rock at one of the workers driving a tractor one day, and my father had called me. Someone had seen the phantom bathing in a stock tank up where the cattle ran. Someone else had been out riding a horse and saw him butchering a goat, but that was last year. "He's been here a long time now," my father said, easing himself off the fender. "He's living on food from the golf course."

The Green River Golf Club was just to the east. "How do you know?" I asked. We started walking to the shed where he kept the smudge pots.

"I met one of the cooks. He's seen the guy taking bags out of the dumpster in the back."

"Oh yeah?" I said. My father stopped and sat on the wooden bench near the picnic table where he repaired tractor parts and pruning shears and whatever else needed fixing. In the open door of the shed I saw the smudge pots lined up like one-armed soldiers.

"Remember when he knocked over every single one a those?" my father said, rubbing his shoulder. "Took us all night to fill 'em back up with fuel and he did it again. I wanted to kill him."

"Kill him?" I looked at my father's hand, the wrinkles filled with black rime from the citrus rinds, the dark lines never erased since I'd been a child no matter how hard he scrubbed with cleanser.

"Not kill him," my father said wearily, glancing up at me. I was a cop now. "I was just so damn tired. And the kerosene was running down the irrigation lines. El fantom—like a mocoso, but they say he's a grown man."

Mocoso. A bad little kid. Why would he throw rocks all the time? I said, "Maybe we'll find him tomorrow."

I took all the bagged fertilizer off the truck and into the barn. When I walked back to my car, with the new windshield thick and green in the afternoon light, I stopped at the house, like I did every time. Three rooms. I looked inside the front window at the altar for my mother.

I only remembered the cough. I was about five. She coughed all winter. You could hear it in the front room, where I slept, and from inside the trees when we picked the valencias in January. The crows used to wake us up with those raspy caws, and I thought it was them, but it was my mother. Pneumonia.

The altar had not changed since she died that year. Plastic wisteria blossoms arranged all around her picture, and new roses every day in a vase on the little table underneath, with the veladora glowing faint. He left it lit all day, no matter how many times I told him not to. The flame was little, though, inside the glass. Maybe as big as a grain of rice.

He thought I didn't know about the two babies, but I did.

The long drive into the ranch was lined with pomegranate trees. In spring the flowers were like pink umbrellas hanging everywhere. But now, in November, the old pomegranates were hanging on the branches like dead Christmas ornaments.

There were only about fourteen families left on the ranch. People kept telling my father the owner was going to sell it next year, and someone would build housing tracts all the way up to the hills. "Yorba Linda will be a big city," they said. "The canyon will be full of people instead of cows."

I got on the freeway and the center divider was full of trash and bottles.

"*Keep on truckin, baby,*" the radio said. "*You got to keep on truckin.*"

By the time I pulled into the station, it was "*One toke over the line, sweet Jesus, one toke over the line.*"

The words were still in my head when I got dressed. The tracker was from Oklahoma, and his voice was country. They'd hired him from El Cajon Border Patrol and he'd been here off and on since May, when the deputy got stabbed. George and some deputies had been out on a bunch of occasions, sometimes on motorcycles and horseback, and they hadn't seen anything. So they got Kearney.

He didn't say much, but I heard him tell someone, "I plain love putting together a puzzle like that." They'd been looking at maps for weeks. I couldn't tell what he thought when he glanced at me, so I hadn't said anything except that I used to hunt with my father in the canyons.

"What you hunt?"

"Rabbits."

He had a mustache like a black staple turned upside down. A brimmed hat. They called him a sign-cutter and a man-tracker. Some of the other guys in the locker room joked that he was like Disneyland—Daniel Boone or some shit. He'd been working Border Patrol for seventeen years, tracking Mexicans trying to cross.

He looked at me. "Rabbits. Why?"

I looked back. "Dinner."

Then he nodded. "We ate a lot of rabbits in Oklahoma," he said. "Let's go."

* * *

We got there when the sun was in the eucalyptus windbreak, not twilight yet, and hiked toward Brush Canyon. It was Kearney and four other Border Patrol sign-trackers, three deputies, George, and me. La Palma Road went along the canyon, with the river and freeway west, and the train tracks and hills east.

"He crosses the damn river every time he hits the freeway," someone said. "How the hell does he do it? He fords the river, fords the traffic, all to throw a rock?"

The tracker had seen where he entered the river, and where he left, and he thought the guy was living in Brush Canyon.

We moved up toward the foothills. We were going to stake out the mouth of the canyon and the trail he used lately to get to the freeway or the golf course.

I scratched the cut on my neck, under the bandage. I could smell the cooking fires from the ranch. How many times had the phantom watched my father, or me?

Did he remember my face from when I dug the hole, when I pushed the body into it after I checked for the bullet?

My service revolver was on my hip. I was fifth in line and the foothills loomed up like they had all my life, in fall, the rocks smelling cool, not like summer. The brittlebush and creosote giving off their scent. The animals stirring in late afternoon.

"First camp was Bee Canyon, right?" someone said. "That's where he lit the fire last year."

"What was he doing?"

"Cooking. In a coffee can. Musta got out of control."

"He was camped in Coal Canyon after that. But that one's been empty a long time."

Kearney frowned. No one talked after that.

Kearney was sure it was Brush Canyon. He said the tracks kept leading us away from there—that's what any animal does when it wants the hunter to stay away from the nest or den.

We're just animals, my father said. Except our souls, the priest said. The phantom was a man, but he'd been living like an animal for years. We moved up past the railroad tracks and the rocks smelled of sulfur along the embankment.

He had a knife.

If he saw my face, if he moved toward me, if he started shouting, I would shoot him. He had a knife. He was armed. Justifiable.

I knew the rules. I'd known them last year when the guy kept walking toward me.

Kearney studied the ground every step of the way. He figured the phantom had to leave Brush Canyon on the trail he'd been using for days, and we each had a place to hide. I kept looking up, since Kearney was looking down. Brush Canyon was a jagged arroyo, steep sides and then slopes studded with granite boulders that turned pink now with the sun fading. A few rogue pepper trees, like in every canyon, and no other green because winter rain hadn't started yet.

Was he watching us, all this time? He was a crazy little kid, my father said. Was he laughing? He wouldn't throw a rock down here, because we'd find him then, but he'd stand in the center divider of the 91 where hundreds of people could see him for a few minutes, until he launched it like a Little League pitcher.

The air was purple now, the railroad tracks ran red and shiny as Kool-Aid. This was the time my father used to say I had to head home. "When the silver tracks turn red, or the rocks turn pink, or the river turns black, you better be close to here. Or La Llorona will get you."

We were fanned out on the possible trails, about a hundred yards from the canyon. I lay behind the boulder Kearney had pointed to. The others kept going.

I listened to their footsteps move away.

They knew nothing about La Llorona. She was a beautiful woman who had killed her children over a man, and now she roamed the riverbank searching for them, or for some other kids to replace them. That's what my mother had told me, before she died. She was lying in her bed, and I was six, and she didn't want me wandering.

She didn't know I'd watched in the night after the two babies came out of her, with the old woman from up the ranch to help. My mother was very sick. The babies were born too small, the size of small puppies. They were wrapped together in a white cloth and then my father took the bundle outside to the rose garden and pomegranate tree my mother loved.

They couldn't have been babies yet, with skeletons and hearts, or they would have gone to the priest. But my mother was crying and coughing, and the old woman said in Spanish to my father, "No mas."

And my father said to her, "Don't tell anyone. No one. Those Hernandez women keep saying she's got the evil eye."

By the time I was eight, my father didn't care if I wandered off, as long as I did my work. We'd go up to Brush Canyon, the ranch kids. We dug a deep mine, with hammers and picks and shovels, looking for gold. We found piles of mica—fool's gold we thought we could sell.

The darkness fell completely, and I waited for my eyes to adjust. I heard nothing.

* * *

In Bee Canyon, I'd had nothing to dig with, to bury the guy.

I hadn't gone up there to shoot rabbits. I'd been CHP for about a year then, and I'd come to my father's house on my day off to help him take out two dead lemon trees. Gophers were bad that year.

I was covered with sweat and dirt and crumbled roots that flew up when we finally pulled out the stumps. We chain-sawed the branches and trunk for firewood, and then I piled the green wood on the south side of the house so it could dry out for my father to burn in winter.

I told him I had trouble with the service revolver. It wasn't like the rifle I'd been shooting since I was a kid. "The kick is weird," I said. "And the way you have to look at the target. They keep messing with me at the range. Their favorite word is wetback. *Go back to a hoe if you can't handle a gun.*" I felt the rage rise up in my chest like hot coffee swallowed the wrong way. "I want to tell them I'm not used to shooting something that ain't alive. But I can't say shit. Hueros."

"You been shooting all your life," he said. "A gun's a gun. Go up there in the hills and find something to aim at."

I put my T-shirt back on, even though my skin was sticky, and then my shoulder holster. I grabbed a flannel shirt to cover the holster. I was still sweating when I left the grove.

I walked a couple miles that day, along the river where the wet sand smelled like aspirin from the willows, and then I turned toward the hills. The cattle grazed up there, three thousand acres or so. We had three hundred acres of citrus.

I remember I was already thinking about the phantom when I crossed the tracks, because he'd thrown rocks a couple of times by then and downed the smudge pots. I'd seen a bridge made out of vines and cable over the arroyo under the train tracks, but everyone said that was old, from a Vietnam vet.

I figured I'd get far enough into Bee Canyon so no one would hear me shoot at beer cans set up on a rock.

I found tall Coors cans in the shade under a little pepper tree, like I knew I would. In high school, lots of people came up here to drink beer. Always Coors and Marlboros and weed. The cans were old and faded. Perfect to shoot.

I stuck four fingers into the four sharp tab holes and kept walking. A car was parked in the dirt at the mouth of the canyon. But maybe the people had gone back toward the river. I listened. No laughter from the canyon. It was dim up there now.

I kept going, and then I heard a huffing—*huh, huh, huh.* Breath like a hammer. *Huh, huh, huh.*

Then I heard, "What the fuck! What the fuck you lookin at? What's a nigger doin up here in Orange County!"

I dropped the cans in the sand. I was off-duty. I didn't go on for two hours.

I kept walking, up past a flat section of sand near the deep scour where the rainwater poured down, and then around another boulder.

A white guy with long brown hair hanging down his bare back was straddling a girl. He looked up the canyon. He hadn't seen me. But he stood up.

She looked dead. Dried blood dark under her nose. Denim skirt hiked up around her waist, her legs open, black hair there, her feet black on the bottom. He hunched over and zipped up, the muscles in his back jerking like snakes, and then turned and saw me.

"What the hell?"

My CHP voice came out before I could think. "Sir, I need you to tell me what's going on here."

"You speak English?"

My face burned. "Sir, is this—"

"You're not dark enough to be that nigger's brother. He was right up there. Watching. Freak."

"What's wrong with the young lady?" I hadn't moved. Felt like my feet were sinking into the dirt.

"Young lady? Why you talkin like you're on TV?"

"I'm law enforcement, sir."

"No you're not. You're just nosy."

"Is she okay?"

He laughed. "She was supposed to do a slow ride. Take it easy. But the stupid chick OD'd. Couldn't handle the trip. Couldn't handle the ride, man. Like it's your fuckin business. Wetback." He pushed his hair behind his ears and started walking toward me. He must have been about thirty-five, forty. His skin was lined around his eyes like birds had clawed him deep.

Was he another phantom? Shit. Was he the vet who'd built the bridge?

The girl hadn't moved. What if she was dead? I made my voice louder. "I need you to turn around and walk over to that rock and put your hands on the rock." I didn't have handcuffs. I might have baling wire in my pocket.

"You need to go back to Mexico."

"Sir."

I didn't move. There was no sound except his feet on the sand. Soft like ground corn.

"Sir." He was close enough that I could see his eyes were green.

People said the real phantom was a guy who still wanted to live in the jungle. Maybe if I brought up the war he'd know I respected him.

"Are you a veteran, sir?"

"Fuck Nam. I don't need to be a Vietnam vet to kill somebody."

He was about ten feet from me now. Kill her? Kill me?

Then the girl made a noise. She coughed. Her throat rasped like it was full of sand. He grinned at me and said, "Hey, kid, you just get here from Tijuana? You swum all the way up that river and this is where you made it?"

I looked past him. The girl raised up on one elbow and tried to stand. She scrabbled against the boulder and he turned back fast and covered the ground. He said, "I'm not done with you."

He drew back his arm and punched her in the face. Like she was a man. The sound of her nose breaking. A popping. Then an animal moan—like a coyote, full in the throat—but not her. From above us. The phantom. He moaned again, like he couldn't stand it when the girl fell.

I pulled my service revolver from the shoulder holster under my vest. It was silent now above us. The girl lay still, but her breath was in her throat like a saw blade in wood.

He wouldn't shut up. He just kept talking when he came back toward me. "What the fuck are you gonna do with that? You steal that from a cowboy, Frito? From an American? Ay yi yi yi—you think you're the Frito Bandito?" He was three feet away and reached out his hand. A turquoise ring on his finger. "You better give that to somebody who knows how to use it, chico."

My mother called me chavalito. When I came in at night smelling of the river.

I shot him in the chest like he was the silhouette at the range. But he didn't move sideways. He fell straight back.

No sound from above. The girl pushed up again, on all fours, like a dog. She crouched and swayed and stared at my face, squinting, the blood crusting like dried ketchup under her nose and mouth. Like a movie. I went over to the guy and stared at the hole in his chest. The blood running down his ribs. Different blood.

I looked up to say, "Miss, I'm gonna call—" She ran sideways past me, bumping past the rock.

Then the car started up at the bottom of the canyon and the tires popped over the gravel like firecrackers and I jumped.

I must have stood there for a while, because five flies landed on his chest, green as fake emeralds moving slowly over his blood. I would lose my job over this asshole. I would go to prison.

His shoulder was sweaty and hot. I grasped it to see if the bullet had gone through. It was gone. Went into the soft sand that smelled of animal waste and creosote roots. I'd never find it.

I put the shoulder back down. I didn't look at the open mouth. I didn't have time to go back to the ranch for a shovel. I found a stick and started trying to dig in the damp sand where the water had pooled long ago. Deep enough to keep him from coyotes, was all I thought.

A scraping above me, and granite pebbles falling.

A pick slid down the steep hillside and landed a few feet away. Homemade. Metal wired to a piece of crudely sanded wood. Like someone had thrown an anchor overboard.

Once it was all the way night, I thought that if he came my way, down this trail that led to the east, to the golf course, I would grab him, take the knife, cuff him, and keep my face down. It was dark. He wouldn't see me.

But he never came. He knew exactly where we were and what we were doing.

I'd slept, off and on, hearing small rustlings of rabbits and birds in the darkness. Twice I heard metal scrape against rock. One of the other men.

The phantom hadn't gone toward the river, or the free-way, or the golf course. He was probably watching us, even now at daybreak, when the sun rose over the Chino Hills and the brush glittered with dew like glass shards.

Kearney and George and the others came down the trail and I fell in. We drank some water and ate some stuff they'd packed, and then we fanned out to look for fresh signs. Foot-prints in the moisture, broken stems, all the things Kearney had used for years to track Mexicans on the border. Mexicans trying to swim up the rivers and walk over the desert. Beaners. Wetbacks.

I was out of breath. Hungry. Bending down so far my back hurt, remembering the short-handled hoe my father kept— the one he'd brought from Red Camp and propped in the cor-ner of the porch so he wouldn't forget it. He was awake, a few miles away, brewing his coffee in the dented aluminum pot, making sure the veladora was lit, looking out the window at the pomegranate tree. He didn't know I was here—so close to him.

"Hey!" one of the deputies called softly.

Fresh tracks.

We followed for two miles, but we ended up at the mouth of Brush Canyon. Kearney said he knew it all along. He and two guys started up from the bottom, and George circled up and worked his way down. I was behind him, and then one guy hollered out, "There he is!"

We looked down the steep canyon slope. A head popped out of a heap of brush. Black curly hair covered with dust. He was moving.

Everybody drew their guns. I had mine aimed at his back. His shirt was so tattered and patched it was like a weird quilt. He had a knife. He had the pick. I'd left it there when I was done. I'd wiped off my prints with my flannel shirt. His shirt was even worse in front when he turned to see the rest of us.

Don't look at me, I was thinking. Don't do it. Don't look in my eyes and then start yelling about what happened.

He was hunched over. I saw his face. He wasn't some little mocoso. He was a grown man. But the sound he'd made, up in Bee Canyon, when he heard the punch. The bones breaking. He'd been beaten. I'm not through with you. That sound.

But he had a knife. I couldn't move toward him, but if he saw me and shouted, "No! I didn't kill him! He did it!" I'd have to shoot him. Justifiable.

My gun was pointed at his face.

"I quit! I quit!" he screamed, his eyes on the ground. He wouldn't look up.

Kearney holstered his gun. "Come on out, James. We aren't gonna hurt you."

The phantom. He was about five-seven, slight, but it was his face. A little kid. He bowed his head. "I quit," he said.

I holstered my gun and turned around. It felt like someone sitting on my chest, hammering at the bone running down the middle of me. Like I always felt when I'd done something wrong. I looked out over the canyon. Down there were bones, and skeletons, everywhere under the dirt. The babies. The guy. My mother's bones, in the churchyard. The Indians who lived here first. The cows and coyotes and rabbits. The skulls rolling down the arroyos if it ever rained for forty days and forty nights.

They questioned him for a long time.

He was James Horton Jr. He'd been born in Keithville, Louisiana. He was forty-two. He'd been riding the rails since he was twelve.

I pictured the arm throwing the rock at my Nova.

"When I was little, I never had no time to play. I never had a chance to get into mischief, like Dennis the Menace. That's what I was doin with the rocks."

But why throw them at cars?

"The cars were going so fast. They made me mad, because they were going so fast."

Why did he live in the canyons?

He didn't want to be around people.

He ate black walnuts in fall, lemons and oranges, the goat he found dead, and food from the trash.

"You coulda killed someone," one of the deputies said, and I felt the hammering again, lighter, but still there.

"I quit, I quit," he said again softly.

They tested him for insanity, and he pleaded, and I never heard anything about him again.

My father had a heart attack in 1979, and we buried him next to my mother. Our house was empty for a year and then it burned down. They said transients were living there, but Bryant Ranch was already sold by the grandson of the woman who'd built the place and planted all the pomegranate trees.

Last week I saw an ad in the newspaper. *Executives Prefer Bryant Ranch*, it said, with pictures of huge houses. *Close to Brush Canyon Park, Box Canyon Park, and Golf.*

I left my apartment in Santa Ana and drove up there in my old Nova. I'm in the Old Farts Car Club and we restore classics.

I drove along La Palma. The river was much calmer now because of flood control. I used to imagine the phantom in some locked room in a mental ward. No river in his sight. Back then, I kept thinking Louisiana—he must have grown up beside the Mississippi. Huck Finn and shit like that— Dennis the Menace. But I looked up Keithville, and it was near the Red River.

He must have spent years looking out a window somewhere, waiting until he wasn't insane. No rocks. No water. No hiding except under a bed, when people came and scared you and said, "I'm not done with you yet."

I drove up to Bee Canyon, but it was just a scar in the hills. There were bones in every canyon of the world.

The big gray and beige and rust stuccoed houses, the roads and sidewalks and the same plants over and over. Purple agapanthus, society garlic that stunk up the median, and fountain grass, which my father always thought was a weed. The only people walking were two women in workout clothes with iPods.

It was late morning, and I still worked the evening shift, so I drove as close as I could to the Santa Ana River, off and on the freeways. The water was wild and free in the canyon, and then corralled with cement banks, tamed by the time it got to Newport and emptied into the ocean.

I drove around Fashion Island, and the South Coast Plaza. No island. No coast. Just rooms. Big rooms. Asphalt like black carpet around them.

On the way back, I drove up into Santiago Canyon, Modjeska Canyon, and I ended up in Santa Ana. The canyon turned into flatlands covered with rooms. My three rooms. The same number my father had.

I didn't want people around me either.

I liked working at night.

I partnered with Carl McGaugh for the last three years. He was only twenty-five. Didn't say much. His dad was Irish.

I drove. Driving the freeways was like swimming in the river, the currents and the way you had to move. But the freeways were choked with traffic all the time now. The phantom wouldn't have any trouble getting onto the median. He could walk through the stopped cars easy. But if he stood up with a rock, somebody would shoot him. In a heartbeat. Because what people cared most about was their vehicles. Their Beemers and Hummers and Acuras. Their property. No room for mischief when someone would pull out a semiautomatic weapon from the passenger seat for any reason at all.

DOWN IN CAPISTRANO

BY ROBERT S. LEVINSON

San Juan Capistrano

Ondel Cream, the chief deputy working the overnight shift at the Orange County Central Men's Jail in Santa Ana, owed Judge Oliver Wendell Knott a favor, which is why the judge was able to slip in after hours without a security search or a need to sign the visitor's log, a phony Vandyke beard and wraparound sunglasses sheltering his identity from the security cameras.

"Least I can ever do for you, Your Honor," Ondel said for the third or fourth time while guiding the judge to one of the second-floor Module-R conference rooms reserved for pretrial maximum-security inmates and sexual predators, where he'd stashed Quentin Lomax twelve minutes earlier, wrists cuffed to the anchored cast-iron table, ankles secured to the cast-iron chair.

Ondel said, "What you went and done for my baby brother Marcus, a righteous act not another judge woulda done," his hoarse baritone echoing in concert with the squeak of his rubber-soled combat boots along a dimly lit corridor that reeked of a disinfectant not strong enough to entirely eliminate the layers of prisoner sweat insulting the judge's nose.

Judge Knott smiled benignly, wished the deputy would shut up, but he knew better than to destroy the mood or otherwise disrupt the bond that grew between them after he'd sized up the deputy as somebody he could manipulate to his advantage and dismissed the drunk driving charge hanging over Ondel Cream's brother.

He said, not for the first time, "Marcus struck me as a young man who deserved a second chance more than a third strike," and, adding a fresh bit of friendship massage, "especially given an upstanding, God-fearing sibling like you to keep him grounded on the road to good citizenship."

"Amen, Judge, sir, amen to that, and you seeing it for the truth. Marcus, he ain't had nothing hard to drink ever since, but only once where I needed to slap him around some to keep a shot-a the hard stuff from cursing his lips."

They reached the conference room.

Before turning the key in the lock, Ondel assured him, "You'll be safe as my own son in there, Judge, what with Lomax secured tighter than a virgin's precious jewel. It's a precaution worth taking, since no telling what all could happen if that murdering cuss was crazy enough and free enough to go for your jugular."

"Lomax hasn't been tried and convicted yet in my courtroom, Ondel, so fairness dictates we withhold judgment until all the evidence is in and a jury renders its verdict."

"What you say, Judge, but you might sing a different song if you saw him up close here, days in and out, and listened to his mouthings. Ain't for no reason at all he's kept in solitary, in the block reserved for the worst of the worst. And even the worst of the worst, they scared of Lomax just being so close to themselves. Mark my words, no jury is ever not gonna escape seeing that . . . Fifteen minutes, you said you need?"

"Maybe twenty, but certainly no longer."

The deputy raised his wristwatch to his eyes and squinted after the time. "Need to get Lomax back where he belongs before the next bed check, so that works out fine. I'll be outside keeping guard, so knock if you finish up your business early or need me any reason at all, Your Honor. A shout and I'll come running."

Quentin Lomax eased back as far as the security restraints allowed and studied the judge through deep-rooted black eyes fired by a mixture of curiosity and contempt. They seemed a mismatch with the oversized features of his pockmarked face and a wrestler's body stretching the limits of his orange jumpsuit.

"I don't know you from spit or why you're here all dressed up like it's Halloween, thinking the beard's fooling anybody," he said. "Trick or treat or whatever in hell's going on, you're getting not a word from me without my lawyer, so who in hell are you anyway?"

The judge stroked his fingers over the Vandyke to strengthen the spirit gum holding it in place, removed the sunglasses and parked them inside the breast pocket of his jacket.

He flicked a smile and said, "If you're a praying man, I'd be inclined to say I'm the answer to your prayers, Mr. Lomax."

"And if I ain't?"

"I'd say the same thing."

"That sort of gag goes with the whiskers . . . or you on something, mister? I don't know what you're talking about."

"Of course you do, Mr. Lomax. We both know the murder you're about to stand trial for was not your first murder, only your sloppiest. A particularly bloody crime you won't slip out from under, the way you have more than a few times in the past."

"Hurry this up, will ya? I gotta piss real bad."

"Your lawyer, Mr. Amos Alonzo Waldorf, will be up to his usual courtroom stall tactics, but in the end they'll all be struck down, one after the next, and, it follows, justice will prevail. You'll be judged guilty and sentenced to death by lethal injection. Appeals will keep you alive for some years. They'll be struck down one after the next, and in time your mother will cry over your grave, but—"

"Leave my mother out of this!"

Lomax's face turned a fiery red. He pushed up from the chair and, shouting curses, aimed a headbutt at the judge, falling short by two or three feet because of the cuffs and leg irons. He dropped back into the chair, struggling for breath, his eyes promising some future menace.

Knott, who'd stayed still as a statue through the attack, answered him with a smile. "May I continue?"

"Screw you. I want my lawyer."

"As I was about to say, it doesn't have to be like that, Mr. Lomax. You take my offer seriously, you'll be a free man before you know it, out from under the shadow of prosecution. Back to making regular visits to your mother at the Sunny Acres nursing home. All your other habits, good and bad."

"Who are you to talk? My judge?"

"Yes. Your jury and executioner as well, if it comes to that. Are you ready to listen?"

"What the hell. Spill it."

When the judge was finished, Lomax said, "That's all of it? I send him sailing over the edge, this Arthur Six guy, and—"

"Exactly, Mr. Lomax. Arthur Six dies, you will go free," Judge Knott said, making it sound like an elementary exercise in justice. "The Arthur Six jury made a mockery of my courtroom when it bought into the so-called Unwritten Law invoked by his crafty lawyers, who cloaked Six in sympathy, laid the blame on the victims, and convinced enough of the jurors to cause a hung jury."

"My legal beagle's no amateur, so maybe I take my chances with a jury. They vote my way—what then? It becomes my turn. You set me up for a whack, send me sailing over the edge?"

"You keep your end of the bargain, Mr. Lomax, I'll keep mine."

"How much time I got before you need my answer?"

"Until I reach the door and call for the guard," the judge said, rising.

At Central Justice Center in Santa Ana later that week, the judge flipped through some legal paperwork before he spit a little cough into his fist and announced, "Allowing that the defendant has never been tried, much less convicted, of the multitudinous crimes the district attorney maintains were of his doing, the court denies the prosecution's motion to remand the defendant to custody. Bail is set at . . ."

Lomax missed how much he'd have to fork over for his freedom, too busy bear hugging his attorney, like it was Amos Alzono Waldorf who'd pulled it off, at the same time thinking how Judge Knott had delivered on his part of their deal, how now it was Quentin Lomax's turn.

He already knew where to find Arthur Six.

The judge had seen to that.

Six was down south in San Juan Capistrano, at the mission, working as a gardener and handyman in exchange for room and board in the friars' quarters; hiding his history as an accused murderer under an assumed name, John Brown; Lomax chuckled every time he thought about it on the train ride down, trying to figure how much imagination it took to come up with an alias like John Brown, as in not very much imagination at all.

Stepping off the Amtrak at the station, he considered what name he might pick for himself, it ever came to that, not all that convinced he'd want to give up Quentin Lomax, mainly because that would also mean giving up the rep he'd worked damn hard to achieve over all these years with clients who paid top dollar to get the kind of contract service that would never track back to them.

Even that last friggin contract.

A fluke he got caught, but no way he'd let it go to touch tag with the people who'd put their confidence in him, paid him the cash money.

One of the reasons he gave in to Judge Knott, to prevent something being said in open court that would implicate them.

Sail Arthur Six, a.k.a. John Brown, over the edge?

A cheap price to pay for the privilege.

Lomax fell in with the tourists window-shopping the antique stores and souvenir shops along the main drag leading to Mission San Juan Capistrano. He bought himself through the gate for seven bucks and split from the pack to go looking for Six, confident someone who couldn't do better than John Brown for an alias was no master of disguise.

He found Six after fifteen minutes of wandering around what the tour brochure said was ten acres of gardens. Six was on his knees, pulling weeds and puttering around inside a vegetable garden. Except for the Charlie Chaplin–Hitler kind of mustache sitting slightly crooked under his eagle beak of a nose and dirt smears on his forehead and cheeks where he had been swiping off sweat with his muddy gloves, he looked exactly like his mug shot.

"Growing tomatoes, looks like," Lomax said, starting up small talk while heading toward Six from the sheltered archway, a distance of about twenty feet along the adobe path.

In no hurry.

Checking his bomber jacket pocket for the switchblade he planned to exercise on Six's throat.

Saying, "Always taste better off the vine; what other vegetables?"

"Fruit," Six said, sizing him up. "Tomatoes are a fruit, not a vegetable. Nothing a lot of people realize, but they are."

"I learn something new every day . . . Sounds like you know your fruits," Lomax said.

"And vegetables. Over there, peas. There, carrots. Two favorites of the friars. This is their private garden, where the flower gardens, the bougainvilleas, and the water lilies floating in the Moorish fountain center of the patio area are also meant to be enjoyed by one and all, the visitors like you."

"Corn?" Lomax searched over his shoulders for signs of tourist traffic.

Nothing.

He fingered the switchblade, figuring to have Six sailing over the edge in another minute, minute and a half, himself out and gone, back to the Amtrak station and waiting for his train to L.A. before anyone stumbled into the body.

Six said, "The brothers eat store-bought corn now, after growing it for a while a lot of years ago. They love it, but don't like the way the stalks grow and, they say, distract from the beauty, the peace and solitude of the mission." He planted his trowel in a water channel and, rising, brushed himself off and stashed his gloves in his overalls.

There wasn't a lot to him, maybe 120 pounds stretched over two or three inches less than six feet. A strong breeze might be able to carry him to the Pacific, Lomax decided.

Only a few yards from him now, he tightened his grip on the switchblade, saying, "I thought I'd see the swallows they're always writing about. How the swallows been coming to Mission San Juan Capistrano year in and year out, every year, for hundreds of years."

"That happens in March, not this time of year," Six replied. "And it's not happening so much in March anymore, either, though no one knows why they stopped coming." He held out his left palm like a traffic cop, adding, "And you can stop right there, no funny moves, you know what's good for you."

He raised his other arm to give Lomax a better look at the .22 caliber automatic he had aimed at him, its blue steel barrel reflecting the bright sunlight.

"What's that all about?" Lomax asked, hanging onto his cool, fishing for time while his mind raced after a way to do Six before he could squeeze the trigger, the look on Six's face telling him the poor schnook was working on a different unwritten law here, the law of survival, and would have no problem adding a third corpse to his count. "Some kind of joke you like to play on strangers who stray off the guided tour?"

"Nothing personal. A matter of life and death. Quentin Lomax dies so that Arthur Six can go on living. Simple as that."

Right then, hearing Six speak his name, Lomax recognized that Judge Knott had played him for a sap. Set him up. He said, "You know who I am."

"Yes, and don't move another inch, or else. I know how to shoot this thing. See? The safety is off and all."

"You were expecting me."

"I was. You take a pretty nice picture, by the way, although your smile leaves a lot to be desired. Braces growing up, they would have helped."

"Braces cost money . . . So, you also know what brought me down to Capistrano?"

"A ruse. The judge said you'd be real easy for him to trick. He was right as rain."

"Who are you? Einstein? Thinking no one will ever come along and see through that stupid mustache you grew like a vegetable, raise a holy stink about you being here, Mr. Arthur Six with that dumb-ass John Brown name?"

"The law says I'm innocent until I'm proven guilty. Besides, I'm in a place where kindness, love, and forgiveness are the rule."

"And killing me, they'll love and forgive you for that?"

"The way it looks—got attacked by this loony, speaking gibberish and pointing a gun at me for no reason at all. We got to fighting, the gun went off, and—"

"John!" A friar in a hooded cassock called for Arthur Six from across the courtyard, distracting him.

Lomax leaped forward, barreling hard into Six, wrestling him to the ground.

Six bear-hugged Lomax as they rolled in the dirt, knocking over the seed packages on sticks set in the ground to spot the lima beans, the potatoes.

Lomax was too strong for him.

He broke free and forged possession of the .22, gripped it by its pearl handle, and stuck the automatic under Six's chin. Said, "You want to keep your head attached to your body, say whatever it takes to make Friar Tuck go away, unless you want me using him for target practice."

"Then what?" Six struggled for breath; barely able to get the question out.

"What do you think?"

"You look surprised to see me, Your Honor."

"Surprised to see you inside my home, Mr. Lomax, enjoying the comforts of my bar," Judge Knott said, his face a study in irritation and no small amount of concern; eyes blinking furiously.

"French windows. You should remember to always shut and lock 'em up tight if you're going out. Otherwise, they're an open invitation to burglars, or worse . . . The mixed nuts on the stale side; you might want to do something about that too, next time you go grocery shopping."

"Full of handy hints. A regular Martha Stewart, are you?"

"Hardly. Martha Stewart, she served time, not me. Prison's not where I'm heading, if your word's better'n your bowl of mixed nuts."

"Given this unexpected visit—shall I assume that you've upheld your part of our arrangement?"

"Days ago."

"I've seen nothing about Arthur Six reported on the news."

"Or John Brown, dumb alias he picked. And you won't, never. I taught him the Jimmy Hoffa trick."

The judge half-smiled, nodded understanding. "Excellent," he said. "Then you're free to assume your case will be fast-tracked by me out of my courtroom and the charges dropped by the district attorney once and for good. My early congratulations to you, Mr. Lomax."

"How many strings you pulling to make that happen, Your Honor?"

"Mr. Lomax, do I ask you how you conduct your business?"

"No offense. Only curious. Wondering if it's as many strings as for Arthur Six."

"For Arthur Six? Precisely what is it you think you know, Mr. Lomax?"

"Only what Six thought he knew and was saying to me before words failed him along with everything else."

"Care to share?"

"Six told me you got him a hung jury, not his lawyer, by the way you kept shutting down the DA's people and holding onto his leash through intimidation; said you told him you would keep the DA from following through on retrying his sorry ass if he was game for doing something for you in trade."

"Did he say what the trade might be?"

"Nah, like it was some giant, friggin state secret between you and him, but he said he wrote it all down and gave it to someone he trusted to pass on to the news bloodhounds if it ever turned out you broke your word to him and didn't make the charge blow away for good, or if something happened to him, like it was about to."

"Such poppycock. Who would take the word of an absent, accused murderer facing a retrial for killing his wife and her lover over that of a distinguished jurist, an Orange County Superior Court judge who has served with honor and distinction for twenty-four years?"

"I suppose anybody who decided to run against you in next year's election, figuring a little scandal is good for the ballot box, but I can see by looking at you that ain't gonna be the case, right, Your Honor?"

Judge Knott gave Lomax the reassurances he wanted, several times, Lomax putting the question to him from different directions until, professing satisfaction, he allowed their conversation to dwindle into small talk. He poured himself another scotch, picked his way through the nut bowl, and left the same way he had entered, making a show of shutting the French window and testing the safety lock. A conspiratorial wink and an animated thumbs-up became the last the judge saw of him before he disappeared into the moonless night.

The judge spent a motionless minute before he blew a fat breath across the room and followed it to the bar.

A tall vodka helped him collect his nerves; then another before he reached after his cell phone and had the service connect him with Mission San Juan Capistrano; asked the birdlike soprano who answered the call if he might speak with John Brown.

No, sorry, she said.

Dear John disappeared earlier in the week without notice.

No telling when he might be back, if ever, God bless him.

The judge's next call was to the district atorney at his private number.

It was time to collect on a few past favors due.

He wanted the book closed on Six, wanted Six out of his courtroom as well as his life, should the media ever come around asking embarrassing questions, like why so many postponements on a trial date or why no bench warrant issued for the arrest of a defendant who'd obviously fled. And he had to make good on his deal with Lomax, construct a wall of comfort between them until he could make other arrangements.

"Spence, it's Ollie Knott here," he said into the phone, and after some pleasantries, "Spence, I need a little help from my friend . . ."

A week later, Lomax was in the courtroom with his impeccably groomed showboat of an $800-an-hour lawyer, Amos Alonzo Waldorf, Esq., exuding a cocky confidence from a back row seat as the judge mechanically breezed through the first call on a morning calendar bursting with the usual run of motions and pleadings until Mary Rose Treeloar, the greenest lawyer on the DA's staff, rose to request a dismissal.

A sleepy-eyed, overweight brunette in a cheap pinstriped suit that told everything there was to know about her pay grade, Mary Rose was facing the judge for the first time.

Her stammer betrayed her unfamiliarity with the Arthur Six case as she alternated reading from her yellow pad and fumbling after documents in a modest stack of manila file folders with twitchy smiles for Judge Knott that seemed to beg for his understanding.

The judge made a show of asking tough questions, an interrogation that soon had the young, inexperienced DA on the edge of tears. He had bet himself he would have her crying outright before second morning call, at the same time lamenting the sad quality of the lawyers being turned out nowadays by even the highest-rated universities. She wasn't the first to be put to his test. She wouldn't be his last.

He scored earlier than expected.

He had the tears spilling over her cheeks shortly before he eased his reign of terror, accepted the DA's decision against retrying Arthur Six, and removed the trial date from his calendar, saying, "I am similarly convinced the lack of any additional evidence against Mr. Six suggests we would only be tossing substantially more good money after bad and wasting valuable time that can be put to better use by this court."

Turning contemptuous eyes on Fix's preening lawyer, who was smiling and nodding approval as if he had brought about this happy turn, Judge Knott observed for the record, "I didn't entirely buy into your shoddy excuse for your client's absence, sir. His face was not one I needed to see again and further delays would have changed nothing, but I strongly urge you to never again let something like this occur in my courtroom."

Next, the judge moved up hearing a dismissal motion from Amos Alonzo Waldorf to just before his toilet break, instead of waiting until after lunch, where it was listed on the day's calendar.

This threw Mary Rose into a mild asthma attack.

When she finished gasping for air, she requested that the matter be delayed until after the lunch break, as scheduled, or, that failing, second call.

She said, "I got assigned only this morning, the absolute last minute, Your Honor," her voice an exercise in fear. "I haven't had enough time as of yet to completely review the Lomax files and compile my notes and—"

Judge Knott shut Mary Rose down with a school crossing guard's gesture, looked at her like he was examining a wart. "All interested parties are present and accounted for, Miss Treeloar. Request denied, and I suggest in the future you work longer and harder on your preparation skills."

He struck a pose, his elbows on the bench, hands forming a pyramid, as Waldorf marched forward, adjusted his $3,000 Armani suit jacket, fussed a bit with his understated silk tie and matching pocket handkerchief, and launched into a catalog of reasons and citations for dismissing the murder charge against his client, the put-upon and wrongfully accused Mr. Quentin Lomax, making a crown jewel of every word he spoke.

Mary Rose stammered and stuttered through a set of responses that earned frequent yawns from the judge. He knocked them down, one after another, before hammering her quiet, declaring, "Miss Treeloar, Mr. Waldorf's persuasive arguments coupled with your ineptness oblige me to find in his favor. Motion to dismiss granted."

Mary Rose promptly suffered another asthma attack.

Lomax pulled Waldorf to him and planted a fat kiss on the lawyer's mouth.

A few nights later, the look on Judge Knott's face reminded Lomax of that girl lawyer he had turned into hamburger, the poor kid in a zombie-state and sucking up the oxygen, her skin the color of chalk when the paramedics rolled her out of the courtroom. Knott looked scared, wearing his nerves like a heavy-duty aftershave, like he knew what had brought Lomax uninvited into his home again; like he knew it wasn't just for another taste of his expensive hooch or another trip through the nut bowl.

"Glad to see you did something about the locks on those French windows, Your Honor, but you shouldn't-a stopped there," Lomax said. "This place is easy pickings even for an amateur; easier to crack than an egg."

The judge, his composure back in harness, replied, "Having concluded our business, I did not expect another visit from you, Mr. Lomax."

"Not exactly concluded, though. Some loose ends."

"How so these loose ends?" He soldiered across the den, maneuvered behind the bar, helped himself to a vodka, and offered a pour to Lomax.

"Stickin with the scotch," Lomax said. "I don't ever mix my liquors, any more than I ever mix business with pleasure . . . Cheers!" He clanked glasses with the judge.

"And these loose ends of yours, are they business or pleasure, Mr. Lomax?"

Lomax blew out an untranslatable exclamation. "You got me there, Your Honor. Now I think about it, a little-a both. You call it. Which you wanna hear first?"

"You choose," Judge Knott answered, circling back around

the bar and settling in one of the leather recliners facing the giant plasma TV screen occupying most of the paneled wall across from the stone-faced fireplace. He used the remote to turn on the picture and mute the sound.

"That old movies channel, huh? Me too, whenever I got time," Lomax said. "The flick where Jimmy Cagney's in the joint, listening to his boyhood chum, the priest, trying to talk him into something. Never get tired of watching that one whenever it's on."

"Pat O'Brien."

"As the priest, yeah, sort of like you'll be now, while I need to confess something to you." Lomax moved his eyes away from the judge and focused on his drink. "It's like this, Your Honor—what I said to you before about Arthur Six telling me he gave a letter to a friend, for the friend to make public if you didn't square your deal with him?"

"Go on."

"Was a lie I invented. Insurance you would go ahead and square your deal with Arthur Six, get him off the hook on the murder-one charges. You came through with flying colors, so points for that. Any man who finds himself with a cheating bitch of a wife, he deserves all the sympathy and understanding he can get."

The judge couldn't hide his annoyance. "That was definitely none of your business, Mr. Lomax. Our agreement called for you to deal with Mr. Six in a forceful manner that would allow me to unburden you of a trial and conviction of murder. Not Arthur Six, Mr. Lomax. You."

"Except you made it my business, Your Honor, which gets us to my second lie, where I said Arthur Six didn't tell me what the deal was he made with you? He did, though. How he was supposed to kill me when I caught up with him down in Capistrano? How you had it all arranged with him? That wasn't a very nice trick to play on me, Your Honor, not so very nice at all."

The judge sprang to his feet, fists clenched and pounding the air, his head spinning out of control. Shrieking, "There are lies and then there are damned lies! That's a damned lie Six fed you, Mr. Lomax, clearly to save his own skin. Our deal involved a reasonable sum of money to be paid me for my co-operation in the courtroom, on Arthur Six's promise he would kill no more, never again. Were he here now, I would call him a liar to his face." He sank back into the recliner.

"Why not?" Lomax said. He pointed to the archway that led to the central corridor, calling, "C'mon out and show your face, Artie."

Arthur Six materialized to the invitation.

Judge Knott groaned.

Lomax laughed. "What say, Artie? Which one of you's been playing the truth for a sucker?"

"You heard it all already, Quentin. That answer's in my checkbook. A big fat goose egg for a balance, not a golden goose. What little I had all went for lawyers already, why I was going to need a public defender if a new trial came about."

"Him, Judge Knott, having you send me sailing over the edge?"

"An answer to my prayer, the judge's offer. Before I knew you, Quentin, or I never would've gone along in the first place."

"This is so much damned nonsense," the judge said, rising. "What's done is done. You're both out from under, free men, and that's what should matter most to you."

"Until when?" Lomax said. "For how long? Until you can line up your next patsies, who'll come after me and Artie so you can protect your precious reputation?"

"I'll give you my word," the judge said.

"Why's that? Run out of two dollar bills?" Lomax advanced on the judge with the open switchblade he'd held out of sight until now. "You let me down, so I gotta put you down like the dog you are."

He flew the blade across Judge Knott's neck, opening a river of blood that the judge covered with both hands seconds before his legs gave out. He dropped to the floor, knees first, then over into a fetal position.

"And that's that," Lomax said. "We're outta here, Artie."

"Not exactly," Six said. He had pulled his .22 automatic from somewhere and was aiming it at Lomax. "Fair's fair, Quentin. The judge ultimately honored the arrangement he and I had, so I would feel less of a man, truly guilty, if I were to ignore my responsibility toward him. It would be a sin I'd carry into the confessional, and with me for the rest of my life."

"Jesus, Artie, you wouldn't, would you?"

"What do you think?" Arthur Six said.

DIVERTERS

BY ROB ROBERGE

Tustin

The day had started out with me shitting blood. A little later, I was shivering in Doc's passenger seat under the warm July California sun, asking Doc about the blood while we were on the way to Tustin to see this friend of his who was supposed to help us get some morphine.

Doc and I called each other friends, but we both knew without saying that we were drug buddies. That if I didn't have the five hundred bucks in my pocket to pry this hospice-care friend of his from her ethics long enough to give us some terminal cancer patient's painkillers, Doc would be in this car alone, or with some other human ATM machine. He had the connection, I had the money—and this made us, however temporarily, partners in the world.

I was worried the blood could be an ulcer, maybe something more serious. Lately, I hadn't been able to get much more than Vicodin for my habit, and it had been corroding away at my stomach, a million tiny pickaxes mining the walls of my guts, so I figured it had caused an ulcer, caused me to rip and bleed into myself and leak slowly away from the inside out. But, too, my mind slid easily to thoughts of cancer and that I could be dying, at least dying faster or in a different way than from addiction. I'd asked my girlfriend Amber and she figured it was nothing. So I asked Doc, "Is blood out of your ass always bad news?"

"It's never good news," he said.

"I didn't ask if it was ever good."

"It's not ever good," he said.

I took a deep breath. I had the start of what would be full-blown dope sickness in a few hours. The metallic taste at the back of my mouth, the chills. Soon there'd be sweats. Then puke and diarrhea and my body making a tortured fist of itself. I needed exactly what we were going to get. While, of course, realizing it was what we were going to get that caused this. Every day becomes the same cycle of desperate need met with desperate opposition and sickness. I couldn't tell today from tomorrow anymore than you can tell the sea from the horizon in a marine-layer fog. It all just blurs together.

"But is it *always* bad?"

"Not always," he said. "But it's never good, so disavow yourself of that silliness right now."

I looked at him.

He said, "This is your ass and your blood, I'm guessing?"

Sometimes things are simple. Doc was called Doc because he used to be a doctor. Maybe he still was—I wasn't sure, but I knew he wasn't allowed to practice medicine, at least not in California. He wrote some bad scripts, and he ended up losing his license. I think it may only have been suspended. But if anyone official was checking on him, he wasn't living too cleanly. He'd been able to hook me up until the day before with a pretty steady flow of Vicodin, but that only kept me going and didn't really make me high anymore. Without it, I was sick—a shivering noxious presence to all who had the bad luck or bad sense to enter the debris field I'd made of my life. With it, I could function, more or less, get to another day of clawing myself through the hours, wishing the next day would be better, but not seeing any reason it would be. I looked out the window at the towns under the 22 freeway. We'd left Long Beach maybe twenty minutes before and now we were passing the cluster of suburban sprawl of north Orange County, flashing by under an army of tall palms, blown by the offshore winds. It was a beautiful place, even from the freeway. Rooftops of homes glided under us to the right—to the left, a series of car dealerships in Garden Grove, and just east of them, out of sight from the freeway, a series of Vietnamese pho joints and body-piercing parlors in strip malls.

I met Doc when he was still able to get OxyContin, eighty milligrams for a while and then forties, but eventually his source dried up. Oxy was a dream for a newly off-the-wagon user like me—a time-released chemical equivalent of heroin, without the messy, sloppy, desperate need to fix with needles. Crush a couple of eighty milligrams to start your high right off, and then top them off with a couple of unbroken eighties for the time-release, and you could live your life in comfort and at something resembling peace. But as they always do, the drugs had stopped working and then, worse, they dried up and the mirage of beauty and ease they gave, they took away with them.

Right now, though, Doc had talked about an old friend he used to work with who could hook us up with some morphine and maybe more in Tustin and was I in? I heard *morphine* and said yes and committed my last five hundred bucks from a poker win a few nights before. Normally I need a lot more info, but most of Doc's friends, even the addicts, were very white collar. They were all liars and cheats, but generally not as dangerous as street dope fiends. Plus, we were talking about morphine. The risk-reward was too good and I just jumped without a second thought, quick as a seismograph at ground zero.

Doc said, "You and Amber been, you know, doing anything?"

"What?"

"From what I hear, strippers like to strap one on now and again."

Amber did, in fact, like to strap one on now and again. And that had caused some blood, but only a little, and only right after. Not for days at a time afterward. "Dude, that's a stereotype," I said.

"I'm your doctor."

"You're not my doctor."

"Well, I'm *a* doctor," he said.

"Are you?"

"Nevertheless," he said, "I have been an internist. I have a certain amount of experience with insertables. I've seen an astounding amount of things up guy's assholes. And women's assholes. You can tell me. Plus, I need to know the facts to know if this blood is an issue. "

"Okay, fine," I said. "Yes, she has fucked me with a strap-on. Happy?"

"Don't get so defensive, man. I'm your doctor."

I let it slip that time.

Doc said, "When was the last time?"

"For the blood?"

"No," he said, smiling. "When you let your pervert girl-friend sodomize you." I looked at him and he smiled and laughed. "You need to lighten up." He was driving and not looking at the road much as he hunted for his smokes in the backseat. I gripped the door handle and flashed visions of car wrecks and blood. Being a passenger scared the shit out of me—if I had any, I would have taken a few Valium before getting in the car. He said, "Everybody loves something up their ass during sex."

"Really?"

"It can sure as hell seem that way when you work the ER."

"I can't talk to you at all, man."

"C'mon," he said, "I'm trying to help. When was the last . . . penetration?"

"Weeks ago."

"Okay," he said. "And this blood?"

"The last few days."

"Today?"

I nodded.

"Well, it's not that," he said. "Are you shitting blood? Or is there blood *in* your stool?"

"What's the difference?"

"Color."

"What?"

"It's an issue. What color is the blood?"

"Red," I replied. "Blood colored."

Doc nodded. He put in a CD—Jonathan Richman and the Modern Lovers' *Rockin' and Romance*. He cracked the window and lit an American Spirit, then offered me one.

I shook my head. I had quit smoking almost ten years before. One of the hardest things I ever did. Doc had quit for years and only recently started again since his divorce. I really would have liked one then, but I held out. "Shit causes cancer, dude."

"Media hype," Doc said. "And red isn't the only color blood can be. Especially on the inside."

"So is red good?"

"Nothing is good," Doc said. "No blood in your shit is good. That's our goal. Our vision. An America with no blood in our shit. That's the ticket I'm running on. The no-blood-in-your-ass ticket."

"Red is less bad?"

"That is true," he said. "Red is much less bad. If the blood in your stool is a greasy-looking dark red, almost black, *that* is a major and immediate concern."

"And this?"

He shrugged. "Probably nothing. How many Vicodin a day are you taking?"

I was, until a week ago, taking about thirty, but I was stealing, when I could, from Doc's stash, when he had a stash, so I went with a low estimate. Our supply had run out five days ago and I'd halved my intake from twenty, to ten, to five, to only three the day before. My eyes felt like sandpaper and the suffocating heat in my head made every pump of my heart throb painfully all over my body. Like every nerve ending burned with Fourth of July sparklers. "Ten to twenty if I can. Less, lately."

"That's probably it right there," he said.

Jonathan was singing about his jeans and how they were a-fraying as I looked out the window at the blur of objects racing by.

I knew I couldn't continue on the way I was going. My short-range plan involved the morphine and, after that, a meeting with this guy Leroy Marcus about some pot he wanted me to sell. The morphine was supposed to be my last for a while—the plan was to use it and slowly wean myself off, taking Vicodin when I had to, in order to detox as painlessly as possible and start clean. Go back to meetings. Be humble and start over. I'd done it before. I could do it again.

I had, at that point, quit various opiates somewhere between thirty and fifty times in my life. Which meant thirty to fifty intentional detoxes. Withdrawals that made you sorry for ever being born—which sometimes seemed the point of the whole thing. The self-loathing burning hot enough to make the sorrows you suffered from withdrawal seem something like justice for the liar and cheat you'd allowed yourself to become. The twisted core of wrongness at your center everywhere you went was something that made suffering seem valid and just, in some way.

"I can't drop all five hundred on the morphine," I said.

"You have to."

"I can't. I need at least a couple hundred for tonight."

Doc said, "You got a game?"

I shook my head. "You know Leroy Marcus?"

"That 'roid rage guy?"

Leroy had an earned reputation as a guy you didn't want to fuck with. He'd been a boxer and had ended up recently with an ultimate fighting obsession. Leroy liked violence—seemed to like getting hurt as much as he liked hurting people, which made dealing with him an uneasy proposition at best. Someone who's not afraid of getting hurt, someone who actually welcomes the pain and raw savagery of the fight, is not someone you want to face off with. My dad told me when I was a kid, you never throw a punch unless you're willing to kill the guy—because he might be willing to kill you. Leroy probably got the same lesson somewhere along the line. But he threw punches and I didn't.

"That's him," I said.

"What the fuck do you have going with that beast?"

"A pot deal," I said. "I need at least two hundred to sell some medical-quality shit he has."

"You smoking pot?"

I shook my head. "Pot's dollar signs to me. I'm trying to make some money."

"Pot's legal now, dude."

"Not legal," I said.

"More or less. Any fuck off the street can get a script for it. How you going to make money?"

"Buying a couple hundred off him and selling it to a buddy in Long Beach for about double. Quick cash. No risk."

"You can't trust Leroy. There's plenty of risk just walking in his door."

That was true enough. "I need money," I said.

Doc smoked the end of his cigarette and rubbed it out on the outside of his door—the side of his car was streaked with the ends of his butts. He'd pinch out the tobacco and let the filters pile up at his feet.

"We're scoring morphine—a real fucking drug—in Tustin," he said.

"Are we?"

"We are."

I felt the sickness overcoming me. "We better be."

"My point is," Doc said, "we'll get enough to make some money off it, if you want."

I had tried over the years to make money with heroin, with Dilaudid, with OxyContin, and a variety of other opiates. All I ever did was end up doing them all, either fast or slowly. But they never made it, for me, from *intent to deal* to ever actually dealing.

Doc said, "What if we spend your whole five hundred bucks on the painkillers?"

"Then I'll do them."

He looked hard at me.

I said, "I'll do half of them."

"Right, but what if you let me tuck a couple hundred aside and deal that."

"For both of us?"

"Of course for both of us, man," he said. "Who you going to trust to make a buck? Me, or Leroy Marcus?"

Neither of you, I thought. *Leroy's a brutal beast of a business-man and you're a dope fiend.* But given the choice, I answered honestly. "I'd rather be in business with you."

Doc merged off 22 onto 55 South, where it splits going to Riverside one way and Orange County the other, and we were headed toward Tustin, just a few miles away. We seemed to have reached some tacit agreement about the extra two hundred and the profit on the deal.

"So, tell me about your connection," I said.

"She's a hospice worker with a terminal case."

"And?"

"She's a diverter. She's helping us out."

Diverter is the medical term, and the narc term, for a medical professional who diverts pain meds from the people who need them. The language of distance and euphemism. They're thieves, and people like me and Doc pay them to steal from people in pain. I try not to have any more illusions about what I do. I used to be able to lie about it—to others, to myself. But after seven years clean, it's hard to see this as anything but a hideous failure for me as a human being. My next drug posses-sion case puts me at what's known at the SAP pits, SAP be-ing short for Substance Abuse Program. I can't do this much longer—one way or the other.

"How terminal?" I asked him.

"What?"

"How terminal a case?"

"There aren't degrees of terminal," Doc said. "Trust me, I'm a doctor."

"I mean how close to dead is this person?" I don't know why it mattered to me, but it did. As if the closer to dead they were, the less I'd be ripping them off, somehow.

"Close enough to be designated terminal and have 24/7 hospice care," Doc said. "That's usually pretty late in the game."

I nodded.

Doc said, "And it usually means a *lot* of pain meds."

The drug talk, along with my system being weaned off meds the last few days, started to make me feel cravings that hurt. But they were cravings with hope—that tingle when you're close to the drugs, in both time and distance. "Any chance for Dilaudids?"

Doc shrugged as we reached the two Santa Ana/Tustin exits for 17th Street. The second exit heads south toward Tustin, and we took that one. "Hard to say," Doc said, lighting another cigarette. "Pain-management theory these days shies away from Dilaudids. But we should get plenty of morphine."

When I still shot up, which I hadn't done in this last slip from sobriety, so it had been over seven years before, Dilaudids were like gold. Generally, they're about five to eight times more powerful than morphine, and you don't need to cook them—you can do what's known as a cold shake. Which is pretty much what it sounds like. You put a pill in some distilled water and shake it until it dissolves, and you're ready to put it in the cotton and up the syringe and go.

"Listen," Doc said, "there's something difficult we might have to do."

"Difficult how?"

"It's a relatively new procedure. I haven't asked Sandra if he's on it or not, but this guy may have a permanent morphine vial implanted near the base of his spine."

"Lucky bastard," I said, and I sort of meant it.

"It's the wave of the future. Going to hurt people like you

and me. Pills and shit like that are going the way of the horse-less carriage."

"I don't follow."

"All drugs are going to be time-released," Doc said. "Soon, they're won't be any pills to steal."

"You said there'd be morphine at this place, right?"

"Right," Doc said. "But, worst case scenario, you are going to have to cut the vial out of this guy."

"I thought cancer patients had IV drips and patches and stuff."

"They do, but in addition to that, depending on how far gone he is, he might have this semipermanent vial."

"Why do I have to cut it out?"

"Well, no one's saying for sure it's there."

"*If* it's there, why the fuck am *I* doing the cutting?"

Doc shrugged. "Because I don't want to."

And that was that—his connection, his call. "But he may not have one of these, right?"

"He may, he may not. But you might want to wish he does—concentrated morphine drip."

"I'm not cutting open some poor fuck who's about to die," I said.

"Well, let's hope it doesn't come to that. I was just warning you about some of the potential difficulties."

I shook my head and looked at the faces of the other people driving out on the freeway. I wondered what they were talking about. What they were thinking they might have to do in the next half hour and how sick they made themselves.

As we got off the freeway, I realized how tense I was, realized I hadn't been taking regular breaths, realized I'd actually been holding my breath. I tried to take in a few deep breaths while Doc swung across four lanes of 17th Street.

"Be careful," I warned.

"It's important to blend in," Doc said. "Cops pull over people like you and me when they're doing the speed limit. People drive like maniacs here. So should we, if we want to be left alone." Someone honked and Doc gave them the finger.

I turned around and looked at the WELCOME TO TUS-TIN sign behind us . . . This side was for the people just leaving Tustin and it read: Work Where You Must But Live and Shop in Tustin!

"Ah, yes," Doc said. "Rustin' in Tustin."

"You from here?"

"That I am. And a more dull town, you'd be hard pressed to find."

"Good punk scene here," I said. "Wasn't there?" I was from the East Coast and most of my knowledge of the West Coast scene had come from fanzines like Forced Exposure and Flipside.

"True," Doc replied. "The old Safari Sam's in Huntington Beach saved our lives. But before that it was strip malls and before that it was orange groves." He pointed out the window at the strip malls, banks, and yogurt shops that tumored all over state roads from here to Florida and back. "Thirty-five years ago, when I was a kid, this was ten miles of orange groves."

A Vons slid by on our right. I took nervous breaths and felt my heart beat like a rabbit's in my chest. A church with a high-peaked roof stood on our left with an announcement out front: WHY DO THEY WANT US DEAD? What the Bible says sbout Islam.

Doc said, "Almost there."

I nodded and made several more attempts at a deep breath.

He took a left on Mauve and a sign reading NOT A THROUGH STREET greeted us as we headed down to the second-to-last house on the right. There was a Toyota in the driveway and we pulled up next to it, blocking one of the garage sides. I pointed, said, "What if someone needs to get out?"

Doc shook his head. "No one needs to get out. Look. This is a call I only get a couple times a year—the situation has to be perfect. We are going into this house and we are going to score, okay?"

"Okay."

"Like I said, this is rare. The patient is alone, they probably don't have much family, they may have none. My connection pretty much has the run of the place. It's like an opiate candy store in there and we are here to clean them out, understand?"

It was starting to sound too good, but it also had a momentum that I couldn't pull against. Plus, I needed to get high pretty soon or I'd be a wreck. I wasn't in a position to argue.

"Give me the money," Doc said.

I reached into my front pocket, took out a rolled wad of moist bills, and gave them to him.

Doc said, "Dude, you carry your money like a ten-year-old."

"Sorry."

"You have to stop apologizing for everything too."

"Uhm . . . sorry?"

He counted out the bills and folded and rearranged them.

"Tell you what. After we make a few bucks here—will you use a fucking proper billfold if I buy you one?"

"Is that like a wallet?"

He shook his head. "The way you carry money, no one's ever going to take you seriously."

"People take money seriously—they don't seem to care how it's folded."

"You're wrong," Doc said. He lit a cigarette, took a deep drag. Then a second. Then he put the cigarette out. He turned to me. "If anyone asks, you are my assistant."

"Who's asking here?"

"Inside. There should only be Sandra, my friend. But *if* someone is here . . . family, friend, what*ever*. I am a medical professional Sandra called for an opinion and you are my assistant. Got it?"

I nodded, looked down at my torn jeans and Chuck Taylors held together with electrical tape on the right toe, and thought, *Yeah, medical assistant.*

"Great," Doc said. "Let's do this."

The place looked like the *Brady Bunch* house. Midcentury modern blighted by a 1970s renovation and then left to domestic ghost town since. Doc's friend Sandra met us at the front door. She wore blue scrubs, with one of those infantilizing tops that nurses and hospital workers all wear these days. The shirt was loitered with Cookie Monsters and Ernies and Berts and some Muppet I didn't recognize that I figured might be Elmo. I shifted my carry bag to my other hand.

"He's asleep," Sandra said quickly, and before I knew it we were in the house, the quiet suburbia of Tustin a whisper of lawn sprinklers and muffled TVs behind the closed door.

Doc introduced me and we shook hands. Sandra wore a stethoscope draped over her shoulders the way people do in movies. I wondered when they stopped wearing them with the earpieces around their neck, the way they did when I was a kid and my mom was an ER nurse. I used to spend the midnight-to-7 a.m. shift with her on nights she couldn't get our neighbor Doris to watch me and my sister.

The house smelled like the ERs of my childhood—the vague mix of cleaning fluids and urine and medicine and latex and rubbing alcohol. The latex and alcohol gave me the start of a hard-on and I thought about Amber and her latex nurse outfit. Doc grabbed two lollipops out of Sandra's pocket and gave me one.

"Sandra and I have some business to attend to."

She gestured upstairs. They headed up, with Doc telling me to wait for them.

"Is there a bathroom down here?" I asked.

Sandra told me to go into the living room and keep going to the right and back.

Which would have been fine, except the living room was where her patient happened to be. I was alone in a room with a dying stranger. The poor bastard. I walked into the room slowly, afraid to startle the guy. There was a stairwell to my right, where Doc had followed Sandra upstairs to wherever they were now, their talk muffled behind walls and hard to distinguish under the gentle drone of an oxygen machine.

As I walked forward, the main floor opened to a kitchen on the left and a huge sunken living room to the right. He was on a hospital-type bed in the middle of the room, facing away from me and toward a big-screen TV that was tuned to some talking heads, but the sound was muted. The oxygen machine droned on, interrupted by the beeps and peeps of a series of diagnostic indicators reading out numbers that were completely meaningless to me.

The man was on his back, his head turned painfully to the side. A tube ran into his mouth. He was motionless, except for a mindless chewing of the tube. His eyes were open, but he didn't seem to register that I was there. His catheter bag seemed dangerously full and I made a mental note to mention that to Sandra when she came back down. It looked like it was going to spill onto the floor.

I walked by, careful not to step on any of the various wires and tubes on my way to the bathroom.

I closed the door behind me and searched the medicine cabinet. This, too, was mostly a time capsule from 1972. There was a container of Alberto VO5 hair treatment. A glass bottle of Listerine. A jar of Brylcreem. There didn't seem to be much of anything worth taking, or anything from this century, aside from a bottle with two Xanax that I emptied on the spot. I took a couple of deep breaths and felt the candy Doc had given me in my pocket. I took it out, realizing it was a fentanyl lollipop.

It was supposed to be cherry, but it was really just some odd vaguely red flavor. I licked it for about ten seconds before chewing it to pieces, sliding it down my throat, and waiting for whatever relief it might offer. I sat on the closed toilet lid and read through a series of forgettable *New Yorker* cartoons. I closed my eyes and let the back of my head rest on the cool tile and waited for the drugs to unclench me. Soon, soon, *soon*, I told myself. I tried to take deep breaths, and before long I found myself breathing in synch with the oxygen apparatus out in the other room. I opened my eyes. The bathroom was small and dusty. The tub was filled with cobwebs. There was a door that led to a side yard and, out of habit, I made sure it was locked. I took some more breaths and waited for the drugs to have some effect. I left the bathroom, hoping that Doc and Sharon would have returned to save me from being alone with the dying man.

This is where drugs and straight people's image of drugs tend to part ways: in rooms where life and death are at center stage. This guy, mind-numbed and clearly on his way out, probably would have cut a deal with whatever he believed in just to get a few more days of life—of a life like mine. That's just fact. It's not to make me think—think about how wrong what I'm doing is, think about the various paths we follow in life, think about what a stupid man I am for allowing this blessing of life to drift so far away from me. It simply IS.

My life was shit and I'd been there before. All my yesterdays and all my tomorrows were lining up the same—that's what drugs do to you. They give you this illusion of control. I'd been through it enough to know it was fake. Any decent track record of clean time fucks your relapses. It's hard to see them as anything but the worst idea you've grabbed onto in quite a while.

The guy on the bed would have cut any deal with any devil in the world to trade places with me. The sick thing, and I knew it was sick, was part of me would have traded with him for that steady morphine drip, quietly escorting me out of this life and into something quiet and peaceful, maybe.

He had no chance. I had, depending on the studies you read, probably about a 2 to 3 percent chance to clean up if it was court-ordered, maybe a double-digit chance if I went in myself. I was the walking dead, but that was a lot better than him there in his living room, mindlessly chomping on the sad, gummed tube.

I could still hear Doc and Sandra upstairs—they seemed to maybe be fucking, or at least in a conversational intimacy that suggested fucking. This brought my loneliness crashing down. I hate being left by myself in rooms, being alone where I don't know anyone. But it could have been worse—at least the dying guy couldn't talk. And this was a true blessing—he couldn't move those wet, sad eyes of his to focus on me. If, for a second, I thought he could see me going through his meds, going through what was left of his life so I could get high, I think one of the last things he might have seen was me killing myself. At least I hope it would have been.

On a tray next to the bed was a box that looked like it had scripts in it. Score. They were fentanyl patches. The box had been opened, but there were several others under the bed. I grabbed five boxes. I tried several times to carry a sixth, but I dropped them all when I added one more, so I went with five and brought them back to my carrying bag.

Like so much crap in America, the packaging was obscene and unnecessary. The boxes held six patches each. I tore open the boxes, trying to be quiet, as I wasn't sure if this was part of the deal with Sandra or not, and neatly stacked the patches until I had thirty of them ready for my bag. I would have taken more—would have taken every single one I could find—but I didn't want to fuck up our connection for the future. I'd love to be able to say I was thinking about the dying guy—and it does happen, the groundswell of a decent human surfacing in me from time to time, often enough to not seem like a miracle—but the truth is, in that moment, I'd forgotten about him and his need for his own painkillers. He didn't exist to me.

I chewed another of the fentanyl lollipops I found. They seemed pretty useless. I wondered if they'd put this guy on Oxy or anything good, pillwise, before they had him on the patches and the pops.

Inside the kitchen, next to the coffee cups, I discovered a cabinet filled with bottles of pills. The usual useless suspects— Advil, Tylenol, gaggles of vitamins, and, scattered inside the cabinet, the snake-oil desperation of shark's fin and whale cartilage and shit like that. I pocketed a bottle with about ten ten-milligram Vicodin and kept scrambling through the cabinet until I found something worthwhile in a near-full jar of eighty-milligram OxyContin. I felt myself smile. I took two of the eighty-milligram tablets, crushing one and allowing the other to slide down my throat and release itself over time.

There was nothing else of value in the cabinet. I swapped the contents of the Advil and OxyContin bottles and kept the Advil in my pocket.

Back in the living room, I looked closely in the guy's eyes. Nothing registered. He was alive—that's what the machines seemed to be saying—but there wasn't much going on. I wondered, again, if I could cut him to get that vial out. I supposed I could—people could do all sorts of things they didn't want to do in life. Just not think about it, and get it done. It didn't have to be any more complicated than cutting into a steak, so long as you turned your brain off.

I sat on the couch and looked through a *TV Guide*. I had no idea about any of the celebrities or shows—that's another thing dope does. The outside world of news and talk just goes away. You can't tell anyone a single current event, even if they offer you a million dollars. The world fades and recedes. I glanced around. There was an antique musket over the fireplace. Everything about the house felt old. Murder mysteries piled up by the end table. This guy, or maybe Sandra, really liked mysteries. There had to be a hundred new hardcovers in that room alone. There was Luna's great *Penthouse* CD open on the stereo—so, evidence of someone not old too. I suspected the CD was in the machine and I really wanted to hear it, but I didn't want to do anything wrong, so I didn't hit play.

I listened more to what Doc and Sandra might be doing. If they were fucking, they were being fairly quiet about it. I fingered the fentanyl patches in my pocket. I wanted to ask

Doc how much longer we'd have to wait. I was starting to get nervous. We'd been there for twenty-five minutes and I had no idea if this guy ever had visitors and, if he did, when they might be coming by.

In any event, all this was Doc's call. I was just along for the ride. I went back into the bathroom, still feeling vaguely sick. Not dope sick anymore—the fentanyl and OxyContin had trickled some help into my blood and brain—but sick from the familiar nerves of being somewhere I didn't belong. The fear of being caught pressed on me like a vice. The fear of having to cut that guy open to get the morphine vial. But if I had to do it, I would.

I started running the bath. When the water first came out, it was rust brown, and then slowly started to clear. The fentanyl patches work better if you're warm. I put one on my right arm and one each on my right and left thigh. I took some deep breaths and made the temperature as hot as I could stand it and lowered myself in. Then I took two more eighty-milligram OxyContin.

Twenty minutes later I was nodding off. It felt so good, a warm waking dream, that I was worried I might be close to overdosing. I felt this incredible warmth inside me—it was like my heart was a glowing road flare and my bones were hollowed-out bird bones. Balsa wood. I could have weighed ten pounds, the way I felt. Behind closed eyes I had firework displays blasting in slow motion. My head rolled from one side to the other and it didn't seem connected by anything thicker than dental floss.

I heard the voices out in the living room. Yelling. A man's voice I didn't recognize.

"I said, who the fuck is this?" he screamed.

I heard Sandra's voice. "He's a doctor I'm consulting, Rick."

And I thought, *Rick? Who the hell is Rick?*

Rick yelled, "Consulting? Is that what the fuck you were doing? Consulting?"

She started to talk again, but the man named Rick said, "Get the fuck downstairs—do you understand?"

I stood on legs that could barely hold me up and banged into the towel rack and knew instantly the noise was too loud—Rick had to hear it even over his yelling. My bag was in there with me, along with twenty-seven patches and the bottle of OxyContin I'd taken and my clothes. I had a few lollipops. I thought about Doc, but didn't figure I could help him any. It was one of those situations where my presence could only add to the trouble.

Behind that door. Rick. Doc. Sandra. The dying man, helpless to do anything about the anger that swirled around him.

And what would adding me do to the situation? It couldn't make it better.

I got dressed as quietly and as quickly as I could, without drying off. My clothes stuck to me and I held my arm out to the wall to keep myself upright. I double-checked my bag and made sure I had all the drugs.

The guy kicked the door in as I was trying to reach for it.

"And who the fuck is this wet fucking junkie?"

I closed my eyes for a moment.

"Back in the fucking room, junkie." Rick had a gun.

The three fentanyl patches clung wetly to me and itched under my clothing. I looked at the side exit and noticed the doorjamb was all but destroyed by termites; it didn't look like anybody had used the door in a while and it didn't look like I'd be using it now, either.

I came back into the living room. Rick had Doc and Sandra in front of the TV and told me to stand with them.

"Dude, you took a bath?" Doc said.

I nodded, not wanting or feeling much need to explain.

Rick pointed with his gun hand at Doc. "So, you're a doctor?"

Doc nodded.

Rick said, "So am I. And THIS," he said, waving the gun around, "is *my* hospice connection." He looked hard at Sandra. "Or did someone forget that?"

"I'm sorry, Rick."

"Shut the fuck up!" he yelled.

He wasn't on dope—he paced and chewed his lips and had picker scabs. All speed and meth shit. I can't take speed freaks—they pounce on everything, darty and unpredictable as bats at sunset.

He walked back and forth. "Yeah, I've done fucking seventy-two-hour fucking shifts sewing up idiots like you, you careless fucks. Fucking zombies. You BUY this shit from me, you don't take it, is that understood? You better believe that's mother-fucking understood."

He rambled on for a bit, not even looking at us, just screaming, while the oxygen tank and the machines did their job.

"You want to know something about our fucking insides?" Rick said. "My first day in ER they tell me to sew this guy up. They needed to get at the liver and you know what they fucking do to get at a liver? They take the fucking twenty-five feet of your guts and they put them in a silver tray next to you. Upper, lower intestine, all out and throbbing in a bowl, still connected to you but outside your fucking wrecked body, while the doctors fix you idiots. And then they tell me to put it back together and you know how we do that? We just moth-erfucking DUMP the guts back in, all thirty, forty feet of guts, any old place, and sew the fucker up. It takes about five days, and they're all back to where they're supposed to be."

I was still kind of nodding, having real trouble seeing where the guy was headed with all this. He was reading in my brain like those poetry magnets that kids put together on fridges. Words not adding up to anything. He seemed careless and floppy with the gun and I thought about my dad, a state trooper who had killed at least one man, who I saw kill my dog when he was mad at me when I was a child. Shot my dog in the head and made me bury it as punishment. I thought of that man whose toxic blood ran through my veins and I tried to remember if you rushed guns or knives, and I figured it had to be guns because you'd run away from a knife, for sure.

Rick was in front of the dying man's bed, now pointing the gun back and forth at all three of us like carny ducks he was getting a bead on. "And you motherfuckers want me to put you back together after you rip me off?"

I still had no idea what he was getting at, but I figured, I'll try to get this gun and if he kills me, that's cool. Maybe this is where I die. Everything slowed down. My blood felt like roof-ing tar. All I saw was that gun and the hands that held it and everything else went away. I figured if I was going to let this fucker shoot me, well, so what? I just didn't care.

That's when I jumped into his chest, head down. I slammed him over the side bar of the dying man's bed and started punching his sides. I know I hit Rick, but I also hit the bed rails, and I hit IV tubes, and I punched the dying man's chest, and one landed hideously on his ventilator tube. Rick clawed at my back. I felt that he had both hands on my back, which meant he didn't have the gun. I smelled piss from the catheter bag spilling to the hardwood floor, and a moment later Rick and I were sloshing in it, the dying man's bed rolling off sideways like a drifting luxury liner, me still punching at Rick's guts, because that's where you hurt a man. Idiots punch heads. I'm not tough, but I know that much. I kneed him in the balls repeatedly until he was making sounds like a little kid and spit bubbled slowly from his mouth. I did it hard enough for my knee and thigh to start hurting.

By the time Doc pulled me off of him, I think I was ready to kill the guy. I never saw that coming. I was willing to let him kill me, but I hadn't anticipated the savage rush I was still feeling. I was briefly sickened by the notion that my father, in all his animal brutality, would have been, for once, proud of me. I felt like puking in a corner.

Doc held the gun and Sandra busily tried to reattach the tubes and wires I had ripped out of her patient, whose machines, I now noticed, were all going faster and louder than before. I didn't know if the guy was worse off, or if I was just in some adrenaline-fueled space where noises were louder. Rick was at my feet clutching his balls in a puddle of the dying man's piss. I was drenched from the piss, from the tub, and from sweat, which flowed out of me like my pores had tripled in size.

Doc said, "Sandra, we're going to take what we came for."

She nodded. "What about Rick?"

"We could call the cops after we leave," I suggested.

Sandra shook her head. "If he talks, cops are going to start asking me questions." She paused. "And then they'll talk to you."

We should kill him, I thought. This is not a thread to leave loose. My father would have killed him.

I said, "Maybe you don't know us as well as you really do. When Rick wakes up, you tell him we're strangers."

Doc turned to me. "He'll come looking for us."

I said what I was thinking: "It's that or we kill him. And the biggest idiot cop on the planet would connect the dots to us in one interview with her." This was when it occurred to me that if we killed Rick, we'd have to kill Sandra. But that would still leave way too much connective tissue from us to this scene. And I couldn't believe I was even thinking about it. I at least had enough sense to pull back. Rick rolled around semiconscious on the floor. Doc kicked him in the thigh. Then again.

"Fucker." Doc shook his head. "Let's get the fuck out of here."

I got my bag. Doc put the gun in his pants and started to collect more of the patches and pills from Sandra, who I'm guessing already had the money, or else she was too scared to ask about it.

Regardless, I went out the side door I'd noticed earlier. Doc followed me. I walked by the recycling and garbage cans and out the side yard gate. The driveway had a newer Lincoln next to Doc's car. Rick's car, I logged, in case I ever saw it again. I stopped, glanced left, away from the dead end and toward 17th Street, my hair still wet and the sun warming me as I peered down the street and then walked toward Doc's car, trying hard to look like what I was. A man stepping into the passenger side of a car on a beautiful day.

We got in. Doc took a deep breath and then another and had both hands on the wheel without starting the car. He lit a cigarette and said, "Dude, you were a fucking hero in there."

I didn't look in his eyes. Lawn sprinklers whirled on at the neighbor's house. He fired the ignition and we pulled out of the driveway, away from the Lincoln I hoped to never seen again in my life.

Doc said it again. "Dude, you are fucking heroic."

And this time, just to shut him up, just so I'd never have to hear it again, I said, "Yeah."

A GOOD DAY'S WORK

BY NATHAN WALPOW

Seal Beach

Rae was Hank's daughter. She had it and she flaunted it, and though some of it was starting to sag, when you're on the downside of your sixties and living in Leisure World, you can let stuff like that pass.

So when Hank suggested walking to the pier, and that Rae—who'd been staying with him for a month or so—would pick us up and have lunch with us and drive us back, I couldn't say no. Sheila was still my world, but a guy can have fantasies. So I told Hank yes and we met at the giant metal globe out by the guard gate and crossed to the other side of Seal Beach Boulevard, by the Naval Weapons Station. We figured they were up to something diabolical over there, like in that movie *The Mist* that Hank got on Netflix, where the military types open a rift to another dimension and giant insects show up and eat everyone. We thought it would be fun watching three-foot dragonflies chasing down the ladies from the quilting club.

Someone coming the other way might've thought we were brothers. It was more than just the old-white-haired-man thing. Our faces were the same shape and our eyes the same watery blue and our mustaches were like caterpillars from the same batch. Every once in a while we'd catch someone looking. I'd never had a brother, and it was kind of fun having at least a pretend one.

Maybe a quarter mile along some moron had taped a campaign sign to the fence that kept the riffraff out of the naval base and the overgrown cockroaches in. The senatorial election propaganda had started showing up lately, on bumpers and stuck in lawns and stapled to light poles. I planned on voting for Roger Elliot. He wasn't much of anything, but his heart seemed in the right place.

The other guy, Tim Swift, was a right-wing maniac better suited for a turn-of-the-century hanging judgeship than the U.S. Senate. Which was how he'd gotten elected to Congress for eleven terms in Orange County. But I guessed it wasn't enough for him, because since he'd gotten himself nominated for senator, he'd ramped up the Neanderthal stuff. Truth be told, the guy scared me, especially after that reporter got roughed up. Swift was playing for keeps.

The sign taped to the fence was his. *A Real American*, it said, like Roger Elliot was only playing one on TV. I muttered, "Goddamn politicians."

Hank looked at the sign. Something started to come over his face, but he got hold of it before I could figure out what it was. I said, "What?" and he said it was nothing and that we should pick up the pace.

Things were a little off the rest of the way down the boulevard and onto Electric Avenue, like I'd stepped over some line I didn't know about. But just before we hit Main Street he looked at me and said, "Sorry I got weird. Some shit I'm dealing with."

I almost asked if it was about what had happened back in '92. Which he didn't know I knew about. Instead I said, "Want to talk about it?"

"Nah. No big deal. Getting-old shit. If it ain't one thing it's another."

"You can say that again."

We turned the corner. More foot traffic there on Main. Lots of kids out of school for the summer, yelling and screaming and running around like wild Indians. Lots of young ladies with skimpy outfits. We dodged the kids and took in the view. Just a couple of old coots out for a walk.

After a while we passed the Jack Haley Community Safety Building and stepped onto the pier. My back was hurting a little and my legs a lot, but I didn't mind. It seemed right. Pain I'd earned, as opposed to the gallbladder I was missing through no fault of my own.

About a third of the way to the end we were suddenly surrounded by kids. Dozens of them, ranging from maybe eight to twelve, boys and girls, all wearing blue bathing suits. All shapes, all sizes, though a few of the girls were starting to develop and looked sort of out of place. There were a couple of adults mixed in, hollering instructions. The whole kit and caboodle swept by us and moved on down the pier. Then they stopped, gathering round one of the adults, listening in varying degrees to what he had to say, and we caught up.

One of the boys caught my eye. He was bigger than the rest. Taller than most, and fat. He had a big stomach and creases in his sides where the top half of his flab met the bottom. He was gingerly walking barefoot along the planks where all the other kids were scampering carefree. He had a little friend, a skinny kid, urging him along. "You're gonna have to," the friend said, and the chubby one shook his head. Poor kid. His parents signed him up for swim camp when he wanted nothing else than to sit in his room eating Fiddle Faddle.

We moved on to where most of the fisherman were stationed. Then there were splashes behind us. The kids, bless their hearts, were climbing over the rail and jumping into the water. "Feet together, arms at your sides!" one of the adults yelled. They continued leaping, at least fifteen feet down into the depths, boys and girls, in ones and in twos, some slicing right in and some splashing. They'd pop up and shriek and bob in the water, and they'd look up for their buddies and urge them in.

Over on the other side of the pier, the fat kid's friend was pulling on his arm.

"Hey!" It was Hank.

I turned back to him. "Yeah?"

"Come on. Let's grab some coffee."

There was a Ruby's at the end of the pier. Assembly-line Americana. We went in and came out a couple of minutes later with our coffees. Passed the fishermen again. Got to where the kids had gathered. Most had jumped, and were paddling in toward the shore. The stragglers were making a big show of leaping in, acting like they were about to and pulling back at the last minute.

The fat kid was still there too. He'd been deserted by his little friend. One of the adults, a guy in his twenties, was eyeing him, like he knew he had to deal with him but was hoping he'd disappear first. Then he sighed and meandered over. "Chuck!"

The kid looked around, like maybe there was another Chuck to take the heat. No luck. He turned to the grown-up. "I don't want to."

"We went through this yesterday. You have to. Look, it's easy. All those little kids did it. All those *girls* did it. You're not going to let them show you up, are you?"

"Nope."

"Then get your big old butt over there and jump on in."

Chuck took a step. Then another. Two more, and he was

even with the counselor or lifeguard or whatever he was. He stopped and said, "Do I *hafta?*"

"Yes, you—"

"No, you don't," I said, inserting myself between Chuck and the grownup, whose name, according to his badge, was *BILL JAMISON*.

"I'll handle this, sir," he said.

"You've been handling it, and you're doing a miserable job of it."

"Sir, please. We're trained in—"

"Shaming kids into jumping way down into the ocean by saying the girls do it? That doesn't sound like very good training to me."

Chuck detected a possible reprieve. He shuffled sideways toward the shore.

"Chuck Pemberton, you stay put," Bill Jamison ordered. To me, "Look, they know they have to do this when they sign up. It's no big deal, really. All the kids do it." A sick little giggle. "I haven't lost one yet."

"That supposed to be funny?"

"Shit," Hank said. "I'm gonna call Rae. Get our asses out of here before you get us arrested."

Bill Jamison had his hand on the whistle around his neck like he was going to call time-out. "Sir," he said, "these children are none of your business. And I don't think it's right for you to be hanging around like this."

"Hanging around? *Hanging around?* Are you playing the child molester card?"

"Well, I—Shit."

Mission accomplished. Chuck was in full flight toward shore, his chunky frame bouncing along like a cartoon character. Bill Jamison tossed me a truly fine dirty look and took chase.

I turned to Hank. "And that is a good day's work. Call Rae."

We'd lived in Seal Beach before, around 1980, when Sheila's job at the bank took her to Orange County. We moved to Laguna when things got good, and then to Garden Grove when they got not so good. But she always talked about moving back to Seal Beach. Which was a fine ambition. Nice little beach town, clean air, tucked into the armpit—and I mean that in a good way—of Orange County.

First time we lived there, I was friends with Ralph O'Brien. Who got mixed up with a girl half his age. I saved him from his wife finding out, and he owed me one. After we moved I'd still see him a few times a year, and when we came back it was a lot more than that. He'd gotten himself elected to the city council, which meant I learned a lot more than I needed to about Seal Beach politics. He was also still married to the wife, so I figured he was right about still owing me one.

I called him and said it was time I collected. He said, "Anything," and I told him what I wanted. He said I was out of my fucking mind. Then he said if anyone ever found out where I'd gotten the address he'd cut my balls off. And that he'd call back within the hour. Ralph knew about Jody. Knew that was what was driving me.

He called back as promised and half an hour later I was at a house on Balboa Drive. It had signs for Roger Elliot all over the place. Stuck in the lawn, in the front window, stapled to the mailbox post.

I rang the bell and a man answered. He had what we used to call an Ivy League look, hair cut short, button-down shirt, khaki pants. He looked me over and said, "Yes?"

"You Chuck's father?"

"You from the swim camp?"

"Not exactly."

"Look, I already talked to him about it. He'll do as he's supposed to." Then he realized I was a little old to be from the swim camp and his eyes narrowed. "Who are you?"

"I'm the guy who let your kid get away with not doing as he was supposed to."

"What—"

"Look, Mr. Pemberton, you don't know me from Adam, and I'm fine to keep it that way. But I've got something to say, and I'm going to say it, and if you care about your kid you'll listen. Don't make him do things he's scared to."

"You'd better get out of here before I call the police."

"I'll be gone before they get here. Now listen. The kid doesn't want to do something dangerous, something scary, don't make him."

Some maniac was on his stoop, with no one else around. "Sure, sure," he said. "Whatever you say."

"You don't sound like you mean it."

"Who *are* you?"

"A concerned neighbor. Remember. No scary stuff if he doesn't want to. No man stuff if he doesn't want to."

I did a one-eighty and went down the walk and I heard the door close behind me. I was guessing he was still just inside it. Thinking about what I'd said. That was all I could ask for.

Jody was eleven when he went to sleepaway camp. He didn't want to go. He said the woods and the animals scared him. But I thought it was time he learned to deal with his fears. Sheila wanted to let him stay home. I compromised. Said if he felt the same way after three days, I'd let him come home. It only took two for the bee to find him. We didn't know he was allergic to bee stings.

Thirty years on, I'd never really gotten over it. Sheila'd done better, far as I could tell, and she kept me together for all those years I acted like a prick. Supported me when I couldn't keep a job.

Eventually we bought the apartment in Mutual 14—they call it a co-op, but an apartment's all it is—and there we were, sixty-six apiece and in a retirement community, and I finally started to let it go. Being there with all those old folks, with my own mortality looming, I'd been able to put things into a little perspective. The thing with Chuck's father was my first episode since we'd been there.

When I got home Sheila knew something had happened. She asked if I wanted her to stay home from her painting club. Leisure World had a wagonload of clubs. Dance clubs, hobby clubs, nationality clubs, religion clubs, about six dozen fucking clubs.

I put on a happy face and said I'd be fine. She didn't believe me, but she knew not to push. So she went to her club.

But I wasn't fine. I was eating myself up from inside. Making myself sick. I went outside for some air. Before I knew it I'd wandered down the road to Hank's.

He let me in and went for a couple of beers and when we were all arranged in the living room he said, "Something eating you?"

Before I knew it I'd told him the whole Jody story. When I was done, I guess he felt obligated to reveal something to me. He said, "I've got something to tell you too."

"I know," I replied.

"Know what?"

"What you're about to tell me."

"Since when?"

"First time I met you."

"How?"

"Because when you were in the news everyone told me I looked like you. So I had your face in my head. When I saw you—"

"No one here knows."

"At Leisure World."

He nodded. "Except Rae, of course."

"No reason that should change. Hell, I doubt more than a few even heard of you. The timing. How'd you manage that?"

"Pure dumb luck, I guess."

The timeline of Terry Bouton's—that was Hank's real name—arrest and trial for killing Allison Lopez Bouton, his second wife, pretty much paralleled that of the cops who beat the shit out of Rodney King. The case against him was sloppy, and he got off. It would have caused a lot more of an uproar were it not for the timing. His verdict came in an hour after the cops', and there was no room on the news for Hank, not with L.A. in flames.

Life and death were on my mind. "Did you do it?"

He leaned back, leaned forward. Took a long pull on his beer.

"Stupid question," I said. "Forget I asked."

"It was an accident," he said.

"Look, let's just let the last minute or so—"

"I found her with another guy."

"Hank—"

"But when I busted in . . . he was . . . hell, my wife, for Christ's sake. I just . . ."

"Look, I—"

"I nearly shot him too."

"How come you didn't?"

"Because the bastard jumped up and said neither one of us wanted people to find out what happened there that night. He said he knew a lot of lawyers. He said if I didn't bring him into it he'd be sure I got off."

"And you believed him?"

"Didn't have anything to lose. I got a fair trial, they'd've fried me."

Sounds at the door interrupted. It was Rae. She came in, put down her purse, looked at the two of us.

"He knows," Hank said.

"I thought he might," she replied. "What's he going to do about it?"

"Ask him."

"What are you going to do about it?"

"Nothing." To Hank, "Nothing's different." I stood up. "Thanks for the beer."

I went home and waited for Sheila to arrive and make everything better.

I didn't see Hank the next day, or the one after. The one after that, not until 10 at night. There was a bang at the door. I figured it was him. Most people at Leisure World knock politely if they have the gumption to show up unannounced that late.

I pulled the door open and he rushed past me, with Rae in his wake. They waited until I closed the door, then Hank gestured toward the bedroom.

"Out," I said. "At a play. With the theater club."

"He tried to kill me."

"Who did?"

"The guy we were talking about the other day. Had someone try and run me over. In the parking lot at Spaghettini's."

I turned to Rae. "That how you see it?"

"Asshole came out of nowhere and nearly clipped him."

"What kind of car?"

"It was dark. How do I know?"

"It was a big old Lincoln," Hank said.

"Deliberate?" I asked.

"Could've been," Rae said. "Could've not."

Back to Hank. "Were you loaded?"

"I had a couple of drinks."

"Four," Rae said. "You had four."

"Probably nothing," I said. "A drunk driver. There's a million of 'em out there."

"What if he sends someone else?" Hank said.

"He's not going to send someone else. I don't think he sent anyone in the first place. Just lock your doors. I'm sure everything'll be fine."

"You don't understand."

"What don't I understand?"

"It's Tim Swift."

"What is?"

"The guy, for Christ's sake. The one who was with Allison. He's running for Senate now. You've seen what a whackjob he's turned into."

I remembered watching Channel 6. What that reporter looked like after the little "misunderstanding" at the Swift news conference. "Can't argue with that."

"He can't afford to have me floating around. I'm a loose end."

Key in the lock. "That's Sheila," I said. "She doesn't need to know about this."

The door opened. In came Sheila. She took in the three of us. "What's happening?"

"Hank's got a gas leak. He came to borrow a wrench."

She didn't believe me and knew she wasn't supposed to. "Did you leave all the windows open to let the gas out?"

"No," Rae said. "Come on, Dad. We should get back there and make sure the windows are open, before we blow ourselves all to hell." She grabbed his arm and hustled him out of there. The door shut and I locked it and turned around.

"He forgot his wrench," Sheila said.

"Damn."

"You want to tell me about it?"

"Not sure. Let me sleep on it."

I woke at first light, with a sick feeling in my gut. Like I'd had too much caffeine without any food to absorb it.

Something was missing.

It took me a minute. The crows. That time of morning, they ought to be cawing their damn heads off. But they weren't, and none of the other birds were on duty either.

I slid out of bed, pulled on some clothes, slipped out the door. It was only a few steps before I rounded the curve and saw Hank's place. There were three cop cars. Two LW security vehicles. Paramedics. A couple of neighbors standing around gawking. Across the street, someone's visiting grandbaby was squalling its fool head off. The kind of thing living at Leisure World was supposed to eliminate.

Rae was talking to a couple of cops. She spotted me and ran over. "They—"

"What's going on?" I said, real loud. "What's the matter?" I put my arms around her, whispered, "Act dumb." She stared up at me. "You don't know anything. Got it?"

Nothing.

"Rae. I need you to focus. You don't know anything. It's important. One of the cops is coming over. I need you to get it."

She straightened her spine. "I got it."

The cop came near. He was young and he had a mustache and he thought he was hot shit. I asked, "What happened, officer? Is Hank all right?"

"Who are you?"

"A friend."

"Well, friend, why don't you just step over there and wait. We'll get to you soon enough."

"Certainly, officer." I put my hands on Rae's upper arms. Squeezed. "You going to be all right?"

A tiny nod. "Uh-huh."

"Okay, good. You need anything, you know you can count on Sheila and me."

"Sir . . ."

"Right. Over with the others." I stepped away and began to concoct some useless information to share with the police.

Someone had managed to get past the guard gate and jimmied Hank's lock and shot him twice. He'd evidently used a silencer, because Rae, sound asleep in her room, didn't find him until some time later.

It wasn't going to be long before the police figured out who Hank was. I figured I had a couple of hours head start.

Rae showed up a little after 9. "Last cop just left."

"Good."

"We have to get the son of a bitch."

"And we will."

Sheila poured her coffee and we sat at the little table in

the kitchen. When Sheila's back was turned Rae gave me a look. "She knows everything," I said.

"I'm very sorry," Sheila said.

"Thank you," Rae said.

"And now I'm going to leave you two to . . . to do whatever you're going to do."

Once she was out the door Rae said, "First, you need to know this. Allison. She stole him from my mom. So I hated her. She deserved what she got. But Dad didn't kill her. She was dead when he got there."

"Swift killed her?"

"Yes."

"Why?"

"Dad never knew. But Swift had been drinking. Maybe it was an accident. Or maybe she was going to declare her love to the whole world, and Swift couldn't have that."

"Then why did Hank stand trial?"

She took a deep breath. Looked away. "Blackmail."

I thought about it. Took a few seconds before things fell into place. "He was willing to shut up for a big chunk of cash. But without a presumed murderer, the cops would've dug deeper. They would have found out it was Swift."

She turned back to me. "Swift says to him, yeah, I'll give you the money, but you have to let the cops think you did it. Then I'll make sure you get off. Which I guess he could do. He had people in his pocket. And while the heat was on Dad, he covered his tracks."

"Swift could have double-crossed him. Let him stand trial, not interfere, and get him convicted."

"If he had, Dad would've told the real story."

"Who'd have believed him?"

"He had a picture."

"He just happened to have a camera with him?"

"He was done with her. He was going to divorce her and get back with my mom. He was going to take a picture of them together, and then he was going to use it to get a divorce, and if she complained he was going to let everyone see Swift fucking around. Which Allison didn't want, because she'd gone and fallen in love with the asshole."

"But he didn't get back with your mother."

"It didn't work out."

She slumped in her seat and stared at me with eyes half open. "You don't seem surprised."

"About your dad blackmailing that shit Swift? I'm not. Not really."

"How come?"

"You're not going to like it."

"Tell me."

I stood up. Went and leaned on the kitchen counter. "I thought he'd done it. Gotten away with murder. Up until you told me different a couple of minutes ago. So if I was ready to think him a murderer, then what's a little blackmail?"

"You thought he did it, but you palled around with him anyway?"

What was I supposed to say? That I still figured I'd killed my son, and I felt some kind of weird kinship with someone who'd killed his wife? She didn't need to hear that. "I liked him. I got past his past."

Did she believe me? Maybe she did. It didn't really matter.

"So now what do we do?" she asked.

"What happened to the picture?"

"He sent it to Swift after he got off and got the money. The negative too."

"How honorable."

"That's the kind of guy Dad was."

"That's the kind of guy I am too. But . . ."

"But what?"

"But self-preservation. If you're dealing with straight shooters, you shoot straight. If you're dealing with scum . . ."

"You think he kept a copy?"

"I would have."

"Then let's go look."

There was nothing in the bedrooms. Nothing in the living room. We moved into the kitchen. "There a junk drawer?" I asked.

She pointed. "Top one on the right."

It looked promising. All sorts of crap. Take-out menus, pieces of string, toaster instructions. Little bits of plastic that had broken off things. Random tools, including a utility knife. Which I discovered when the blade sliced my pinkie open. I jerked my hand out and wailed and bled all over the counter.

Rae hauled me into the bathroom. She put pressure on and washed the finger and poured hydrogen peroxide over it. After a few minutes the flow turned to an ooze. She went into the medicine cabinet for bandages.

"Just like mine," I said. "Pills for everything."

She bandaged me up. Stared at my hand. Then at the medicine cabinet. Tried to retreat from the reality in which her father had been murdered. "I guess we won't be needing these anymore," she said, grabbing a bunch of the prescription bottles and tossing them at the wastebasket. But she took too many. One fell to the floor. Another into the sink. As she bent for the one on the floor my eyes went to the one in the sink. Which didn't have pills in it.

I grabbed it and struggled with the childproof cap until

Rae saw what was up and snatched it from my hand. She flipped it open and poured the contents into my palm.

A key. A safe-deposit key.

"Where did he do his banking?" I said.

We tore open a box of canceled checks and I practiced his signature. My cut finger made it harder. But I didn't think it had to be really close. Who's going to expect one geezer was trying to get into another's box? Especially when the first geezer looks a lot like the photo on the second's driver's license? Which we grabbed before we headed for the bank.

I was right about the lack of scrutiny. The kid manning the safe-deposit station barely looked at the license or the signature. Two minutes later I was sitting in a little room, alone with the box.

I pulled out some thin gloves I'd found under the kitchen sink. Sooner or later they'd figure out someone had gotten into Hank's box a couple of hours after he left the planet. I didn't want them to know it was me. Good thing I watched *CSI*.

The photo was in an envelope under everything else. A much younger Tim Swift standing next to a bed on which a body lay. You could see the face.

Perfect.

I had Rae make the delivery. The man at its destination would remember me, and I'd be in Seal Beach for a while. Sooner or later he'd run into me, and questions might be asked. I didn't need them. But he hadn't seen Rae before. And I was certain she'd be leaving town soon.

But I watched from across the street. When she knocked on the door, Chuck answered. He had a package of CornNuts in his hand.

She asked him something and he shook his head. So she said something else and handed him the envelope with the photo. She spoke again. He nodded. She left.

When she was back in the car she said, "Daddy'll be home in a bit."

"Then our work is done."

I'm guessing some of the Elliot people wanted to let it out immediately. Cooler heads prevailed, and it broke just in time for the evening news cycle. By 8 that night Tim Swift was in custody.

He was out the next morning. His campaign spokesman got on TV and whined about photo manipulation and smear campaigns. The local news people and the cable networks went bananas. Implication and innuendo filled the air. A former staffer came forward and said she'd had an affair with Swift six years back. The TV people all went hysterical.

By late that evening the Swift for Senate campaign had been suspended.

There was no service for Hank. We never saw Rae again, at least not in the flesh. I did spot her a few weeks later on TV, the day Tim Swift gave up his House seat. A reporter asked her how she felt about it and Rae gave him a look that would curdle milk.

Two months later we sold the place at Leisure World. Rented an apartment a lot closer to the water. The sea air is good for us, and so are the younger folks in the building. One couple has a boy of ten or eleven. In the right kind of light, at the right time of day, he reminds me of Jody. And that, I've been pleased to discover, makes me feel just fine.

PART II

EVERY MOVE YOU MAKE

CRAZY FOR YOU

BY BARBARA DeMARCO-BARRETT

Costa Mesa

When I moved into Levi's apartment in the converted motel on Placentia Avenue, the blue neon "i" of the *Placent_a Arms* sign was burned out. I worried it was an omen, a feng shui gaffe. It made me think too damn much of placenta, birthing, that whole entire mess—not a good thing when the sight of blood makes you faint. I've grown used to most things, and I figured I'd grow used to the sign, if I didn't leave Levi or go crazy first. But I hadn't grown used to it, and I was still here. It was going on three months and my feeling of foreboding had only increased.

The Arms, a chipping aqua U-shaped construction, was clean enough, but Levi's apartment above the fray on the second story, right-hand corner, was growing smaller and duller by the day. So was Westside Costa Mesa, once idyllic cattle grazing land, then an agricultural haven. Now, about the only things that grew wildly were the illegal immigrant population, low-income housing, and Latino gangs. So different from where I was from. If I spoke the language it might be different, or if I was brunette. But I was blond, the only gringa in our apartment complex.

I pulled a folding chair onto the balcony and lit a hand-rolled cigarette, the only tobacco I could afford these days. In the Arms' courtyard just below sat a square swimming pool that had seen better days. Sorry little children with loser parents—why else would they be living at the Placent_a Arms?—splashed in its murky depths. Even the mourning doves inhabiting the adjacent kumquat tree seemed weary of the pool, but then Southern California was mired in a ubiquitous drought and the pool must've been better than nothing, I suppose. Although you can make yourself believe pretty much anything if your life depends on it.

At night, after a drink or two, as you watched the lights beneath the water, all blue and tropical, it was easy to trick yourself into thinking you were at some lush Orange County resort and were one of the beautiful people. The reverie never lasted long, though, because one drunk resident or another would start singing off-key—Barry Manilow, Aerosmith, pop Latino—reminding you that you were *not* in posh Newport Beach, the next city over, or in Laguna Beach, just down the coast, but in lovely Costa Misery. My sister Leonora, a nurse, left home back east to work for a plastic surgeon—the perks included discounted *enhancements*—and I followed when I quit my teaching job, all because of Levi.

Levi was sixteen when we met, seventeen when we started spending time together—backstage, on the football field, in cars. I was Levi's drama teacher, thirty-three years old, but young-looking for my age. My friends called him jailbait, this sleek pretty boy with sea-foam green eyes and abs to die for. I lusted after the kid, but when my soon-to-be-ex husband caught us in my car in the parking lot outside Bob's Big Boy and threatened to have me fired, I decided I needed my job teaching more than I needed Levi, resigned, and moved here. I saw what happened to other teachers who crossed the line, who forgot they were teachers and not teenagers.

A year later, when Levi turned eighteen, he quit school and found me. He was of age, but still too young for me. I was still living with Leonora and her three dogs, substitute teach-ing in Costa Misery, along bus routes. The trip cross-country had killed my beater and I let my driver's license expire. The better school districts never seemed to have an opening and I didn't want a full-time gig at just any school. Levi had already rented the furnished apartment at the Arms and I planned on spending just a few days, thinking this would help to get him out of my system. But he guilt-tripped me into moving in, said he wouldn't even be out here if not for me.

"Mimi, the guy's a loser," Leonora said. "You can do bet-ter." But I was addicted to Levi's body, his skin that felt like silk, and tired of being one of Leonora's pack.

My stomach growled. I lit another cigarette and looked at my watch. Five o'clock. Levi would be home soon. I went inside to throw something together for dinner.

Levi worked as a handyman. Ten bucks an hour, some-times more. Not what he thought he was worth, but it paid the rent, bought the beer. He told me stories about the rich people's houses where he spent his days—brushing the walls of a nursery with designer paint or retiling a hot tub. He de-scribed how, at one home, the outdoor pool connected with the interior of the house through a manmade cave with faux boulders you had to swim through. So Orange County.

Another client owned two houses side by side—one of them they lived in and the other one was the kids' playhouse. *Playhouse!* Homeless people lined up at church soup kitchens and lived in parks and alleys around the town. Life was indeed unfair. And I was a little envious. Some people in Orange County had too much, while others had so damn little.

On the west side, everyone—the Latinos, the working-class heroes, even the dogs—was, for the most part, lackluster. There were artists who added color, I suppose, but every day

I read the police files in the *Daily Pilot,* and so much of the crime in coastal Orange County happened right around where I lived. Here were the factories, auto shops, taquerías, and lavanderias, and so many of us were scraping by, but on the east side that bordered Newport Beach, that's where the real money was, that's where the Orange County life that I had imagined and fantasized about resided. I'd been to Disneyland but never got why they called it the Happiest Place on Earth, not with all those screaming children and tourists with blue-white legs and lunky cameras strangling their necks. But a house on the east side, now that would make for a happy day, every day.

Levi came home from installing shelves in what he said looked like the kitchen of a TV cooking show: marble—not granite—countertops, Viking stovetop, a fridge the size of our bathroom. He rambled on about how the homeowner didn't even have a wife. I was standing at the stove, stirring Arborio rice, adding vegetable broth every few minutes, to make risotto. What you pay for at a restaurant when you order risotto is not the ingredients, but the time it takes for some sadly underpaid restaurant worker to make the rice swell all plumplike. Biscuits, which I had flattened with my marble pastry roller—my most prized kitchen implement—and baked in the dollhouse-sized oven with a stovetop that only had three working burners, were cooling on the rack.

Levi could see I was down, so he kissed my cheek hard and wrapped his arms around me from behind. After a day among kids who treat substitute teachers like dog doo, Levi's touch was heaven. He snaked his hand beneath my skirt and found my sweet spot. I wanted to shoo him away—you can't leave risotto for *one minute*—but once Levi got on a certain track, there was no stopping him.

Levi liked to give me pleasure, or maybe he knew this was

the main thing he had to offer, so he got on his knees and buried his face down *there* and I about went nuts, but kept stirring until I just couldn't take it anymore. I let the spoon clatter to the counter and dropped to the aqua and white linoleum. I pulled Levi down with me. It didn't take us long, which is another thing I liked about Levi—he wasn't one of those guys who needed to linger and stretch it out.

We finished, and I washed my hands before returning to my risotto, but it was too late. The pot of rice was one sticky clod. I dumped it into the sink. Levi cracked two beers and ordered a pizza. While we waited, we went out onto the balcony. We drank our beers and watched the pool where a lone pink inner tube floated.

"Get this, Mimi," he said. "The house I was at today, it also has a three-car garage. Three fucking cars! And there's just one dude who lives there, with his kids."

"Where's the wife?" I asked, taking a swig.

He shook his head. "Died from cancer or something—and not long ago. There's fucking art all over the place and expensive dishes are stacked in a monster cabinet the length of our living room wall. His brats have these little motorized cars they drive around the neighborhood. They live on this dead end—a *cul de sac*. Old money Costa Mesa, looks like. People have got serious funds over there. More than they need."

"Some people have all the luck."

"We deserve that kind of life," he said.

"Everyone thinks they do."

"But we *really* do. His fucking housecleaner knows more about his stuff and what he has than he does. He has so much crap he wouldn't miss a few things disappearing."

"I hate it when you sound stupid," I said. "You think you can just help yourself? Is that what you're saying?"

Levi shrugged, took a long pull off the bottle, and slipped out of his red leather cowboy boots, setting them inside our apartment doorway. He pulled off his T-shirt. He was still that sleek boy, a beauty. His curly brown hair was streaked blond and he had just the right amount of growth on his face. His teeth were white-white and his bare feet were perfect. He could be a model, that's how handsome he was. Feet and teeth, I always say, have got to be superior. His physique made me overlook the fact that he wasn't the brightest bulb in the room.

"Shepard needs a nanny for his kids, pretty much right away," Levi said. "Someone smart enough to tutor. He's running an ad but says he can't find the right person."

"I'm a teacher," I reminded him, "not a nanny."

"But you *could* be a nanny . . . for a time. Then we'd both be working there."

"You think he'd go for a fricken handyman and his older girlfriend both working for him? Please."

"Don't call me a handyman," he snapped.

"That's what you are, babe."

He looked hurt. "I aspire to more."

"Sure you do," I said. "I just don't like where you're headed with this." I stroked his chest and tickled his nipples, which always put him in a good mood.

"Shepard would like you, Mimi. I told him about you. He seems lonely. I mean, who wouldn't be, your wife up and dies and leaves you with little kids? But once he sees a pretty young thing like you, his day's suddenly gonna seem a lot brighter. Don't you want to brighten up a widower's day?"

"I'm not that young."

"You're the sexiest thing going," he said, running his fingers along my collarbone. "We could both be working there."

"And then?"

"Who knows? But you deserve better'n this," he said, his hands describing an arc about him, his voice going low. "You think all the rich fucks in this town work for what they have? A lot of them got old money. Inheritances. Bank accounts handed down. Or they have great gigs, businesses that haul ass. We weren't lucky that way. Shit, Shepard has an entire goddamn library! He's old, Mimi, but he has money."

"Levi, you're scaring me."

"Don't be scared, baby. How about I just introduce you to him?" He put his hands on my shoulders and looked down at me with his seawater eyes. "C'mon, Mimi. As long as you don't like him *that* way, and why would you?—he's not *me*—it could be fun."

"Ripping off your employer . . . fun, huh?"

He shrugged. "Like I said, it'd be better'n this."

We turned our attention back to the pool and that pink inner tube bobbing about when a pizza boy came whistling into the courtyard, looking like a waiter holding a tray with that flat box poised on his fingers.

"We'd need a plan," I said, as the pizza boy looked up, trilled the fingers of his other hand like we were in some Hollywood musical, and headed for the cement stairway.

"Mims, I'm all about planning," Levi replied, pulling a twenty from his pocket.

The stinking economy, even here in glorious Orange County, had pushed substitute teaching gigs further and further apart, so the next day, around lunchtime, I was sitting on the balcony smoking a hand-rolled and scanning the classifieds. A cherry pie cooled on the counter. I had to do something fast to rescue my financial situation. Levi's truck skidded in. He threw a veggie bologna sandwich together—white bread from Trader Joe's, Dijon mustard, and four slices of fake lunchmeat—and said he was taking me with him to Shepard's house, ten minutes away.

I climbed into his truck, a major gas hog, which you just about needed a ladder to get into. As we passed Latinas with long black braids that touched their waists who pushed strollers, and homeless guys wearing tattered backpacks, he said, "Um, by the way, Shepard thinks you're my older sister, so just play it cool."

"Excuse me?"

"I decided he wouldn't like the idea of you being my girlfriend."

"Sometimes you fucking make me wonder."

He nodded, keeping his eyes fixed on the road. "I just thought of it. Brilliant, huh?"

"Yeah, right. Incredible genius you got goin' in that head of yours."

But as we crossed over Newport Boulevard, leaving the not-so-good side of town for the lush, moneyed side where tall eucalyptus swayed in the faint ocean breeze, Costa Misery segued to Piece of Heaven, California, with its cute cottages, palm trees, rosebushes, magenta bougainvillea, and Jaguars, BMWs, and hybrids.

We pulled into his boss's driveway. A tall husky guy in khakis and a polo shirt, with short graying hair, futzed in the garage. He was a bit thick in the middle and wore conservative beige shoes.

"You owe me big time," I said, pushing open the door as Mr. Orange County Republican approached us.

"That a promise?" he responded, as I jumped from the cab.

The guy had probably been a hottie once and was hand-some in an almost-fifty way, but he was *so* not my type. He held out his hand. "You must be Levi's sister," he said, giving me a warm handshake. "He didn't tell me you were so pretty."

"He's been forgetting to take his ginkgo biloba," I countered, playing it off, but I was charmed. And it takes a lot to charm me.

Levi laughed as if I were the funniest older sister in the entire universe.

"You two get acquainted," said Levi. "The back fence is calling me."

Shepard gave him the thumbs-up sign and said, "Shall we go inside?" Shepard's eyes were friendly as he gestured me in and hit the electric garage door button. "The kids are at school, but I'll show you around so you can see where you'd be spending your days."

I forced a smile, tried to look interested.

"School's out tomorrow," he said. "I need someone who can be a nanny *and* a teacher. Only occasional sleepovers, when I'm out of town." He had a gap between his front teeth, which were white and even. I had a boyfriend once with a gap I loved to tongue.

"Your brother said you're a teacher."

Brother? Then I remembered.

"I was, back east," I said. "Taught drama and English. I've been substitute teaching since I moved here. Not a lot of work these days for teachers without seniority."

"That's too bad," he said, touching my shoulder to direct me into the living room. He must have noticed how my gaze fell on the baby grand because he said, "You play?"

"Used to."

"Like riding a bicycle, don't you think? You're welcome to
. . ." He nodded toward it.

"Ah, no, maybe another time." Being able to play piano
impressed people, but it didn't impress me. You could learn
anything if you wanted to.

"Your brother said you like to bake."

"I'm obsessed with making pies." When we have extra
money, I almost added.

"You're welcome to bake here, anytime. I can't remember
the last time a pie came out of that oven. Just give me a list;
I'll buy you what you need."

If it were possible to fall in love with a house, I was falling—
hard—especially for the kitchen. With that kitchen, I could
bake a million pies and never grow bored.

"Like something? Coffee? A soda?" he asked, sticking a
glass into the opening of the fridge's front panel. He pushed a
button. Ice dropped and chinked into the glass.

"Diet Coke?"

"Sure thing," he said, taking one from the fridge. He
moved toward the cabinet.

"No glass," I said, so he tore a paper towel from the roll
and wiped the top of the can clean before handing it to me.
No one had ever done that before, and I swear, he looked different after that. Charming.

We talked about my background and his needs, and an
hour later, when the kids were dropped off, he gave them big
bear hugs and introduced us. "Bella and Dante, this is Mimi.
She might be helping out. Want to show her your rooms?"
The kids appraised me like I was a new piece of furniture, and
then Bella took my hand.

"My room first," she said. Her little brother led the way,
running his Hot Wheels police car along the wall.

They showed me their rooms and I liked them. Levi stuck in his head and said he had to run off for a while, and when he returned at 5:00, he seemed hyper, strange, and rushed me to go.

As we pulled away from the curb and headed down the tree-lined street, Levi said: "He's not bad, right?"

"He was fine," I replied, almost adding, *He was more than fine*. "And you're lowdown." I had never felt so cold toward Levi. But he didn't seem to notice.

"He tell you what he does for a living? I think he's a developer or something."

"Something like that," I said.

"Major bucks."

"Construction's taking a dive."

"He tell you that? Don't believe it," he said, turning onto a street with houses behind high walls, pulling over and putting the truck in park. He scooched over to me, took me in his arms, and started kissing my neck. Melted me every time. Stupid guys who were cute made the best lovers. It was the truly smart ones you had to watch out for, who could fracture your heart with one skewered word.

"C'mon, baby, don't be mad. It's a way for us to get ahead."

"But his kids weren't brats. They were sweet."

He pulled a blanket from under the seat, covered us as he pushed me down with kisses, and said, "After this, we'll go eat. I'm starving."

We sat across from each other at Wahoo's Fish Tacos, a popular haunt on Placentia, down the street from where we lived. The exterior was covered with chipping teal paint. Surf stickers smattered the windows. The menu offered Mexican entrees that weren't gourmet, but were good enough, priced for artists and people on limited incomes, and for rich Orange Countians who wanted to feel they were getting away with something. As he talked about what we'd do with the money—a new truck for him, a kitchen for me—you'd think I was one hungry fish, the way I went for it. I must have been beyond bored. We'd go slow and easy, figure things out, and when we had all the pieces, we'd make our play, he said. But I had a bad feeling.

Levi started staying up late, figuring out where we'd escape to once we had a few of Shepard's more high-end belongings that Levi would give to a friend of a friend who would split the proceeds. I did a bit of research and learned that Shepard had paintings and antiques worth thousands. He had one Chagall lithograph, *The Artist with a Goat, #1026,* that was worth thirty grand. Even inane simple drawings of dolphins that lined the hallway by that overrated Laguna Beach artist, Wyland, sold for three grand apiece. Levi's idea was we'd leave Costa Misery for Mexico. No one can find you down there, he said.

A week into my new nannyhood, as Levi and I were wrapping it up for the day and I was saying goodbye to the children, Shepard said, "The kids are going to their aunt's. Why don't I take you out to dinner, my thanks for coming to our rescue."

Levi didn't miss a beat. "Go ahead, sis," he said. "It'd be fun for you."

Sis?

I scanned what I was wearing—jeans, a purple pullover, lowtop red Converse. "I'm not exactly dressed up."

"You'd look gorgeous in a flour sack," said Shepard.

Levi winked at me. I shrugged. "Okay, then."

Levi hurried off a little too quickly with a nonchalant wave.

"Let's have a taste before we go," said Shepard. "Pick anything you like from the wine cellar and I'll meet you out by the pool."

The cellar was a converted closet off the kitchen with a slate floor and thermostat that said fifty-three degrees. I chose a 1987 Tondonia because I liked the name. He carried our glasses to the back patio that overlooked the pool. This pool was a million times better than the one at the Arms.

"I could get used to this," I said, after we clinked glasses.

"I hope you do," he said, his voice all syrupy and warm, like the wine.

Soon Shepard and I were in his Jag cruising up Newport Boulevard to Habana, a Cuban restaurant in a funky open-air mall with an oil-drum waterfall and tattooed, pierced hipsters. Habana was dark, lit only with candles. You could barely see who was sitting next to you, but the waiter could see well enough to recognize Shepard and make a big deal, and it was different being with someone before whom people groveled.

Shepard ordered a bottle of Barolo red, which he explained was the king of wines. We toasted and he said to order whatever tickled my fancy. Those were his words. During dinner, a second bottle of wine arrived and for dessert we shared a Cuban flan. Our fingers brushed against one another.

"We're delighted you came to us, Mimi. The children like you very much."

"They're sweethearts," I said.

"Actually, to be honest, I'm the happiest." He stroked my arm and focused on it as if it were a great treasure. "You've got great skin."

"This light would make anyone look good," I said, feeling guilty over how much I enjoyed his attention. Then I thought, *What the hell. Levi got me into this*, and I gave in. Right then and there I felt myself loosen and open to Shepard. When his hand found mine, I let it. And when he brought my hand to his lips, I let him. We left the restaurant and returned to his Jag, his arm laced around my shoulder. He opened the passenger door and I slid onto the butter-soft leather seats that reclined at the touch of a button. He got in and buzzed down the windows. He turned to kiss me and I kissed him back, tongued that gap in his front teeth. The wine was talking; I've always been an easy drunk. His hand found its way under my pullover and then he was in my jeans. I pressed against his fingers and before long I shuddered. Who cared if he was a conservative and a bit too husky—he had the touch of an angel and I liked how sweet and considerate he was. He was different from anyone I'd ever been with. Maybe older guys with money could afford to be patient, considerate.

"What about you?" I asked into his neck, rubbing him down there.

"There's time for that," he said, gently removing my hand and kissing it.

When I got home, Levi wanted to know where we went and what we did. He wasn't so laid-back about it anymore. I didn't tell him everything, and I distracted him with sex. It always worked. I had to keep my O.C. Republican a secret for now.

But things had changed and Levi knew it. Now when we arrived at work in the morning, there was no mistaking the glimmer in Shepard's eyes. He'd hang around the house to have coffee with me before taking off. On occasion, when everyone was out of the house, we'd fool around.

"The dude fucking likes you," Levi said a week later, his eyes flashing. We were in his truck, at a stop light.

"What are you talking about?"

"He's been asking me all about you. He's in love with you."

"He can't be," I said, secretly wishing it were so.

"Hey, it could be good for us," he scowled.

"What do you mean?"

"Shit, what could be better for us than if he wanted to marry you?"

"Excuse me?"

"It wouldn't have to change things between us. No one's as great for you as I am. You'd never go for someone that old. And if you did, I'd kill you." He laughed, then added, "You'd just have to live with him for a time. It would help us pull off our plan."

"You're talking too crazy for me," I said, as we crossed over Newport Boulevard and Piece of Heaven turned back into Costa Misery, with its pawnshops, its dive bars. But that night, after Levi went back out to do who knows what—he wouldn't say—I stood on the balcony and smoked a hand-rolled. As the lit murky water below pulled my focus, the sounds of the compound drew close—TV, a neighbor singing off-key, kids screaming—and my own version of an old Animals song spun an endless loop in my brain: *I gotta get outa this place, if it's the last thing I ever do.*

The next day, after Shepard's sister picked up his kids for an overnight, he said, "Let me take you to the fair. You've been to the Orange County Fair, right?"

"Um, no," I answered. I'd left Bumfuck where "hooptedoo-dle" was a favorite expression, and I had no desire to return.

"Then you got to let me take you."

"Fairs are a Republican thing."

"Pshaw!" he said, tucking in his turquoise polo shirt with a tiny alligator over the left breast.

"Shouldn't you take your kids?"

"They've been, and I'll take them again before it ends. Tonight it will be just you and me. How about it?"

I said yes. I said yes to everything—to Levi and his schemes, now to Shepard.

I went to freshen up.

Levi called from another job while I was in the bathroom; Shepard had run out of work for him. I told him I had to work late. I'd been spending more and more time at Shepard's and less and less time at our sorry excuse for a home. It was getting to Levi. I knew because when he talked about Shepard, he no longer used his name.

"The motherfucker tell you anything interesting?" or "What's up with the motherfucker?" I found a bindle with white powder in Levi's things. His skin was becoming all mottled and he was losing weight. He denied using crank, said he had gotten it for a friend, but he was short-tempered and negative. Now I just wanted to escape with Shepard, go someplace where Levi couldn't find me.

Shepard and I walked hand in hand to his dusty blue Jag and moments later were gliding down Broadway to Newport and up to Del Mar, his hand on my knee, my hand on his thigh, to where the dark sky was lit up all red from the lights on the rides and the midway. The Ferris wheel spun lazily around, its colorful, happy life temporary—like mine, I feared. This happiness wouldn't last—it couldn't; it hadn't been a part of the plan for me to fall for an Orange County Republican. Levi would never let me have Shepard. I wanted to confess and tell him what Levi was planning, but I didn't know how I could put it where he wouldn't just fire me and tell me to be on my way.

We parked and walked toward the lights, toward the Tilt-a-Whirl and the rollercoaster with purple neon cutting the black sky, teenagers on all sides of us running amok, clutching cheap stuffed animals and stalks of cotton candy. Shepard bought us caramel apples, fried Twinkies, and roasted corn on the cob. We got wristbands and drank draft beer.

It was going on 11:00 and the fairgoers were pouring through the gates, probably to get a jump on the freeways. Shepard and I moved against the flow, heading toward the livestock area, past Hercules, the giant horse, llama stalls, and a corral where the pig races took place. He said he'd been coming here since he was a kid. Fair diehards moseyed about. My phone rang—Levi's ringtone—but I ignored it, and I feared it. Levi said he could always find me. Something about the GPS positioning on my phone and how he'd rigged it. Cell phones didn't make you freer—they made your whereabouts known, and I didn't like it one bit, this hold Levi had on me.

Couples lingered in the shadows. Shadows scared me. I worried Levi might be hiding in them. Lately everything got on his nerves and he suspected everyone. He'd screamed at the next-door neighbor to quit his fool singing. He'd even pierced the pink inner tube in the pool because he no longer liked seeing it floating there.

Shepard directed me to the metal bleachers around the cattle arena. He picked me up, set me on one so our faces were level, and kissed me. "You make me so happy," he said.

This tall bulky man had grown on me. He pulled a little robin's egg–blue box from his pocket and flipped it open. A diamond solitaire.

He took the ring from the box and slid it on my finger. "You will, won't you?" he said. "Marry me?"

* * *

Levi was leaning over the railing of the balcony, smoking with one of his lowlife loser buddies, when I arrived home at midnight. I'd taken off the ring and sequestered it at the bottom of my tampon holder.

The light from the water bounced off Levi and his buddy whose name I forgot. I gave them a half-hearted wave. Levi nodded and smiled his lizard-cold smile.

"Where've you been?" he asked, flicking his cigarette butt down into the pool as his buddy took off.

"Had to stay with the kids until Shepard got home." I took a cigarette from Levi's pack on the cement floor.

"Fuck you did," he said.

I gave him a long look. It was always better to say less than more.

"Where's the ring?" he said.

"What ring?"

"Mimi, this'll only work if you're straight with me about the motherfucker."

I went to go into the apartment, but he grabbed my arm. "I'm gonna tell him all about you, Mimi. You weren't supposed to fall in love with the asshole. You love *me*, remember?"

I wrenched my arm away and hurried inside. I poured a glass of water, trying to think.

Levi hurried in behind me. "Don't fucking walk away from me, Mimi."

"I'll do what I want."

"Fuck you will." He pulled me to him, pressed his mouth against mine, hiked his hand up my top. "C'mon, baby, what happened to us?"

I pulled free. "Leave me alone, you asshole."

"I own you," he said. "I came all the way out here to find you and claim you and now you're mine."

"Whatever drug you're doing, it's making you crazy."

"Crazy for you," he said, grabbing me with one hand and undoing his belt buckle with the other.

I'd never given into a man forcing me and I wasn't about to now. I tried pushing him away, but his grip on my arm only grew tighter.

"You always liked it with me before," he said. "Mr. O.C. motherfucker better'n me now, Mimi?" His face looked strained, a Halloween mask. "He won't want you when I tell him who you really are, when I tell him everything you planned. He'll take his ring back and then where will you be?"

"What I planned?"

He jammed his hand down my pants and hurt me and that's when something snapped. My prized marble roller sat on the counter behind me, where it always was. I felt for it with my free hand and almost had it, but it slipped away. My hand landed on Levi's hammer. I brought it around and cracked it against his skull as hard as I could. His sea-foam green eyes went wide, as if he were seeing me for the first time. Then he crumpled to the linoleum. A trickle of blood issued from his ear.

"Levi!" I gasped. "Shit!"

The way his eyes gazed into the living room without blinking gave him a peaceful look I had never seen.

I tried to think. Should I pack up my things, including my pastry roller, and split? I considered cleaning my fingerprints off everything in the apartment, but I wouldn't be able to get rid of every little hair, every little cell of mine that had flaked off. I knew about DNA. I could be easily tied to Levi, even without a car or California driver's license. Even without my name on the month-to-month lease or on bills; I still received my mail at Leonora's. To the mostly Latino transient residents, I must've looked like any other gringa. But I talked to Levi on my cell phone all the time. I could even be tied to him through Shepard. They would visit Levi's former employer and find me there, loving my new life.

No, I couldn't simply leave.

I pulled down the shades and locked the door. I wiped my fingerprints off the hammer after placing it near Levi. I turned on the shower as hot as I could stand, peeled off my clothes, and stepped in. This would calm me and help me think.

As the scalding water poured down my face, it came to me, what I would say and do: *I came home, Levi was here with a drug-dealing buddy, I took a shower and heard something. When I got out of the shower, I found my boyfriend on the floor.*

I turned off the water, wrapped myself in a towel, and jumped into my role. I hurried out to the kitchen, as if I'd heard something bad and found Levi hurt on the kitchen floor. I bent down to see what was wrong. Water puddled about me and mixed with Levi's blood. I ran screaming from the apartment onto the balcony. As I started down the steps, the towel slipped from my body, and I let it. I was a crazy naked lady. Residents—men in underwear and T-shirts and women in nightgowns—started emerging from their hovels.

"Call the police!" I made a good hysteric. Someone had done my poor boyfriend in.

Women called in Spanish to each other. More than once I heard the word "loco." A short dark woman with gold front teeth wrapped me in a Mexican blanket, patted my wet hair, and cooed to me in Spanish. The sirens grew closer. A crowd had gathered around us and upstairs at the doorway to the apartment.

There would be an investigation, but after a while I would be cleared. No one ever saw us fight. There was no insurance settlement coming. Why would I kill my boyfriend? The authorities would search instead for the lowlife who did him—or not. Probably not. Who cared about one more druggie dude going bye-bye? My first chance I would call Shepard, tell him details about what happened that he would have heard about on the news. I would tell him how Levi made me say I was his sister, had threatened my life even, had never wanted me to fall for him. I would remind Shepard that I loved him, every inch of him. Shepard believed in me, would never think I could do something like this.

I knew how to be patient. Shepard and Piece of Heaven, California, would eventually be mine, and before long, the ring would be back on my finger.

THE TOLL

BY DAN DULING

Laguna Beach

Robbie froze as he felt a cold, metallic object press into the back of his neck. He realized what it was. The barrel of a handgun. This night was not turning out the way he'd hoped.

It had been the longest six months of Robbie's life. Hiding out in a rented room in a crappy apartment building in the unincorporated part of East Orange County just off the 241 toll road, waiting for the heat to die down back in Laguna Beach, the town he'd grown up in, the town he could no longer afford to live in, the town he wanted to get back to as soon as possible. All he wanted was another chance.

When the call had come from Michele late that August afternoon, he was stoked. She wouldn't elaborate on the phone, but she had a job for him. That was all he needed to know.

It was a little after 3 o'clock the next afternoon when he hopped in his two-tone—rust and primer—road-weary Corolla and headed toward Laguna. He didn't like the sound the battered Toyota was making—bearing or ball joint?—as he pulled up alongside the 241 toll plaza and heaved a handful of coins at the bin. Car repairs were going to have to wait.

"Fuckin toll roads," he muttered as a BMW with a *FasTrak* transponder raced by him. He grimaced. *That's what this place is all about now. They make you pay to get where you're going and pay to come back. It's all about the cash.* He'd been around long enough to know the difference between the old money that seeded this area and the new, stupid money that was spoiling it for everybody.

Robbie had grown up in Laguna and graduated from Laguna Beach High back when their teams were still called the Artists, not the newly minted Breakers. After school, he'd been eager to get away from the domestic horror show at home, but he'd always assumed he'd stay local and figure out a way to coexist among the filthy rich and infamous who were determined to price him out of his hometown market. For somebody with no real sense of direction or ambition, Robbie quickly learned the score.

Influence, that's what it was all about. And most of the locals didn't really want to get their own hands dirty when it came to passing along "financial or psychological incentives" to make things work. Robbie was happy to do what he was told without leaving a trail. He thought of himself as smart enough to know better, pissed off enough to not give a shit, and savvy enough to get his assignments done without making the O.C. *Register's* back pages.

Bottom line, between 2002 and 2007, if Michele and Jeff had a case in Laguna they didn't want to go to trial, or a business dispute or vendetta that needed settling the old-fashioned way, Robbie had a hand in the "mediation." And there were plenty of opportunities: planning commissioners trying to play both sides, hotshot developers eager to flip properties before the next landslide, mayors caught with their hands in the till, lawsuit-happy execs with a taste for the strange, or city council members laboring under the notion that they were appointed to think for themselves.

This was no longer the sleepy little coastal hideaway that had bored him to tears—not to mention various pharmaceutical diversions—during his teen years. No, now even a teardown shack a mile from the beach would run you a minimum of a million bucks. Face it, the only thing tennis pro Lindsay Davenport, the dude who played Freddy Krueger in the *Nightmare on Elm Street* movies, and the guy who made those *Girls Gone Wild* videos had in common was they all made the kind of "fuck you" money it now took to call Laguna Beach home.

Robbie had to laugh as he cruised past that BMW pulled over to the side of the 241 by a state trooper. Tickets on a toll road! He leaned back and shook his head. *They know how to hit you where it hurts. In the fuckin' wallet.*

Next stop, the toll plaza for the 133 South. More coins in the basket for the privilege of heading west. Looking around, Robbie remembered when this area was all orange groves and strawberry fields, not corporate headquarters, industrial parks, and high-end playgrounds for shopaholics. What Robbie saw now was the reassurance of returning job security.

He'd learned his lesson: *Don't let it get personal. Never lose your cool. You're a messenger, that's all.* He wasn't about to forget these past six months of purgatory, going stir-crazy and watching his meager savings run out in the middle of nowhere. All because he got a little too rough and didn't cover his tracks well enough after a job.

That wouldn't happen again. And when Michele had finally called, Robbie knew he'd be on probation for a while, but that was okay. He wouldn't let them down.

Just past the 405, the toll road portion of the 133 ended and he cruised into Laguna Canyon. After his "sabbatical," it was like he was seeing the place with fresh eyes. When he was growing up, this was an eight-mile, funky two-lane road that twisted toward the Pacific like a sidewinder on peyote. Now there were four lanes most of the way and shuttles from the Act V parking lot a mile from downtown. But on an August day like this, it was still stop-and-go from El Toro Road on into town where finding a parking place for less than ten bucks still felt like winning the lottery.

So, the Corolla inched along that final mile, until, at last, he cruised past the grounds of the arts festivals—the Sawdust Festival and Art-A-Fair on the left, the Festival of Arts on the right—a mere six blocks from the "T" where the Pacific Coast Highway briefly parallels the Main Beach boardwalk and Laguna's famous "window to the sea." With its surf, sand, volleyball and basketball courts, and a relatively unobstructed view of the Pacific, Main Beach owed its existence to a movement to stop its development back in the 1960s. Its preservation was made possible by the Festival of Arts with funds skimmed off thirty years of ticket sales to the Pageant of the Masters. As always, money talked, and that only-in-Orange-County theatrical show with its "living pictures" still pulled in crowds from all over the world every summer. And as long as it did, the city made certain it got its cut.

Once, when he was nine, Robbie had volunteered as a cast member in the Pageant. As a porcelain figurine. As crazy as it sounded, that summer was just about his only decent childhood memory, a brief refuge from the endless fights, the drunken beatings and humiliations at home. Now, as he passed the front entrance of the Festival of Arts with its banners and gated grounds filled with artists' displays, Robbie remembered how, back in high school, he'd thought about becoming an artist. Laguna certainly had enough of them. But even then he knew himself well enough to know it wasn't in the cards. Instead, he'd just drifted after school, a loner with no real sense of direction.

Michele and her husband Jeff, lawyers and partners in their own two-person legal firm, had originally hired him to run errands and do odd jobs. They liked that Robbie didn't ask too many questions and he paid attention to details. When had his work for them turned from just being a gofer to the more delicate tasks of money drops and eventually "enhanced mediation"? It had been a natural progression, with Robbie quickly developing a feel and taste for anonymous intimidation. Most of his targets were basically small-town cowards who were deathly afraid of having their dirty laundry aired in the pages of the *Coastline Pilot*. But Robbie didn't really care why Jeff and Michele had him do what he did. As far as he was concerned, he got paid to turn "no" into "yes, of course, it'll never happen again" by whatever means was necessary.

The Corolla angled into the left lane, and when the light changed, he turned onto Forest Avenue and cruised past the lumberyard parking lot, City Hall, and the fire station. There wasn't much of a chance to build any momentum before climbing the steep "blind crest" hill up to Park Aveune, but he was pleased that the old Toyota managed it without much complaint. Turning left on Park, Robbie slowed just a bit as he drove past the high school. Was he kidding himself that his time there hadn't been so bad after all? *Is this what nostalgia feels like? If it is, it really sucks.*

Park Avenue continued its winding ascent up through the canyons and steep turns that eventually led to Thurston Middle School and Top of the World, that elite enclave of homes with multimillion-dollar views overlooking Laguna Canyon. Everywhere he looked, Robbie saw new houses under construction. He'd watched most of the homes on these same hills burn to the ground in the Laguna Canyon fires in the fall of '93, but you'd never know it now. Taking a left at the middle school, Robbie made his way through the maze of houses to Skyline Drive.

Parking on the street across from another mansion-in-progress construction site, Robbie walked to the front door of Michele and Jeff's house, a California modern, split-level bunker of interlocking concrete and glass boxes. Checking his watch, Robbie rang the bell on the bronze and wood double doors. After a moment, a guy Robbie had never seen before, about six-two, 240, opened the door and peered down at him. Tan and ripped, the guy looked to be in his twenties. Robbie noted that he was barefoot and wearing a Hawaiian print shirt and shorts.

"Michele's expecting me," Robbie said, trying to cover his surprise.

"You Robbie?" the bodybuilder said. When Robbie nodded, the guy took a moment to size him up, then opened the door. "Michele's in the living room."

Robbie wracked his brain trying to think of a way to ask the guy who the hell he was. As he entered the hall, he gave up and simply muttered, "And who are you?" The guy turned and smiled. "I'm Terry."

"You work for Michele and Jeff?"

"Michele."

Terry stepped aside and Robbie stopped short as his eyes met Michele's. She was sitting next to the wall of windows in the living room. In a wheelchair with a cast on her leg. She smiled.

"Terry's my physical therapist."

"What happened?" Robbie couldn't hide his concern. He

guessed Michele was probably in her late fifties by now, but she'd always kept herself in shape. She was attractive in her self-assurance, well built, solid, comfortable in her skin.

"Tennis. Leg one way, knee the other. Cast for another week. I figure three months rehab minimum."

"Ouch." Robbie felt completely tongue-tied.

"Want something to drink?"

"No thanks."

"Terry, could you give us a few minutes?"

"Sure. If you need anything, just let me know."

When Terry was gone, Michele gestured for Robbie to join her by the windows. As he sat down next to her, he suddenly felt like a kid in the principal's office.

"It's good to see you," she said quietly.

"You too," he stammered. "How's Jeff?"

"Jeff's Jeff," she offered flatly. "He's down at the festival. Got juried in again for his watercolors."

"No kidding," Robbie said, nodding.

"He's doing the meet-and-greet on the grounds today, always trying to drum up new business."

There was a pause, then Robbie asked, "You guys are good?" God, that sounded even dumber than he'd feared.

"Robbie . . ." She looked at him, sighed, and smiled wanly. "Let's just say we have a very spiritual relationship. Every day we learn to live with less . . ."

He looked at her, confused. "I don't . . ."

"Nevermind." She smiled. "It's Jeff who needs your help. And we both agreed it was a safe way to ease you back into the swing of things."

"I really appreciate that. I've been goin a bit stir-crazy."

"Well, that's all behind you now. And the guy you put in the hospital . . . well, let's just say he's got other things to worry about these days. Like a company in Chapter 11 and a palace in foreclosure."

"Look, I . . ."

Michele smiled. "It's okay, Robbie. Everybody gets a mulligan. And I think you've learned your lesson."

"Yeah . . . yeah."

She picked up a file and handed it to him. Opening it, he looked at a couple of grainy photos of a guy crossing a street. "Who's this?"

"His name's Madison. He's going after Jeff. Wants to extort two hundred grand to keep quiet."

"About what? What's he got?"

"We're not sure. But Jeff's arranged a meet with him. Tonight on the fire road up above the festival. You know where I'm talking about?"

"That dirt road that goes up behind Tivoli Terrace with the great view of Main Beach and the police shooting range?"

She smiled. "Nice recall."

"I used to hike up there to clear my head."

Michele leaned forward. "They're supposed to meet at midnight at the little turnout overlooking the shooting range. This file has all you'll need to know about Madison to put the fear of God into him. His kids' names and ages, where they go to school, what picture's hanging on the wall in his bedroom. And if that doesn't scare him off, you have my blessing to ruffle his feathers a bit. Just no easily visible bruising."

"Jeff going to be there?"

"No. You're going to get there early and surprise this arrogant little asshole. See, Madison's a ceramics exhibitor at the festival. It seems he and Jeff have at least one thing in common. They like to pretend that art can save them from their fundamental boorishness. News flash: it can't."

Robbie studied the file to cover his nervousness. "So, I guess you and Jeff are—"

"Robbie . . . Jeff's a lawyer; I'm a lawyer; we're partners. If I took him to court, I could wipe him out, but we'd poison the well in the process . . ." She pointed to the file. "You know, there's hardly any moon tonight and that fire road can be a bit treacherous and steep in places. I'd hate to think Madison might fall and hurt himself."

"Right." Robbie grinned. He was relieved she was changing the subject.

"Study his file. If you can reason with him, so much the better. If not . . ."

"Midnight," said Robbie, savoring the thought.

"I recommend you park above the shooting range and cut across. And get there early."

"Not to worry." Robbie rose, holding the file.

"Aren't you forgetting something?"

"What?"

"Your fee?"

Robbie almost blushed. "Right, right . . . Actually, I could use the cash, but I figure there'll be more where this one came from. So let's just call this one 'pro bono.' How's that sound?"

She smiled. "Come here." Robbie moved to her and bent down. With one hand, she pulled his face to hers and lightly kissed him on the cheek. "It's good to have you back."

"It's good to be back."

Terry opened the door for Robbie as he headed to his car.

Robbie spent the afternoon getting ready for his midnight rendezvous with Madison. At the Ralph's on Glenneyre, he bought a recycled canvas grocery bag, six bars of Zest soap, a Coke Zero, and a deli sandwich.

Back in town, he turned off Broadway and headed up the steep hill on Acacia, then a hard right on High Drive and another right onto Poplar. He followed it to Harold Drive at the turnaround next to the access road entrance leading down to the LBPD shooting range. Parking on Harold, Robbie walked over to the heavy chain hanging across the access road entrance and read the sign.

No Trespassing. Authorized Vehicles Only. Unauthorized vehicles and pedestrians subject to prosecution and fine: joggers, hikers, walkers, skateboarders, bicyclists. Laguna Beach Police Department. Do Not Enter.

He looked across the gulley and spotted the fire road and the overlook. Maybe a quarter of a mile down this side past the range and up the other side. Chaparral and scrub brush all around. Not much cover, but all he really needed was the dark later on.

Surveying the turnaround, he could see maybe a half-dozen houses. No signs of life. He could hear a blues band playing on the festival grounds below. And he knew there'd be another Pageant performance that night. Plenty of distractions. He went back and sat in the Corolla and read through the Madison file. He imagined the look on the guy's face when a stranger wearing a ski mask got the drop on him. *Sweet.*

Robbie drank his soda, took a few bites of his sandwich, unwrapped five of the bars of Zest, and tied them into the canvas bag. It had a nice heft. *Who needs a sap when you've got soap?* You could break a rib and barely leave a bruise.

It was already starting to get dark. Robbie drove around

the neighborhood, then back down to PCH. He was suddenly aware of how pathetic the Toyota looked as he cruised through town. For now, it was all he could afford, but as soon as he was flush again, he'd get something less conspicuous and a whole lot more reliable.

At a quarter to 9, he pulled back up to the turnaround near the entrance to the shooting range. In the canyon below, the Pageant was underway. The production shops next to the Irvine Bowl blocked his view of the theater, but Robbie could hear the orchestra and the audience applauding the *tableaux vivants* onstage.

The curtain fell on Leonardo da Vinci's *The Last Supper*, the traditional Pageant finale, just before 10:30. Time to go. Grabbing the soap bag, he loped across the turnaround, stepped over the chain across the entrance to the access road, and disappeared. He crossed the dark, empty shooting range five minutes later, reached the bottom of the ravine five minutes after that, and began the slippery ascent up the shadowy hillside. Footing was surprisingly treacherous, but twenty minutes later, he stepped out onto the fire road. Accustomed to the darkness by now, he located the viewpoint and crouched nearby behind a large chaparral.

As he sat there, he went over in his mind the notes he'd been studying: Madison's family and the little, intimate details that would let the jerk know just how vulnerable he was. Robbie's adrenaline was pumping. He was out of practice. By now, Laguna Canyon Road was full of cars heading home. The festival was shutting down for the night, and the maintenance crew in the Irvine Bowl was almost through cleaning up after the Pageant.

Suddenly, Robbie tensed. He'd heard something. But what? He listened again, then laughed to himself at his nervousness. He checked his watch. Three minutes to midnight. He closed his eyes and strained to hear any activity below.

Five minutes later, he heard footsteps coming up the rutted dirt road. It had to be Madison . . . But wait. Something was wrong. He could make out more than one voice. Madison wasn't alone. Michele hadn't said anything about this. The voices were getting closer. In another minute, two shadowy figures came over the crest and meandered toward the overlook. Robbie adjusted his position to get a better view. They were walking arm in arm, whispering to one another. It was a man and a woman! The man seemed to have a parcel under one arm. As Robbie watched, the man shook the bag and flipped it out. It was a blanket. Spreading it in the darkened clearing, he turned to embrace the woman. Robbie strained to make out their hushed whispers. Could this just be a coincidence? A couple looking for a place to make out at the exact wrong place and time? Robbie cursed his luck. Obviously, they'd scare off Madison. But there was nothing he could do except wait them out.

As Robbie crouched there, helpless, he heard the couple start to undress one another. In the dark, they giggled at their clumsiness. No foreplay, no chit-chat. In another minute, they were groping each other while trying to find a comfortable position on the hard earth. Soon enough, however, discomfort gave way to passion. Amid sighs and gasps, he heard the woman emit a muted squeal.

Robbie sat up and peered down at the shadowy figures. Even in the dark, he was sure he recognized the guy. There was no mistaking his clumsy movements and his labored, rheumy breathing. Jeff.

In that same instant, he felt a cold, metallic object press into the back of his neck. He froze as he realized what it was.

The barrel of a handgun. Jeff had always carried one, but Robbie refused to have anything to do with them. He wasn't afraid of them. He just knew there was no hope for a success- ful negotiation once the guns come out.

Robbie tried ever so gingerly to turn his head in hopes of glimpsing who was behind him. He winced as the barrel jabbed into the base of his skull. The couple, now fully en- gaged, were oblivious.

Responding to the prodding of the barrel, Robbie slowly got to his feet. He felt the figure moving around to stand beside him. Then, in a single motion, the person lifted another pistol in his other hand. Robbie could make out the silhouette of an imposing silencer attached to the barrel of the other weapon. Before Robbie could react, the pistol emitted four dull bursts, and, after two labored gasps, the couple fell silent.

What the fuck was going on?! Robbie turned to look at the assassin, who now leveled the other pistol directly against his forehead. It was too dark to make out a face.

"Nice shooting," said a strangely familiar voice. After a second, Robbie realized where he'd heard it before.

"Terry?" Silence. "What the—?"

His voice was flat and calm. "You shouldn't have tried to blackmail Jeff about his thing with that cute little jewelry maker. You thought if you caught them in the act, they'd pay up. Too bad Jeff never goes anywhere without his piece." Terry flicked the barrel of the smaller pistol as he centered it on Robbie's chest. "And he managed to shoot you before you fin- ished them off . . . Poor Michele."

"Who the fuck are you?" Robbie could barely hear his voice over the pounding in his chest.

"I'm the new you, motherfucker . . ."

Robbie started to lean back, then swung the bag of soap

bars with all his might toward Terry's gun hand. In the blackness, the tinny explosions, like leftover fireworks—two quick bursts followed after about ten seconds by a third—echoed weakly across the canyon.

Michele opened the front door for Terry. She was barefoot, wearing a sheer silk nightshirt. In the hallway behind her, the removable cast was leaned up against the wheelchair. "Don't tell me you forgot your key again," she said as the door swung inward. In the next instant, she did her best to mask her surprise.

Robbie reached out an arm and leaned heavily against the door frame. In his other hand, he held Jeff's pistol. "Terry's not coming home."

Michele's mind was racing and all she could think to say was, "You're hurt."

"I'll live." Robbie pointed the gun at her. As she backed away, he stepped through the door, gritting his teeth, willing himself through the pain. Backing her down the hall, Robbie glanced at the boot cast and wheelchair. "Your knee's better."

"Robbie—"

"Just shut up, Michele . . . I might have expected something like this from Jeff. But I always thought you—"

"You don't know what it's been like."

"I guess not."

"Look, Robbie, we can get through this. We can make this work for both of us. But we've got to get you to—"

"No, we don't."

"You've lost a lot of blood." They were in the living room now. Low lights. Through the panoramic windows, the faint glow of the town below. She tried to scan the room for possible weapons as Robbie moved closer, the gun still leveled at her.

"You had it all figured out. Get rid of Jeff and me . . . clean slate."

"Robbie, it's just you and me now. We could be in Mexico before dawn."

"Right." His attempt at sarcasm hurt like hell.

"I'm worried about you."

"Wouldn't want bloodstains on your furniture."

"Robbie."

"You taught me that it's never personal. Well . . . let me tell you . . ." He lifted his blood-soaked hand from his abdomen and held it out toward her. "This feels personal."

"Let me get something."

"No. It ends here. But first I'm gonna need every cent you've got."

"Of course. It's in the safe." She turned and pointed toward the bedroom hall. When he nodded, she moved in that direction.

"It's in here," Michele said, indicating a walk-in closet in the master bedroom. Pushing back clothes hanging on a rack, she revealed a wall safe. She flicked on an overhead light and punched at the safe's keypad. "We're going to get through this." She looked back at Robbie, who watched her through heavy-lidded eyes, then opened the safe and reached in. "You won't be sorry."

Turning, she pulled out a .22 handgun and swung it toward Robbie. But he was ready, firing three quick bursts at point-blank range, hitting Michele twice in the chest and once in the neck. Her pistol fired wildly, the bullet lodging in a chest of drawers to Robbie's right. She fell to the carpet in front of him. Robbie looked down at her for a moment, closed his eyes, and let out a deep sigh. He noticed blood from his abdomen was now staining his pants leg and overflowing from his sock down his shoe and onto the carpet. Turning, he walked slowly from the room.

At the toll plaza for the 133 North, Robbie turned on the dome light in the Corolla and fumbled in his pocket for the exact change. As he inspected a handful of coins, he looked down at his gut and let out a half-laugh, half-howl. *You forget who you are, you forget what you believe in, but you still remember to pay your toll!* Reaching up, he flicked off the dome light and sat there, breathing slowly, deliberately, trying to ignore the wet, hot black that used to be his midsection. Rolling down the window, he leaned out and flung the handful of change toward the collection bin. It was an awkward toss. The coins clattered to the pavement and his elbow banged against the windowsill. The effort was too much. Robbie leaned back. He wanted his eyes to work, to keep on working. But they were letting him down. The last thing he remembered was reaching over to turn off the Corolla's ignition. The old car was grateful for the rest.

2:45 OUT OF SANTA ANA

BY MARY CASTILLO

Santa Ana

Today, 11:45 a.m.

She could be anywhere by now. She could be standing at the next bus stop, or long gone out of my life.

I should listen to Nana and head back to work. But instead I drive around Santa Ana looking for a little girl in the rain. The few who are out in this weather are huddled under bus stops next to their mothers or grandmothers, looking like pink and purple marshmallows in their puffy rain jackets.

Go back to work. Even though I'll put another month on these boots, I need every cent of my pathetic paycheck as a news assistant with the *Orange County Tribune*.

But I keep driving down East 1st Street toward the freeway as the rain and wind batter my car. Maybe the woman who took Pricila is her aunt and they're on a grand adventure to visit relatives in Mexico. Or Pricila is locked in the cold terror that she'll never see her own nana or mom again.

A few minutes later, I'm dripping water at the front desk of Santa Ana PD.

"How may I help you?" a clerk asks without getting up from her desk.

"I need to report a missing child."

I'm taken behind the counter with Officer Darrin Kravetz into an interview room. His gray eyes are so kind that I can't picture him cornering a suspect in an alley with his gun drawn.

We do fine until he asks for my name.

"Danielle Dawson."

He looks up. "How are you related to the Pricila Ruiz?"

"I'm not. I'm a reporter, I mean news assistant, and Pricila and her grandmother—" I stop myself from saying *hid with us.* Clearing my throat, I say, "They stayed with us last night when ICE raided their home."

"Why didn't her grandmother come in with you?"

"She was arrested an hour ago. Pricila's mother is in jail awaiting her arraignment."

"How do you know Pricila isn't with family or friends?"

"My na— My grandma saw her leave with a woman who was paid to take her away."

He puts down his pen and gives me that look like I'm the kind of person who has left a shopping cart full of her worldly belongings out in front of the station.

"I'm not making this up," I say. "I just want to help a little girl."

"Why?"

Because even at thirty-two, I'll never forget the helplessness of waiting for someone to pick me up from school or feed me dinner. Because my mother left me when the sheriffs came with her eviction notice and the court gave me to my nana and grandpa. Because I might have had a little girl Pricila's age if things had been different.

Officer Kravetz leans back in his seat. "I'm having a hard time following you. Who's the dad? You talk to him?"

"Not really."

Officer Kravetz doesn't like where this is going. "Got a name?"

"Jim Westfall. He's with Immigrations and Customs Enforcement."

The cop's eyebrows arch up and he shakes his head. "You really want me to call an ICE agent and ask about a little girl who an unauthorized immigrant claims is his?"

"He's the dad. Says so on Pricila's birth certificate." Now I'm beginning to wish I'd gone back to work.

"All right." Officer Kravetz says it like I've just sealed a very nasty fate. "Let me call this guy and get to the bottom of it, okay?"

"Okay. Thank you."

"Want anything to drink? Coffee or some water?"

"No thank you."

"Be right back."

He leaves me in the room with the buzzing fluorescent light.

I sit back in my chair. My feet ache with cold and I should've eaten something before I got myself into this. Six months ago, my biggest dilemma was which floor plan to pick for my new town home in Newport Beach. Now I'm sitting in a police station, my boss has been calling my cell nonstop, and I live with my grandmother.

I can't hear anything outside these walls; it's completely soundproof.

Last night, 8:30 p.m.

In Santa Ana there are two types of neighborhoods: the historically significant neighborhoods with names like French Park and Floral Park, and the other neighborhoods. My grandma lives in one of the others.

I turn off North Bristol onto West 3rd and then make a right on Hesperian. Except for Thanksgiving, Christmas, and Easter at Nana's house, the farthest I'd head up on Bristol was the northernmost tip of Nordstrom at South Coast Plaza. Now this is home. Again.

Nana's two-story bungalow stands on the corner. The skeleton of last spring's sweet peas cling to her chain-link fence, and even though she has the space, she still grows her roses and calla lilies in buckets.

As a kid, I used to hide in the avocado tree from my cousins. When you're the only blond, half-white kid in a family of small, brown Mexicans from Jalisco, you know you're a grown-up the moment a white-person joke doesn't punch your flight-or-fight button.

Nana walks out of the kitchen. She's still dressed in her suit but she must have stopped for a pedicure after work. Her toenails are now purple. When she sees it's me, she asks, "Where you been?"

I open my mouth to begin a litany of grievances against my boss when a sharp report shakes the floor. White light bursts through the windows—the kind you see in alien invasion movies—and where there was a quiet street of parked cars and dim porch lights, SUVs and cop cruisers now block us in.

"Did you hear that?" Chachi shouts. My cousins run out of the house to the yard.

Nana shouts at them to come back inside. "Do you want to get shot?"

As a reporter, I should dash out with my press pass, cell phone, and notepad. But the paper doesn't pay me enough and the walls of Nana's aren't even half as thick as the last Harry Potter book. I follow my nose into the kitchen where a vat of posole simmers on the stove. I make myself a bowl, heavy on the hominy. The oily broth scalds my hand. I've been here almost a year and I'm still not accustomed to the almost nightly visits from law enforcement that remind us we live in the "bad" part of town.

Someone bangs on the back door. I turn, about to call Chachi an asshole for scaring me. But a woman stares back at me through the window. Her eyes are almost white with terror and then I see the little girl standing next to her.

I instinctively know to let them in. Without a word, I lead them out of the kitchen and up the stairs to my room. The little girl asks in a voice thin with confusion where they're going and the old lady shushes her. Then the little girl cries out, "Mommy! I want my mommy!"

"Niña, shush!" Her grandma covers her mouth as if the cops outside might hear them. "Está bien. Está bien."

The flashing lights from the police cars dance on the walls and I hear their radios. A dog barks and I think of Jews hiding in attics. My body rocks from the force of my heartbeat.

As they move into my bedroom, I look down on the little girl's head. I hold back from brushing my hand over her French braid because she's not mine to do so.

"Mommy, what's wrong? What's happening?" Pricila asked as her mother pulled her away from the kitchen sink.

"You have to go. Now!"

Nana's hands were wet from washing the dishes. Pricila looked down at the drops they made on the floor.

Mommy pulled her close and held her tight. Then she pushed Pricila away. For a moment, her mother stared into her eyes. Her voice shook when she said, "Go, baby. Go with Nana, okay? I'll catch up with you."

And then that terrible bang happened and Nana pulled Pricila into the yard and they ran in the dark.

They made it to the house next door. Pricila sat at the table, pressed as tightly as she could against her nana. She tried not to look at anyone or wonder where her mommy had gone. She thought about Sleeping Beauty dancing with the animals dressed in the prince's clothes. She thought about her friend Heaven, who brought blue glitter nail polish to school. She wondered if Mommy would still rent her a movie for getting 100s on her spelling tests last month.

"Señora Duran—"

"Por favor, señora, please call me Bettina," Pricila's nana said.

"Bettina," the old lady continued, "are you sure you won't have some posole?"

"No thank you. Coffee is fine."

"Do you have anyplace to go?" the pretty blond lady asked.

Pricila peeked out. The blond lady didn't talk like a princess but she looked like one with curly hair and big brown eyes. She had a deep, serious voice and when she caught Pricila looking at her, she smiled crookedly.

"He'll find us," Nana croaked. "He's the one who did this. To get Pricila. He don't want her. He want to punish my Gina."

Pricila's chest froze with fear as Nana started to cry. The old lady reached out and took her hand.

"Who will find you?" the pretty lady asked.

"El padre de la niña."

The pretty lady frowned. The old lady, who Pricila guessed was her nana, then asked, "He called la migra on you?"

Pricila knew Nana was talking about her daddy. She hadn't seen him in a long time. Mommy said she and Daddy were mad at each other. Even though she said Pricila hadn't done anything, she knew they fought because of her.

"No, no," Nana sniffled. "He is la migra."

"Danielle, take Pricila to watch TV," the old lady said.

Pricila held onto her nana tighter.

"We have some good movies," the pretty lady said.

Pricila breathed in her nana's smell but her nana started to push her away.

"Go, niña," Nana said. "Let me talk to Señora Melendez, okay?"

Pricila shook her head, fighting to stay close to her nana. Her throat burned as she bit down to keep from crying. Another hand touched her back but then pulled away. Pricila could feel it hovering close.

The pretty lady named Danielle leaned in and whispered, "My nana doesn't know this but . . ." She paused and Pricila couldn't help but look into her brown eyes. "I have some chocolate ice cream hidden in the freezer. Would you like some?"

Mommy never let her have ice cream on a school night and only when they could afford it.

"Go on, niña," Nana said. "I'll be right here."

Pressing her chin to her chest, Pricila slid off the chair. Danielle offered her hand and Pricila took it.

Today, 7:45 a.m.

My body tells me I've reached an age where I'll be stiff after a night tossing and turning on my nana's ancient couch. I kept thinking about nine-year-old Pricila Ruiz sleeping in my room.

Before I left for work, Nana gave me the rundown on the raid next door. Even though it was awkward—I've never really spent much time around kids—I was glad to have taken Pricila into the TV room last night so she didn't have to relive the feds breaking down her front door.

My friend Jake, who got me this job, now sits next to me in Warren Ramsey's office. I can see the empty lots that the city bought along Santa Ana Boulevard for a "gateway" to downtown. My Aunt Eloisa's little craftsman bungalow was sold two years ago and then leveled, only to be fenced off. I see the ghost of that house when I drive by it and remember how she'd walk me to the depot to watch the trains.

Warren is the news editor and the one I have to convince to let me branch out from entering calendar items into the system and writing briefs published under my team leader's byline. A story about last night's raid might be a front-page clip and make this whole reporting thing worth it. I've never hustled so hard for so little money, but advertising got hit hard by the economy and this job is better than nothing.

ICE agents arrested Pricila Ruiz's mother, Gina. The little girl's nana, Bettina, claimed the arrest was set up by ICE agent Jim Westfall after Gina threatened to fax a copy of Pricila's birth certificate to his wife's office if he didn't help her get a green card.

Gina had come to the U.S. on a student visa in 1996 to attend USC. Bettina came to the U.S. on a visitor's visa to see Gina graduate magna cum laude and together they stayed. She was doing pretty well with an accounting job at Arthur Andersen that sponsored her work visa. But the company laid her off in 2001 and Gina couldn't get another job with a company that would sponsor her green card. Pricila had just turned a year old.

Bettina said Westfall and his wife couldn't have kids, but I didn't tell Warren that. Westfall promised to marry Gina and streamline her citizenship process so they could be a family. But the divorce and the papers never came to pass and Gina ended it, making threats to force Westfall to at least fix her legal status. He disappeared from Pricila's life and then Gina received a court order to leave the country. She texted West-fall his wife's office fax number, as a reminder of what would happen if he didn't help her. But then ICE agents busted down her door.

I try to catch my breath when I finish my pitch. Jake nods her head at me with approval. She says that my losing my advertising job is good for my karma. I think she likes it now that she makes more money than I do.

Warren sighs and then types something on his keyboard. "Don't go toe-to-toe with this guy," he says, and Jake's knee starts bouncing. "Don't go anywhere near him with this. Jim Westfall gets awards from anti-immigration groups—like the crazy kind—from all around the country."

"But he set up the mother of his child to be deported. I sat with that little girl last night."

Warren gears up to reply but then his phone rings.

"Hold on." He answers his call and tells one of his reporters to stay on the street. Apparently, some guy has been driving around to elementary schools in Santa Ana, trying to get little girls into his car. Warren hangs up.

He leans forward to turn his monitor around. The desk leaves a temporary imprint against his belly. I'm staring at a file photo of Jim Westfall.

I scoot closer. Westfall wears a too-tight white shirt under a flak jacket with big white letters: *ICE*. Behind his sunglasses, I sense the condemning gaze of an inquisitor.

"Okay, so you want to go to this guy, an acknowledged elder-in-training in one of the biggest churches here in Orange County, and ask about how he set up his mistress to be deported?" Warren pauses to let this sink in. "What do you think he'll say to you, if you have the proof?"

"We took on America's Sheriff," Jake chimes in. "We knew he was dirty."

"When the feds had evidence of his wrongdoing," Warren says as he turns his monitor back around. "Okay, here's what we can do. Mario is following the ICE activities—"

"Raids," Jake interrupts.

"Activities," Warren insists. "Maybe Mario can make this part of a larger story."

Mario Landrey is the reporter who covers immigration issues. They call him "Ice, Ice, Baby," and he posts online pictures of himself with agents and their guns. According to Jake, Mario hasn't written one word about the ICE vans parked outside Santa Ana's elementary schools or the day-worker stops. But he's spilled a lot of ink about the arrests of illegals with warrants for drug dealing, rape, and murder. Mario guards his territory like a pit bull.

"Dani should have this story," Jake pleads.

"We have a good relationship with law enforcement and I want to keep it that way," Warren says, standing up to dismiss us. "Even if it's true, Dani's not ready for this kind of story."

I stay in my seat. "But I know the grandmother. She'll talk to me."

"Mario has a lot of connections in the Latino community. He's got the expertise to handle guys like Westfall." Warren grins at me. "Sorry, Dani. Westfall would eat you alive."

My nana calls me. Gina phoned her mother's cell from Central Jail in Santa Ana. She had been questioned and was offered the option of waiving her right to a court hearing, which would've put her on the first bus to Mexico. Gina told them no and now she's waiting to be arraigned.

"Gina and her mother were fighting over the phone so I took the little girl outside to pick lemons." Nana keeps her voice low and I strain to understand her.

"Do you think Gina will get deported?"

"You're the one with the college degree, mi'ja. What do you think?"

"What about Pricila? If she was born here—"

"She'll go with her mama. It's the way things are. You know that."

Anger gathers in my throat, like I'm being suffocated from the inside out. Westfall is a bastard for doing this. No, wait; under his commando posing, he's a *cowardly* bastard for trying to hide his little girl. If people don't want kids, they shouldn't screw around.

It's moments like this that I think I made the right decision when I was twenty-three and starting my advertising career. I'd be like Gina now, irrevocably shackled to a man who might hate me for having his kid. My mother got off easy. Her husband, whose last name I bear, kicked her out when he discovered she'd been sleeping with a fellow grad student. She thinks my real father is a guy from England.

"Is Pricila still there?"

"Yes," Nana sighs. "Ay, Dani, you shouldn't have gotten us involved in this. I had to take the day off and I have briefs to type up for Mr. Levine—"

"You think I should've shooed them from the back door?"

"No, but—"

"I'll come home."

"And do what?"

"Interview the grandmother. I'm a reporter. I'll write a story to help them."

"Don't. You'll only make it worse, mi'ja."

My boss and team leader Jolene buzzes me right after I hang up. Checking the mirror taped to my monitor, affixed there so no one catches me checking job listings online, I see Jolene painting her nails with her phone pressed between her ear and shoulder.

I pull my purse strap over my shoulder and slip out before she hunts me down in the newsroom.

When I turn on Nana's street, there's an unmarked white Suburban parked facing the wrong way in front of her house. The shotgun mounted in the center console is a dead give-away that it's the cops.

As I get out of the car, I sense eyes watching from behind curtains. Even the dogs are quiet as everyone is on full alert that The Man has entered the forest.

Through the screen door, a man I instinctivley know is Jim Westfall turns; my heart freezes when our eyes lock. Bettina is sitting on the couch, her hands behind her back. I make out Nana sitting in Grandpa's chair.

"Wait outside!" Westfall barks.

His partner then walks out and approaches me with his hand hitched on his gun. "Which one works for you?" he asks.

"My grandmother lives here." The wind blows hard against my back and a spray of water dripping off the eaves sprinkles my cheek.

He smiles instead of apologizing for assuming I'm a New-port mommy here to fetch my nanny. "Well, your grandma has been harboring an unauthorized immigrant."

So that's what they call them now, huh?

"We don't card our neighbors when they're afraid to sleep in their own homes."

"You know Bettina Duran?"

"Yeah, she's our neighbor."

"You know where the little girl is?"

"In school, I guess."

He surveys the street from behind his sunglasses. I want

to flash my press badge and yell, *Stop right there, bud, I demand you let my grandma go!*

The screen door hits the front of the house as Westfall walks out with Bettina. She doesn't look at me and I'm hoping Pricila is upstairs.

But she's not. Nana pulls me inside and tells me that a woman with a baby came to the house less than twenty minutes before Westfall showed up. Bettina bundled Pricila in a white coat and her backpack and sent her out the door with her birth certificate and a hundred dollars cash.

"Where did she take her?"

Nana shrugs as she checks her briefcase. "Mexico."

"By herself?"

"This is not our business. Let it go."

"Does Gina know?"

"Yes. That's why they were arguing."

My cell phone buzzes angrily. It's Jolene ordering me back, no doubt. I think about sitting with Pricila in the TV room last night, watching *Justice League* and explaining Wonder Woman to her. Girls these days, they don't even know who Wonder Woman is. Then again, a girl like Pricila has more important things on her mind, like if her mom will be there when she comes home from school.

"Danielle, listen to me. We have no concern in this and we don't want nothing to do with the police. Understand?"

"But they came to us for help! Where are they sending Pricila? What if something happens to her along the way?"

Nana sighs.

"I'm supposed to just let it go, huh?"

"Yes, mi'ja. Let it go."

Today, 1 p.m.

Obviously I refuse, and that's how I wind up in the Santa Ana Police Department.

When Officer Kravetz walks back in, he brings a female officer who looks like she should be running for ASB president.

"Stand up for us, Danielle," he says quietly. All the gentleness is gone in his eyes.

I stand as my heart pounds in my throat.

"Did you find her?"

"Dani, this is Officer Lara. You're under arrest for making a false police report—"

"But I'm not lying. You said you were going to check with her dad and—"

"Turn around, Danielle," Officer Lara orders. When her hand moves to her pepper spray, I do what she says.

The cold handcuffs weigh my hands down and I have to lean forward so I don't fall back. Officer Lara keeps me company while Officer Kravetz leaves the room.

"This is ridiculous. I wasn't lying about Pricila being missing. She's being sent out of this country against her will."

"Well, here's the thing, Dani," Officer Lara snaps, like we're circling each other on the playground. "Jim Westfall doesn't have a daughter and the claims you made about him having a relationship with this woman are pretty underhanded. What are you hoping to gain from all this? A story for the paper?"

Yes. Well, not completely.

"Aren't you going to read me my rights?"

Officer Lara stares at me.

"Do I have to wear an orange jumpsuit?"

Her lips twitch to keep from laughing.

* * *

"If you don't stop crying, I'm going to leave you here," Maya said when Pricila started getting scared again. "They'll put you in jail and you won't see your mom no more."

Pricila flinched when the train's horn shook the ground under her feet. The station was hot and crowded with people who carried boxes tied up with string. Maya told her that she had to hold her coat if she took it off, but she wouldn't help Pricila with her heavy backpack. Her feet squished in her pink boots from a puddle Maya had dragged her through to get on the bus before it left Nana's street.

Even though Maya had a baby, she didn't seem like a mommy. She was mean. Maya pinched her arm through her coat sleeve. It didn't hurt but Pricila felt the pressure all the same and now she was making little squeaking sounds as she tried to stop crying.

"I want to go home," Pricila croaked.

"You can't. Shut up."

"I don't like you."

"I don't like you either."

Pricila almost fell when Maya let her go with a shove. Maya hefted up Baby Carmen and craned her neck to look over the heads of people waiting in line to buy bus tickets.

Pricila thought of all the bad words that Mommy and Nana told her never to say. She called Maya all those names in her head.

The line moved forward and then someone opened the door to the patio. Cold wind swept in and Pricila lifted her face to it, smelling the thick fumes from the train. Then a man smiled at her. She leaned to the right to hide behind Maya's fat butt.

Baby Carmen started whimpering and Maya growled like a dog. She kneeled down and set her backpack on the floor.

"Help me," she said to Pricila. "Open up the zipper."

She did and the train's horn hurt her ears. Maya swatted her hands out of the way.

"Zip it up," Maya ordered impatiently, and then stuck the bottle in Baby Carmen's mouth. But the baby twisted her head away as if Maya had stabbed her with the bottle. "Come on," Maya said. "Just take the fucking thing."

Why had Nana sent her away with Maya? Why hadn't she let her stay with Danielle too? She hadn't caused any trouble.

"Shut up," Maya snapped at a lady in line who was telling her to calm down. "Wait here," she then ordered Pricila.

"Where are you going?"

"I said wait here." People stared at Maya and Pricila heard the lady in line make a comment about her.

Pricila started to follow Maya, afraid to be left alone. She was getting that hurt feeling in her throat again. She wanted her mommy and her nana.

"Are you okay?" The man who had smiled at her now stood next to her. He had big blue eyes and curly black hair. "I'll stay with you until she comes back."

They walk me out of the interview room, presumably to the booking area. My eyes fill with tears, and since I can't bring my hands up to wipe them clear, they spill down my face.

They take me through the station and I burn with humiliation. It's like I'm a prize fish, by the looks of the passing cops. We ride an elevator and it opens to a floor that smells like new carpet, paper, and ink. The men and a few women wear suits with their badges and guns displayed on their belts.

Officer Lara gives me a look that says, *You asked for it.* She opens an office door and two men are standing by a window streaked with rain.

One looks at the other and murmurs something. He gestures to the other officers, who back away and I'm left alone with the Mexican Terminator. His dark face betrays nothing as he walks straight at me. He never drops his stare, even when he moves right into my personal space and stands there with his arms crossed over his chest.

"You made some claims against one of my agents," he says in a hushed voice that's all street.

I fight the urge to step back. "Her grandmother claimed her daughter was set up by your agent. I'm worried about the little girl."

"You have evidence that she's my agent's daughter?"

"I looked for it."

"So you could write a news story that would damage his reputation and my department."

"To help a woman who did nothing wrong but live here illegally and sleep with the wrong guy."

The corner of his mouth tics like he's used to hearing this sort of thing. "Would this kid know you if she saw you?"

I remember Pricila's weight against me as we sat on the couch and ate ice cream. "Yes."

He studies me and I remember why I haven't dated a Latino since I was seventeen. They have a way of making you forget the vow you made in the eighth grade that you'd never be the kind of woman who washes her man's underwear or makes him a plate at parties.

"I'm not going to add to your problems and have you arrested, Danielle. You're a news assistant who's two months behind on your car payment. A Mini Cooper. My sister wants one of those."

"I got laid off," I answer before I realize he has poked into my life. What else does he know?

He reaches for me and I flinch.

He grins as if he likes blondes in shackles. "I'm just going to take off the cuffs."

"What about Pricila? And who are you?"

"Agent Mike Acacio, head of Immigration and Customs Enforcement, Orange County bureau." He takes my arm. His fingers are hot and then, with a twist and snap, my hands are free. "I think I know where Pricila is."

Soon we're in Agent Acacio's car, for which he apologizes. The guys who had it last were doing a stakeout and didn't toss out their soda cans and fast food bags. It smells like stale fried chicken.

We start driving. The rain has let up but the sky is dark and the trees bend in the wind.

"Where are we going?"

"Train depot. You said the little girl left with a woman and a hundred bucks."

I nod.

"More than likely they've got tickets on the 2:45 bus to Los Angeles and then Mexicali."

When I look at him like he's psychic, he shakes his head. "I've been doing this for a while."

"When did you know Jim Westfall was having an affair with an unauthorized immigrant?"

He glares at me. My stomach coils into a knot.

"This is off the record," he says. "I received a faxed birth certificate with his name on it, and when I crossreferenced the list of arrestees, Gina Ruiz's name was on it."

Mike—Agent Acacio—goes on to explain that he had suspicions about Westfall's arrests. I fight back a grin. Gina managed one last strike before Westfall got her. I bet we'd like each other if we ever met.

"Look, we don't make up the laws," Agent Acacio says. "If Miss Ruiz is here illegally, she has to return to Mexico. But I don't let my agents get away with abusing their power."

"So you'll still deport Gina?"

"If the court decides to repatriate her, then she'll be returned to Mexico."

"Doesn't Westfall want to look for his daughter?"

His grip tightens on the steering wheel. I finally notice a wedding ring. "For some people, their kids don't figure into the equation."

"Let's get something to drink. You like strawberry soda?"

Pricila thought about it and nodded. He seemed nice. Even though Mommy and Nana told her never to talk to strangers, they'd let Danielle take her and now Maya. He smiled when he looked at Pricila and he wore Converse shoes like her teacher, Mr. Neil.

"This nice lady here will keep your place in line. We'll come back before your mom does, okay?"

Pricila knew she shouldn't go.

"Here, leave this." He reached for her backpack and helped her arms out of the straps. "We'll bring something back for your mom too. That way she won't be mad at us, okay?"

She looked up at him and then at the café at the other end of the station. As long as they came back, it would be okay. He held out his hand and she took it.

We arrive at the station with an agreement: I'll take Pricila home until the court decides what to do with Gina. Agent Acacio will deal with Westfall. We'll all go on with our business.

When the SUV jerks to a stop, I turn to Agent Acacio.

"I'm sorry, but you know I'm going to talk to my editor after this."

He shrugs like that doesn't mean anything and then jumps out to jog around the steaming hood, but he doesn't open my door. A father carries his daughter to the parking lot and people hurry out to a bus with a sign reading *Mexicali* in the front window.

I reach into my purse, wondering if I have time to call Jake to send a photographer.

At first he held her hand. Pricila tripped when he pulled her toward the doors, away from the café.

"This way, sweetie."

"But the sodas are there," she said, pointing to the café in case he hadn't seen it.

"No, baby, there're better ones this way."

The cold stung her face when he pushed the door open. What if Maya came back before they came back? What if the lady didn't save their place in line? Would Maya slap her?

Pricila wrinkled her nose at the smell of the buses parked alongside the building. She wondered which one she would ride with Maya and Baby Carmen.

He walked faster and she nearly tripped over her own feet to keep up.

"Where are the—"

"Not now." This time he didn't smile. He swooped down and lifted Pricila up in the air. Then he held her against him, one hand under her butt and the other forcing her head down. Her nose bumped against his shoulder and she froze with terror. She wished she hadn't left with him. She wished she had stayed where Maya told her to.

They walked past the big fountain and yellow taxis.

She could hear him breathing and white steam puffed out of his nose. He started running and she squeezed her eyes shut, hoping he wouldn't drop her; hoping Mommy would appear out of nowhere.

He stopped running and she heard keys jangling. A car door opened and he swung her inside. With one glimpse up at him, Pricila realized he didn't look very nice anymore. She opened her mouth to scream but he slammed the door.

Something tells me to look up again. I feel it like a hand grabbing the back of my neck.

I do, and then Pricila glances up over the man's shoulder. Suddenly all these broken pieces pull together in my mind to form a picture. The man driving around Santa Ana, offering rides to little girls. Pricila's white coat.

The doors close behind Agent Acacio as he moves into the train station.

I'm out of the car. Everything in my purse scatters on the sidewalk. My feet pound the asphalt and tires scream as a driver hits the brakes to keep from running me over.

I leap up onto the sidewalk and my wedge boots give out under me. I fall sideways into a puddle of oily water. But I look up when I hear a yelp and then the slamming of a door. He sees me and then ducks into the dented Subaru backed into a parking space. My knee burns and my ankle screams but I get up and hobble the distance to his car.

"Stop! Stop!" I scream so loud it hurts my throat. He starts the car and I slam both fists against the hood.

He revs the engine and the car lurches forward. I lever myself up and my shins crash into the bumper. I snatch my right foot up before it's pulled under the car.

I don't have time to pray. My fingers hook under the hood.

I see the top of Pricila's head over the backseat. He didn't even buckle her in.

I then meet his eyes through the windshield. He grins at me as he guns the car forward, and my first thought as I swing off the hood is that this is going to hurt.

But Agent Acacio shouts for him to stop, and knowing he has a gun, I think that the pain will be worth it.

OLD, COLD HAND

BY LAWRENCE MADDOX

City of Orange

J eannie is celebrating the rites of spring at Lake Mead this weekend," Hudson proclaimed with a deep rumble, taking his eye off me long enough to pack his pipe. "Initiating the drunken mating rituals of the collegiate slut with like-minded male strangers, à la *Girls Gone Wild*, no doubt."

I knew Jeannie. She wasn't a good girl. She liked to spread rumors that she was bedding her professors. I guess in Hudson's case, her immature bragging was true.

"The dickens of it is, Josh, I need to break into her room. Tonight."

"I just don't see you as the love-letter type, Hudson."

"I'm not, damn you." Hudson pawed his trim white beard. "The girl is crazy. She likes to play games that escalate. She sent me these."

Hudson tossed a folder. I pulled out a sheet of paper with porno magazine pictures of a man and woman glued to it.

"Doggy style. Does that have importance?"

"No."

The woman's head had been replaced with the face of a teenage girl, the man's with a gray-bearded geezer. "Hey, Wilford Brimley," I said, recognizing the actor from the diabetes commercials. A voice bubble from the girl said, *Do I get an "A" yet?* Wilford Brimley replied, *No talking in class!*

It was signed, *Studiously yours, Jeannie.*

"That's the first one," Hudson explained. He didn't seem embarrassed at all. I looked through the folder. There were a bunch more, each raunchier than the next.

"You replied in kind?"

"Yes, but mine were more sophisticated."

"And she's threatening you?"

"She's making outrageous demands. She wants honors. A TA position. She wants to hold hands on campus. She says she'll go public. I will not have my reputation tarnished, Josh. It means everything."

I tossed the folder back. "I didn't know you had it in you."

Hudson stopped mid-puff. "What does that mean?"

"Nothing. Well, I mean, with your busy schedule, dating a younger woman who is also a serious head case could be a challenge."

Hudson glared hard before responding. "We weren't dating. We were screwing. Age wasn't an issue."

"I didn't mean that," I said, though that's exactly what I'd meant.

"I intend to have those letters back. Are you in?"

"Look, Hudson, there's no way. It's too crazy. I mean, c'mon. Plus, I've got somebody arriving into town tonight." That was true. I was doing one last interview with Hank Watson for my documentary about former prisoners from the frightful penitentiary in Moundsville, West Virgina.

Hank Watson, charged with burglary, kidnapping, assault. And that's just what got him into Texas' infamous Gatesville reform school as a teen in the '40s. He later graduated to much bigger, deadlier things. Hank needed special handling.

"Tenure reviews are next month," Hudson said.

There it was. Implied, limped around, now it was out on the table.

"I've got to pick someone. Joan is just as qualified, and with those legs, nicer to have around. Frankly, I think I have a shot at her."

"This is unfair. My film went to Sundance."

"You know how many lousy docs play up there? Doesn't mean squat. I was a judge at Sundance. Skied circles around Redford." He waved a beefy, sun-splotched hand at the photos on the wall behind him.

A black-and-white of Hudson with Redford, the Sundance Kid himself, on skis. Hudson was clearly puffing out his chest. It was next to a photo of Hudson holding a big-mouth bass with David Jansen, next to a photo of Hudson karate-chopping James Coburn.

On his bookshelf, enclosed in glass, stood his Academy Award for Best Documentary, *Nineteen Seventy-Something.*

Hudson had the career and the life that had thus far eluded me.

"My point is, as department chair, I do the picking. It's completely autocratic. There are candidates you don't even know about. It doesn't have to be you."

"Don't tell me I'm not good for Chapman. *Freedom Kills* is going to air on PBS. I'm an asset and you know it."

"Chapman is your third university in less than a decade, Josh. You're a newlywed. You don't want to continue dragging that cute little wife of yours around like a bedouin. Orange is a nice little town. Does Sarah know that with tenure, Chapman helps finance the house?"

"We know."

"In this market, you'll clean up. Nothing makes one feel more like a man than buying one's wife a nice house. Except banging twins in said house when wifey goes to spa."

"I got the man thing covered, Hudson," though his words

carried weight. The house, like the career, seemed like a dream that was slipping away. "I just can't help wondering why you're asking me."

"Because you want it bad. I've been in academia for forty years. I can smell you young guns coming a mile away."

"I'm a young gun and I didn't even know it."

"And we both know the other reason."

Now it was my turn to glare. "Other reason?"

"Word gets around, Josh. You and Jeannie?"

"Hold on right there. She's a liar. According to her, she was banging half the faculty, and I don't just mean the male half either."

Hudson cracked a smile. "Of course. Jeannie loved to embellish. I just meant you'd understand my predicament."

"Yeah, I get it. I just haven't taken the plunge like you. So that's why you're asking me?"

Hudson tapped his pipe. "There was love in that little doc of yours. I'd put forth you became enamored of the darkness. Tracking down those ancient ex-cons, getting their nasty little tales, the horrors of the revolution during that prison uprising. You have an interest in things that are out of bounds, young man."

I couldn't deny it. The film, two and a half years in the making, had become an obsession. When nothing else seemed to be working out for me, the doc became my anchor.

I spent months interviewing former inmates of that West Virginia prison, delving into their criminal lives before jail, coaxing out their stories of what they did to survive in hell, and describing in pathetic detail their eked-out existences as old, broken, forgotten men. Three of my subjects had already died. Two by their own hand.

But not Hank Watson. There's a brief montage of him doing his strenuous jail cell work out in the Bakersfield YMCA where he now resides. "Sixty push-ups, sixty seconds," Hank said, looking into the camera. "Just for starters."

I made sure to document my subjects' participation in the bloody prison uprising of 1980 that left twenty guards dead. There had been torture, things done to others that could only have been dreamed up by minds on ice.

There's a good chance Hank had been manning a blow-torch.

"Without tenure, Josh, it only makes sense for you to leave Chapman. Move on when the semester's up."

"Sarah and I were counting on this. You're really sticking it to me, Hudson."

My time spent on *Freedom Kills* had taken its toll on Sarah and me. She had called the engagement off, and she wouldn't put the ring back on until I was done shooting. Hank especially creeped her out.

"Are you in, or are you out after the next semester?"

"Tonight's tough, Hudson," my mind grinding out the possibilities.

Hank Watson, convicted of murder in 1958, was coming over to our apartment. The old friendless relic had appreciated all the attention I'd paid to him. If I asked him to, he'd wait for me in one of those coffee shops in Old Towne spooking the college girls reading Derrida.

"Lifetime employment, Josh. These days, you have to schlep mail to find that."

I could make this work. Sarah and I needed this. I could turn this for good. "It's a deal, Hudson. You're going to owe me."

"Tenure."

"Yeah. Who's driving?"

* * *

Orange was unreal in the spring. It wasn't just the surprise scent of blooming buttercup roses that came rolling into Hudson's open car window as we drove through quaint Old Towne. It was the preserved Americana of it all. Most of the office buildings dated back to the Roaring Twenties. While neighboring Anaheim was a revolving door of strip malls and booty motels, Orange kept its history intact. I'd never seen more antique stores in my life, but they made sense in an antique, lost-in-time town like this.

You could count on things not changing here. Sarah and I loved it.

"Will you man-up and stop calling your wife?" Hudson commanded.

"Don't worry, I didn't tell her I was about to break into a coed's room to steal a batch of love letters."

Sarah was working late at the hospital, and wasn't due back home for hours. I left a message on her cell, hoping I'd be done with Hudson's little B&E before Hank came calling.

The truth was, I didn't want Sarah coming home and finding Hank hanging around. "That twisted old ghost loves you, Josh," she'd said recently. He had become just as obsessed with me as I was about capturing his gruesome stories for the doc. He'd turn up at places I went. I chalked it up to old man loneliness, and he thankfully faded away when we moved to Orange County.

Hudson turned down a tree-lined street sporting a collection of some of Orange's hundred-year-old Victorians. He rolled up to an imposing, unlit two-story with a receded garage tucked away on the side.

I was surprised to see Hudson pull out a key and unlock the garage door.

"I thought we were breaking in."

"We are, you fool. Jeannie gave me a key to the garage so I wouldn't have to park on the street."

"You two were very hush-hush, eh?"

"I'm an old hand at this, Josh. At my age, you'll jump through hoops of fire for a piece of tail a half century your junior."

"I hope to grow up by then."

"Your testicles need to drop first."

The neighborhood was quiet. Operating under moonlight, we carried a ladder out of the garage and around to the back. The turn-of-the-century Victorian, surrounded by cedars, a chestnut, and the ubiquitous jacaranda, had been converted into student housing. "Jeannie said she was going away with all her housemates," Hudson whispered. "I'm sure they're drunk and naked by now."

We placed the ladder against the beige wooden side. "I'll go first," Hudson growled. He spryly scampered to the second story and disappeared inside the bay window. If carrying a ladder and holding Hudson's hand was all I'd have to do, I thought, then this was the right move. I followed him up.

Inside was dark and silent. I could smell patchouli mixed with stale beer. I treaded down the hardwood floor of a hallway, a staircase behind me and three closed doors in front.

"Hudson," I whispered loudly.

No response. He'd only beat me by maybe half a minute, but he was nowhere in sight. He clearly wasn't on the stairs, unless the old fart had fallen over the railing.

If someone appeared, my story would be that I was here to discuss a grade with Jeannie and I'd simply let myself in.

I tried the first door and peered inside. Nobody home. I quietly shut the door. *Where the hell is Hudson?* I went to the second door when my resolve left me. *Something's not right. I'm out of here.*

The door opened before I could turn away.

"What took you so long?" Hudson reprimanded.

I entered the room. Filtered moonlight revealed a scattered mess. I bumped into a chair with jeans tossed over the back. A vanity stood near the door, which Hudson quietly closed behind us. Across the room, a lumpy bed with a full-length mirror at its head.

"How about some light?"

"As you wish."

Jeannie's pretty face was above the edge of the bedsheet, as were her hands, each tied to an opposite post. Her feet were bound similarly.

"Whoa," I muttered, taking a step back. "Is she . . . ?"

"I just want to say it wasn't a rape." His voice stunned me. I turned to face him. He was holding a gun. "I didn't have to force myself, of course. She was willing as always. Things just got a little too rough, and I choked her out." He looked down at his hands. "Didn't know I still had it in me. That kind of power." He shook his head. "The house was empty, except for the two of us, and then it was time for my appointment with you. When I left, my path was clear."

"We better get those letters and take off, then," I lamely offered.

"I don't know where the damn letters are. Doubtless they will turn up. That's why I need you."

"Is this a joke, Hudson?"

"Strip down and get in bed with her."

"Have you forgotten your senility pills?"

"I may be old, but I've lived more life than you. And I will continue to do so while you're buried, unsung, and turning into compost."

I didn't move.

"I'm prepared for this, Josh. Hands on buttons."

"Hudson, stop now. What you did here was clearly an accident. You were in the throes of passion with a woman half your age. A third or so, really, but it doesn't matter. Can you imagine the press?" My mind was working quickly. "It was a crime of passion. They'll paint you as this incredible stud."

Hudson seemed to mull this over. His body sagged, as if someone let all the air out. "You're right. I don't know what I was thinking. I'm through. I might as well go out à la *Entertainment Tonight*. They'll no doubt unearth my Academy Award speech."

"Without a doubt."

"Just turn around and give me a head start. I have some business to clean up."

"Of course, Hudson."

I raised my hands and turned to face Jeannie. I always thought she was pretty, but on closer examination, I realized she was just kind of ordinary. Her youth was the main attraction.

I heard a soft *pop* and fell hard to my knees. It was like every nerve ending in my right foot had been blown apart.

"I have a silencer, Josh. And at the angle I shot you, it would appear as if you pulled the trigger yourself. By accident. A case of nerves, like anyone would have after murdering their unbalanced, immature mistress. And then you cuddled her corpse before blowing your brains out."

I cradled my foot. I was afraid to take my shoe off in case the whole thing fell apart.

"Those rumors Jeannie spread, I guess they were true after all."

"No, they weren't. No one will believe it," I said, shuddering.

"They'll believe it." Hudson stepped closer. "Are you crying, Josh? I always knew you were a pussy. You young Turks can never back up the talk."

I had nothing to say. I was in the most horrible pain of my life, and he was gloating.

"Get undressed and get in bed and I'll do the rest. I've considered having you write a suicide note, but I think things will be self-apparent."

I felt my fingers work the buttons on my shirt. I stood up painfully, balanced on one foot.

"And don't worry about Sarah. I'm a great consoler."

"You won't get away with this." My voice was measured and soft.

"Trousers."

It was hard to pull them over my sneaker. I was taking my time about everything. Slow seconds were all I had.

"Now into the arms of Morpheus," Hudson said.

The bed was surprisingly warm. I got in one knee at a time. I didn't want to touch her cold body. I didn't want to see her dead naked flesh under the sheet.

I heard a crack, and the sound of metal hit the floor, followed by a groan.

I looked around.

Finally.

Hank, baseball bat in hand. He picked up the gun.

Hudson cradled his elbow where Hank had walloped him.

"Put your pants on, boy," Hank said. He tossed the bat to me, kept the gun on Hudson. "Unless you three want your privacy."

It had been a year, and he looked the same. Crew cut. Red neck. Same thick glasses taped in the middle, frames issued by Moundsville thirty years ago. Big ooglie eyes. Slight paunch. Pendleton, same one.

And the veins. They protruded like electrical wires on every visible inch of his creased skin.

"Looks like I done broke up a party."

"Hank," I said. "What took you?"

"It's all right now. Just don't lose your lunch. Already got to clean the blood residues from your leaking hoof." He said *residue* slow, drawn out, like I suppose they did in the '30s in West Texas, where he was from.

"I know you," Hudson said, still painfully clutching his arm. "You're from Josh's documentary."

Hank grinned. "Reckon I am."

Hudson watched me, then looked back to Hank. "What are you doing here?"

"I'm here for my friend Josh. He left me a message."

"Didn't trust you, Hudson, about the tenure. Hank and I were going to keep the letters and you were going to keep your promise." I took a gulp of air.

"You learned something from us old-timers," Hank said appreciatively.

I nodded.

Hudson couldn't take his eyes off Hank. "I'm a killer now too," he said. It was his turn to have a soft, measured, shell-shocked voice.

"Oh yeah? Who'd you kill?"

"Her."

"Her?"

"That's what I said—"

Hank backhanded him.

Hank has big, sharp rings on his fingers. He calls them his class rings, because they "educate others when they be needin' it."

Hank rubbed his hand. "No back talk, and it's 'yes sir' here on out. Now who'd you say you killed?"

"The girl on the bed," Hudson replied through his bloody lips. He pinched his face with effort as he grumbled the word "sir."

I guffawed when I heard him say it.

Hudson shot me a look.

"You don't say," Hank retorted. He lifted up the bedsheet to take a long look.

Hudson shifted uneasily, as if a powerful stranger was checking out his girlfriend on a lonely street corner.

"I know dead, son," Hank intoned. "And she ain't it." He felt her neck. "There's a pulse. Strong too." Hank slapped her lightly. "Wake up, pretty princess."

Hudson turned gray. He fell back against the wall. "What is this?" he gasped. "What the hell is this?"

Hank examined her neck. "You bruised her, but you didn't break the hyoidal bone. That's what shows death by strangulation. Reckon you was too weak." He felt the top of her blonde head. "Bump on her noggin too. That's what knocked her out."

Hank ran a finger down a crack on the mirror, just out of sight below the mattress. "For an old guy, you did a number on her." His laugh was a series of wheezes.

Hudson took a faltering step toward her.

"Jeannie . . ."

"*With the light brown hair,*" Hank sang. He walked over to the minifridge and pocketed the salt shaker sitting on top. "This and some ammonia should wake our sleeping princess right up." He turned to me. "Keep an eye on him. And keep him away from the girl. He's done enough to her."

"Where are you going?" I asked.

"Don't 'plex up, Josh. I'm coming right back." Hank handed me the gun and stepped out of the room.

"We can still get out," Hudson whispered. "You can't trust him. He's an ex-con, full of tricks."

"I can trust *you*?"

"I made a mistake. Jeannie's alive now. Can't you see the ground's shifted?"

I studied him. The man's man took out his pipe.

"Our word against his, Josh. They'll believe any story we agree to. He's a nonbeing."

"And Jeannie?"

"She's alive. She doesn't know anything except we got a little overzealous in the sack. There's been no crime, you idiot. Can't you see?" Hank puffed empty pipe air. "I guess I love her, Josh."

My foot throbbed painfully, but not nearly as bad as when I was pulling my pants off. "You shot me," I whispered. "That's got to be a crime."

"Right," he said. "Right. I'll fix everything, Josh."

I looked at him, but I wasn't seeing him anymore. I was seeing me, in that bed, and Sarah finding out.

And funny enough, I thought of my guys from the doc. My guys, and how they had made the cruel guards plead.

"I'm a legend in my field, Josh. Things will happen for you under my guidance. But we might have to shoot him."

Guidance. I'd so needed it, someone to take an interest. Someone to help me get ahead.

"Don't be buying his wolf ticket, Josh."

Hank strode back in the room, holding a bottle of ammonia. He set it and the salt down on the fridge. "Smelling salts."

Hudson looked sick.

Hank took the gun. "Unless you want to hold onto it."

I considered it. "That's okay."

"Had to drain the weasel too," he explained. "Happens every hour, these days. So what you wanna do, Josh?"

"I guess we call the police," I said half-heartedly.

Hank took a deep breath.

"Josh," Hudson pleaded. "I didn't know what I was doing. Tenure, whatever you want, it's yours. Please." He was sniffling. Minutes ago, he'd called me a pussy.

"I don't know what this 'tender' is he's offering," Hank said. "I found you naked. He was going to smoke your ass, boy. Who knows how this'll all play out." Hank put his hand on my shoulder. "Now, if you could do anything you wanted, anything, what would you do?"

Hudson would've killed me. He had wanted my Sarah. I was still shaking.

I realized someone had shown me the way.

They all had.

You dip into the dark place. You reach out and grab it.

"They should find him in women's clothing," I blurted.

There was a silence in the room.

"Done," Hank said. "Some kind of kinky, left-wing sex-murder-suicide dilly. The reporters will love that." He smirked. "Makes me wish I went to college myself."

Hudson all but peed his pants.

I looked at Jeannie.

Hank nodded in her direction. "She's the price of doing business."

Hudson stepped forward. "You can't touch her. I won't let you."

"I can do anything I want."

"I, I won't let you," Hudson repeated weakly. This may have been his finest moment.

There was a pause, broken by Hank's wheezed laughter. "I

can't keep it up no more. She's dead. Was from the start. Cold as a rack of lamb." He rubbed the back of his creased neck. "Just a little test, Josh. See if you'd turn on ol' Hank." He settled down, then turned to Hudson. "Go through her closet. Pick something pink."

"And frilly," I added.

Later, Hank and I drove his 1972 VW van to Hudson's to retrieve my car. Hank had tended to my foot, but Sarah was going to have to clean it up. I'd have some explaining to do. Hank didn't think I'd need to go to the hospital.

"I just hope I beat Sarah home," I said.

"Sarah already came home."

I looked at Hank. His eyes stared back, distorted and enlarged by his broken, prison-issue glasses.

"She was there when I knocked."

I was clutching my seat.

Hank looked me over. "Look like you seen a ghost, boy."

"You said Sarah . . ."

"Yeah, but she wouldn't let me in. I don't think that wife of yours trusts me."

I exhaled, deeply relieved.

"Anyway," Hank continued. "I know you always like seeing me when I turn up. So there I was, and here I am. You're gonna have to have a talking to her, do something about her attitude."

I was definitely going to have to do *something*.

The house is beautiful, a two-story Craftsman from 1912 with polished hardwood floors you can slide ten feet on in your socks. Sarah briefly tended her rose garden in the back, but the weeds have gained the upper hand since she moved in with her mother in Newport.

There's a guest house in the back, with its own bathroom and even a little yard of its own.

That's where Hank lives.

I couldn't really explain to Sarah why I had allowed Hank to live in the back. Hank and I are like blood brothers now, he explained to me later. We'd both rescued each other, me from certain death, him from loneliness and obscurity. Maybe suicide. Now we got each other's backs, he said.

Sarah thought it particularly bizarre how Hank would sit there cackling on his porch over that old copy of the *Orange County Register*. The one with the headline, *Dress-Clad Prof and Coed in Murder Suicide*.

Blood. The ammonia cleaned up mine.

Now I have something bigger to clean up.

Sarah's four months pregnant, but she won't even talk to me.

I have to fix this, but it's like he's always watching. Always ready.

Still doing his jail cell workout, right there in the middle of Sarah's garden.

I guess that's the beauty of Hank.

I'm going to have to leave the house tonight without Hank following me. I'm meeting an old prison acquaintance of his in Old Towne tonight for a cup of coffee. Benito Scalvo was locked up for over twenty years on a murder-for-hire beef. He's in my doc too. He and Hank have a long-standing prison hate for each other. I want to talk to Benito about that. Benito has no family to speak of, no prospects. Nothing in the world to do.

He was so glad I looked him up.

THE MOVIE GAME

BY DICK LOCHTE

Laguna Niguel

Alfred Hitchcock was definitely some kind of gamesman. Weird, but a gamesman. He had it figured that people came to his films with an attitude, like they were on to his game and daring him to show them some moves they weren't expecting. So he gave them really twisted stuff. Like Janet Leigh getting all cut up in the shower. Or the old dude with his eyes pecked out in *The Birds*. Or, later in his career, in *Frenzy*, when censorship loosened up, the killer breaking the fingers of a naked corpse to get at something she'd been clutching when he strangled her.

But the thing is, he didn't take the game that seriously. As he once famously said to an actress who told him she was worried about how to play a scene: "Ingrid, it's only a movie."

I was slumped behind the wheel of my parked taxi, drowsing over a copy of François Truffaut's conversations with Hitchcock, taking an easy trip through the great director's head. It was a slow night. Lots of slow nights in Laguna Niguel, but there wasn't anything left for me in L.A. and I was living more or less rent-free in my sister and brother-in-law's converted garage in the Hills, making enough behind the wheel to pop for dinner for them every now and then.

I wasn't fooling myself. I knew I was just treading water and I'd have to swim for shore sooner or later. But on nights like that, nice and balmy, with nothing pressing, treading seemed preferable to making waves and attracting sharks. Not that sharks don't find you anyway.

I was in the middle of Hitchcock's description of "Mary Rose," a ghost story he'd considered filming, when the box started squawking and, between squawks, Manny, back at the garage, was repeating a familiar name. Mine. J.D. Marquette.

Manny has a cleft palate and his words have a slushy, lispy sound that I won't try to duplicate in print. "Fare's at a shopping center on La Paz Road, J.D.," he said, adding the name of the center and the exact address. "He'll be in front of Gregory's. Too smashed to drive home."

"Good job, Manny," I said. "I love ferrying drunks."

I turned off the battery-operated book light, a gift from sis, closed the cover on Hitchcock and Truffaut, and went back to work.

That section of La Paz Road is like Mall Town U.S.A. One shopping center right after the other. By light of day, with their too-new, seamless, pastel-colored plaster coats, the structures resemble not very creative film sets, populated by extra players. Those pastels turn circus sinister at night, especially after the shops have started to shutter and most of the extras have headed home.

A big guy staggering around with his collar open and his tie at half mast and four other males, somewhat more sober, were gathered near the entrance to the center, in front of Gregory's Sports Grill. The drunk was the only one of them who looked as if he'd ever played a sport other than foosball. He was big enough to have been a linebacker in his younger days, before he gave it up to booze.

"Glad you made it so fast," a thin guy with glasses said when I got out of the cab. He turned to the ex-linebacker. "Sonny, here's the cab."

"Fuck the cab," the drunk, a.k.a. Sonny, said. "Don't need no fuckin cab."

The thin guy gave me Sonny's address in Monarch Pointe and a pleading look.

I took a step toward the big man. "Come on, sir," I said, taking his elbow. "Time to go home."

He jerked back, face flushed, eyes red as Dracula's. "Don't you touch me. Who the fuck are you?"

"He's the cabbie, Sonny," one of the other guys said. "Gonna drive you home."

Sonny glared at me for a second, then staggered to the side. "Goin home, myself," he muttered. "Doan need help from this long-haired prick."

He did his drunk dance toward the few cars remaining in the parking lot.

The thin guy with glasses ran after him, tried to stop him. Sonny shoved him away, then staggered to a beautiful cream-colored Lexus convertible. He paused, doubled up, and emptied the contents of his stomach over the rear of that lovely vehicle.

Better it than the interior of my cab.

He wiped his mouth on the sleeve of his jacket, then struggled with the car door, got it open, and squeezed behind the wheel.

"Jackass's gonna kill himself," one of the men said.

"Or somebody," I said, as Sonny roared past us, trailing vomit and exhaust.

The thin guy with glasses apologized for wasting my time, gave me two twenties for my trouble. That seemed like a fair enough exchange, even including the *long-haired prick* comment.

I got back in the taxi, folded the twenties, stuck them in

the pocket of my island shirt, and checked in with Manny. "Fare decided to drive himself home."

"Anybody else there need a cab?"

"Doesn't look like it."

"Shit, J.D. We oughta start chargin' these bastards for cancelations," Manny lisped.

"Absolutely," I said. "You got anything else for me?"

"Price of gas, these fuckers should pay."

"Damn straight," I said. "You got another run for me?"

"Naw. It's dead here, J.D."

"Then I think I'll call it a night."

"Wish *I* could," Manny said. "The fuckers."

It wasn't that late. Especially for somebody who gets up around noon. There were a couple of bars near the ocean that still might offer an hour or two of action, such as it was. Probably wouldn't take me that long to blow the forty.

There was no traffic along La Paz. Just the darkness broken by my headlights, the occasional streetlight, and the even more occasional traffic light. I thought about Kelly. There's a scene in *Citizen Kane* where this old guy played by Everett Sloane tells the reporter that when he was a kid he saw this little girl on a ferry, wearing a white dress and carrying a white parasol. He never met her, but as he says, "Not a month goes by when I don't think of her." That was kind of like me and Kelly Raye. Except that we did meet. And we lived together for a while, until I made a mistake and she discovered I wasn't the kind of uncomplicated, dependable young man she thought I was. Funny thing, I was ready to be that guy. But hell, too little and too late. So she was in L.A. and I was in L.N. And not a day went by when I didn't think of her.

I was recalling her birthday two years ago, when I'd just

flown in from New York and . . . Christ! A blonde suddenly leaped out of the shadows on the left, hopped the neutral ground, and ran right in front of my goddamned cab.

I jammed my foot on the brakes and the cab skidded to a stop inches from her, my movie book and lamp sliding to the floor. The seat belt was digging into my shoulder. My hands were locked around the steering wheel.

The blonde was in my headlights. If I'd been going faster than the limit, I'd have hit her. She reached out a hand to touch the cab's hood, maybe to convince herself that it had really stopped.

When I began breathing again, I pried my fingers from the wheel, rolled down the window, and shouted, "What the hell, lady?"

"You're the best," she said, walking around the cab. "I wasn't sure you'd stop. I need a ride and here you are . . ."

She tried to open the rear door and was surprised to find it locked. She frowned, then figured it out. "Aw, crap. You're off duty?"

She was in her late twenties, maybe three or four years younger than me. Dressed California casual, in aqua T-shirt and tight designer jeans. Not spectacular but pretty enough. Straight blond hair. Tanned skin. Good body. Carrying a big floppy purse, the size of a beach bag.

"Please," she said. "I'm desperate. I really fucking need a ride . . . away from here. It's worth fifty dollars."

"Where to?"

She hesitated, then said, "Ritz-Carlton."

Fifty bucks to drive five or six miles. I stared at her, thinking about it.

"A friend drove me here. He . . . didn't want to leave the party. And he didn't want me to leave, either. Understand?"

She looked to our left. I looked there too, and couldn't see anything but the vague shadowy outline of one of those residential complexes with cookie-cutter buildings, heavy on the redwood and stucco. "Please. I really need a lift."

She seemed to be suffering from a lack of sincerity, but fifty bucks was fifty bucks, so I pushed the button that unlocked the doors and she hopped in.

Softened by the age-yellowed bandit barrier, her face looked better than pretty. A hometown beauty contest winner whom the movie cameras didn't love quite enough. In some kind of trouble. She ran her fingers through her hair and let out a long sigh. "You're a lifesaver," she said. Looking to the left again, she added, "Let's went, Cisco."

I stepped on the gas but kept my eye on her in the rearview as she reached into her big bag. She didn't look like carjacker material, but I stopped breathing until her hand reappeared with a cellular. She raised the thin slab to her ear. "You clear?" she asked somebody, leaning forward, tensing. "Great, baby. I'm in a cab," she said. "Right. Amazing luck, huh, a fucking cab out here in the boonies . . . No. Just worry about yourself. I'm golden." She listened for a few beats, then, "Shit. You think?"

She snapped the phone shut.

"Everything okay?" I asked.

Linking eyes with me in the rearview, she said, "I'm not sure. Look, I, ah, didn't mean to offend. The boonies comment."

"Boonies works for me. This is where Republicans come to die."

"You live here long?"

"About a year."

"Before that?"

"L.A."

"Ah. That makes more sense. The hair. I . . ." Her cellular must've vibrated again. "Excuse me," she said and took the call. "Yeah?" Her head dropped and her face hardened. "Woohoo. I'm so scared, you dickless wonder. Eat shit and die." She clicked off the phone. Then she lowered her window and threw the phone out into the night.

"Friend?" I said.

She leaned forward, closer to the plastic guard that separated us, and asked, "Want another fifty?"

"I'm listening."

"Get off this street as soon as you can, stop, and cut the lights."

She looked back to where I'd picked her up, doing a head turn that almost matched Linda Blair's. There was nothing much to see behind us.

In front of us, the neutral ground on the left went on and on. There was a park to our right, separated from the sidewalk by a low white double-rail fence. I could see where the fence ended. I goosed the gas and made the turn into the park on two wheels. Then I made another turn into an empty parking area separated from the road by thick foliage. I braked, killed the engine, and turned off the lights. "This what you had in mind?" I asked.

"Oh yeah, baby," she said. "Perfect. But *I could use a Valium the size of a hockey puck.*"

I turned to look at her. "That's a Woody Allen line, right?"

"*Broadway Danny Rose,*" she said. She leaned forward and squinted at my license information in the moonlight. "J.D. Marquette. So you're into movies, huh, J.D.?"

"I used to have a job that gave me a lot of free time."

"Me too."

"What's your name?" I asked.

"You can call me Nora. Ah, J.D., we may be here a while."

"Yeah?"

"I am paying you a hundred bucks."

"Point made, Nora." I reached down, picked my book and reading light from the floor, and put them into the cab's glove compartment.

"You even read about movies, huh? Maybe we should play the movie game while we wait. It's my favorite."

"I'm not big on games, Nora."

"Oh, come on. You're good. The way you nailed that Woody Allen, maybe too good. I think we should stick to just one genre. All things considered, maybe crime movies."

"I don't play games," I said. "Why don't you just tell me what's going on here?"

"Kind of a crazy story with a crazy twist to it." She was grinning at me.

"That line's from *Double Indemnity*," I said. "Fred Mac-Murray. Now, stop with the bullshit and tell me why we're sitting here in the dark."

"I guess that's not asking too much. My friend . . . his name is Tom Iverson . . . we live in the Florida Keys. Tom has this dumb charter boat thing going. But he does other odds and ends too. So he tells me he's got business here and we'll be spending a few days at the Ritz-Carlton, which sounded like a nice kinda getaway. Only when we arrive, he says the business is with this guy I don't really care for, who's like a freak and a half, you know. Anyway, we go to this . . . Hold on. Car coming."

Nora and I sat silent as a black Escalade floated by, heading south.

When it was well passed, I said, "Okay for us to leave now?"

"No. Not okay. There'll be more and they know I'm in a cab."

"Who's they?"

"Friends of the asshole."

"So, tell me about the asshole."

"His name is Joey Ziegler. A stunt man. You probably saw him in the last *Batman*, the one with the dead Joker guy. I've never exactly warmed to Joey, because he does stuff like grabbing a tit when Tom isn't looking. Anyway, we're bringing Joey a little something Tom picked up in Yucatan, a—"

"*A piece of junk worth half a million*," I said, completing her sentence.

She smiled. "Oops. You do know movies."

"You were feeding me a remake of *Night Moves*. Not a bad film. Gene Hackman as a private eye. Lousy ending. Tell me what really went on back there, Nora. Right now, or I'm tossing you out of the fucking cab."

"Okay, this is the truth, J.D. Wait . . . another car."

This one was a white Escalade. Moving at about fifteen miles per hour. Flashlight beams shot out of its open windows, scanning the foliage on both sides of the road. I didn't think they could see any part of the cab.

"Maybe we should move further back in the park," I suggested when they'd passed.

"Okay. But don't turn on the lights."

I started the engine, backed onto the lane, and began creeping deeper into the park guided by moon glow. We passed a golf course and, eventually, a building in darkness that I assumed was some sort of clubhouse. The lane made a fork, one section continuing on, the other circling the building to a small lot. I took the latter, moving the cab as close to the rear of the building as I could.

"Better," she said. "Maybe we'll make it through the night."

"You were about to tell me the truth."

"Right. My friend John and I have been collecting a few dead presidents selling heroin to Brentwood and Beverly Hills assholes who like to impress their party guests with a special after-dinner treat."

"Where do you get the product?"

"John has a friend who's an army sergeant in—"

She stopped talking because I was shaking my head. "God-damnit. You just can't help yourself, can you?"

"What?" She pretended to be sincerely confused.

"*Who'll Stop the Rain?* Michael Moriarty and Tuesday Weld, with Nick Nolte as the soldier. Not as good as the book. Get out of my cab. I'm finished."

"No, baby," she replied. "I'll say when you're finished." I didn't need much moonlight to see the huge gun she pulled from her bag. "I wouldn't put too much faith in this cheap bandit shield." She tapped the barrel of the gun against the plastic that separated us. "I mean, maybe it might stop a bul-let, but . . . *being as this is a .44 Magnum, the most powerful handgun in the world and would blow your head clean off, you've got to ask yourself one question: do I feel lucky?*"

"Clint Eastwood in *Dirty Harry*," I said, my mouth sud-denly as dry as Clint's delivery. What Nora was holding was a Smith & Wesson Magnum, all right. But it was a 500, bigger and badder than the one in the movie. Enough to take out the bandit shield, me, and the front of the cab.

"Relax, J.D.," she said. "I got no reason to shoot you, long as you behave. In fact, I'm doing you a favor. If you drove out of here right now, with or without me, you'd be a dead man. The difference is: if we're together when they find us, they'll probably just shoot us both. But if I'm not with you, they'll beat you to death trying to find out where you left me."

"Why do they want you? Be straight with me, Nora. No more Yucatán pottery or drugs, huh?"

"My partner Jed and I . . . got into a situation back there."

"What kind of situation?"

"That doesn't matter now," she said. "It happened. We pissed off the wrong guys, the kind who get real biblical when it comes to payback."

"What happened to your partner?"

"He's dead. That call I got was from some zombie, telling me he'd just shot Jed in the face. Like that's supposed to freak me out. Fuck them."

If she wasn't freaked, she was either delusional or suicidal.

Two Escalades full of homicidal assholes out for revenge. Not exactly an everyday occurrence in Orange County. I knew of only one local who might have that kind of entourage, a former Vegas "businessman" who'd retired to the peace and quiet of Laguna Niguel.

"What did you and Jed do to get on the bad side of Caesar Berlucci?" I asked.

"Bad side?" She gave me a nasty smile. "Jed blew that fat wop right out of his Guccis."

"He killed Berlucci? Why would anybody do something that stupid?"

She stopped smiling and tensed. For a second, I thought she was going to use that giant gun. Then she slumped again and I let out the breath I'd been holding.

"It's what we were paid to do," she said.

"Paid by whom?"

"Who the fuck knows? Or cares? The contract comes in. You do the job. Money is money."

"It couldn't have been easy, getting that close to the old man," I said.

"Jed had a golden tongue. Talked us into the compound, won the old bastard over. We would've made it away clean, but Jed got greedy." For a second her eyes sifted toward her big bag, then back at me.

"What went wrong?" I asked.

"Shit happens," she said. "And now we got goombas on our ass."

Yes we did. Two Escalades full, prowling around out there looking for a cab. They'd find out she hadn't made it to the hotel. They would double back and go over the route again. Eventually they'd check out the park and find us.

When they did, Nora, with her ridiculous gigantic gun, which held only five rounds, assuming she hadn't used one or two on Berlucci, would be of no real help. On the other hand, that ridiculous gigantic gun with its five or four or three bullets was more than enough to keep me trapped.

"Okay, what now?" I asked her, while trying to come up with my own answer.

"We wait until morning and people are going to work and there'll be traffic and other cabs on the street. Then we head to L.A. And I pay you for your trouble. And we say goodbye, or . . ."

"Or what?"

"Or we keep going to Mexico and see how much fun we can get into. I've got . . . some money set aside back at the apartment."

"We have a long night before we start thinking about fun," I said.

"We could think about it a little."

"Not with me up here and you back there."

"Come on back. It's nice and comfy."

"What if we have to leave in a hurry?" I asked. "Be less dangerous to do our thinking up here."

"Sometimes danger adds a little something, but I suppose you're right."

Nora had been so sloppy at her chosen profession that I hoped she might change her mind about the gun and put it away. But she kept it pointed in my direction while she got out of the car and joined me on the front seat.

She sat facing me, her back against the door.

She kicked off her sandals, drew her left leg up, and slid it forward until her toes found wiggle room between my back and the car seat. She rested her right leg across my thighs.

"Is the gun necessary?"

"For some reason, I think so," she said. "But we can still fool around."

"Not with a gun in my face. It's much too distracting."

"Then I guess we'll just have to play the movie game instead," Nora said.

"Fun's better than games."

"The gun stays."

I shrugged. "Okay. Games. *It's a nice day for murder.*"

"Cute," Nora said. "But easy. James Cagney. *Angels with Dirty Faces.* Here's one for you: *I guess I've done murder. I won't think about that now.*"

"It's the next line that's the giveaway," I replied. "*I'll think about it tomorrow.* Vivien Leigh in *Gone with the Wind.*" I lowered my hand to her left leg and began rubbing it slowly. "Try this one. *If you're going to murder me . . . don't make it look like something else.*"

Nora frowned. Concentrating. I moved my hand another inch or so up her leg. She said, "I don't know the quote."

"*The Naked Spur.* Robert Ryan."

"A Western? Shit, that's not fair. I don't know Westerns." She was furious, aiming the weapon at my stomach with both hands. She was crazy enough to use it and, I had no doubt, she would eventually. Here. In L.A. or Mexico.

"I didn't complain about *Gone with the Wind*," I said softly.

"That's cause you knew it," she said, pouting. "Give me another and keep it on topic."

I decided to ease the tension with something she was sure to recognize. "*Have you ever done it in an elevator?*"

She grinned. "Glenn Close in *Fatal Attraction*." Happy again, maybe picking up the sexy-psychotic vibe of that movie, she wiggled a little closer. She said, "Here's one from the heart: *It's the first time I've tasted women. They're rather good.*"

I pretended to be puzzled, but in my mind I saw 007 after having just sucked a poisonous spine fish from the flesh of the beautiful Domino. "I give."

She was as gleeful as a little girl. "Sean Connery in *Thunderball*. I can't believe you didn't know that one."

I was leaning forward, my fingers brushing the inside of her thigh. "I didn't see the movie. Where did he . . . taste her?" I asked.

Nora gave me a long look. But she didn't lower the gun. "Your turn," she said. "And this time, make it hard."

"That sounds like a James Bond quote too."

She laughed. "Silly. I meant the movie reference."

"Okay," I said, sliding a little closer. "But instead of a

quote, I'll give you a story. Our hero grows up in the country, leading a good, clean, healthy life, until it's time for him to go to a state college. There, on a Marine ROTC firing range, he discovers that the hunting skills he took for granted back home are pretty damned remarkable. Enough for him to attract the attention of a government agency that dearly needs people who know how to use guns."

"I think I know the movie," she said, "but go on. And don't stop this." She lowered one hand to move mine further up her thigh.

"The agency frees him from his ROTC obligation and agrees to pay his tuition and give him spending money and a car and, in return, he agrees to work for them for four years after he graduates."

"And he becomes a sniper in Vietnam?" Nora asked.

"Not exactly. Not in Vietnam. But his work is government-sanctioned."

"Like James Bond."

"Yes. But not James Bond," I said.

"Got it. Charles Bronson in *The Mechanic*."

"No. The hero of my story is younger than Bronson. And he's based in Los Angeles, pretending to be an accountant for an independent film studio that the government actually owns. And the four years turn into eight. And, about then, he meets this beautiful, wonderful woman and—"

"*The Specialist*, with Sly Stallone and Sharon Stone."

"Let me finish," I said. "I'll make it short. He falls in love. They move in together. He decides to quit the agency, but before he can, she discovers . . . that he's been lying to her, that he's a worthless, self-loathing, piece-of-shit, government-sanctioned, homicidal sociopath."

"I'm still not sure what movie you're talking about." Staring at me, she asked. "Are you crying? Why the hell are you crying?"

"Because life is not a movie, you stupid bitch," I said, bringing my palm up fast off her thigh and shoving her hands and the big heavy Magnum into her face before she could even consider pulling the trigger. Blood flowed from her broken nose. I had the gun by then and banged it against her head twice before she went to sleep.

"I'm in a situation, Henry."

"Who's . . . Jimmy D? Zat you?"

"It's me," I said into my cellular. "Sorry to wake you, but I wasn't sure who else to call."

"No. It's okay." He started hacking and coughing. I heard his wife mumbling something in the background, then him telling her to go back to sleep, that it was business. "Long time between calls, Jimmy. What's the hap?"

I filled him in on everything that had taken place in the last hour or so. He replied by laughing.

"It's not funny, Henry."

"Depends on where you're sitting. The image of you, out in your peaceful, laid-back little town, stuck in the middle of a park with an unconscious hit woman, waiting for morning or a bunch of spaghetti-head yo-yos with guns, whichever comes first . . . it is to laugh, amigo."

"Can you do anything?" I asked. "If not, I'm going to try my luck driving out of here. I'll unload the blonde somewhere along the road."

"If they saw her get into your cab, Jimmy, they got the name and the plate and there's nowhere you can run. Gimme your number and sit tight."

Henry had been my handler. In his fifties, five-seven,

balding, vaguely pear-shaped, totally without conscience, but a straight-shooter and a father figure for all of that. He called back in twenty minutes. "I just spoke with a cretin named Morelli. He says he knows all about you, but he's the kind of braying asshole who, if he knew your name or even the cab company, would have told me just to prove how bright he is. In any case, he says he's willing to forget about you as long as he gets the eighty grand taken from Berlucci's safe. And he wants the woman, of course. You got the money, right?"

"Yeah." I had already investigated Nora's bag. It was loaded with banded fifties. "I imagine it's the full eighty. I'm not going to count it."

"Okay, here's the play. As soon as we hang up, I call Morelli with your exact location. He wants you to leave the broad and the loot right where you are and drive away. Do not look back."

"You sure they'll let me just drive away?"

"You can never be sure, Jimmy. Not when you're dealing with rabid dogs. My guess is they don't want Uncle Sam on their ass. That's the most assurance I can give you."

"Thank you, Henry."

"My pleasure."

The blood from Nora's broken nose had dried on her mouth and chin. She looked like she might be waking up soon. I'd have to hit her again.

"Henry, I'm ready to come back."

"Miss the *La Dolce Vita*, huh?"

"Something like that," I said.

"I'll be waiting with open arms, kid."

I lifted the blonde out of the cab and placed her on the asphalt behind the clubhouse. I put the bag and the money right next to her.

Then I got back into the cab. With the blonde's Magnum on the passenger seat, I left the park and turned right on La Paz. The only vehicle I saw in either direction was an old Chevy truck heading north. I passed it heading south.

But not too far south, maybe half a mile down La Paz to the first cross-street, Kings Road, where I turned right into a block full of middle-class homes. I maneuvered the cab between two sedans parked for the night.

The blonde's Magnum didn't smell as if it had been used, but it held only four shells. Better than bare hands. With the weapon dragging down my Levi's under my shirt, I worked my way back through the park.

They were a noisy bunch. Slamming car doors. Cursing. I was careful moving up behind a tree, Magnum drawn, for a view of the scene at the rear of the golf club building. Six men had come in three cars. The Escalades and a sweet yellow Jaguar convertible with the top down.

I wanted a look at Morelli and his buddies. I figured it was worth the risk to be able to recognize the bozos if they really did have a line on me and decided to do something about it. I had my night vision by then and I studied them as well as I could while they dragged Nora's dead partner, Jed, from the black Escalade.

The guy I picked as Morelli was poking through Nora's bag. Apparently satisfied with its contents, he tossed it into the white Escalade. He was big, bald, almost Mongolian-looking, with a droopy mustache, wearing a black, long-sleeve shirt and pants, with some kind of jewelry around his neck that caught the moonlight. The others were in suits. I noted their hairstyles, facial structures, body movement, as they did the heavy lifting—the departed Jed went behind

the wheel of the Jaguar, the unconscious Nora onto the passenger seat.

I wasn't sure what the plan was, but I figured that last
knockout blow I'd delivered to Nora had been a mercy.

The bald guy with the mustache was definitely Morelli.
He said something that was almost too guttural to be Italian
and, while the others grabbed what looked like short-barrel
Beretta rifles from the rear of the black Escalade, he moved
to Nora.

He rattled off something else in Italian and his boys
laughed. He shook Nora until she awoke with a groan. Her
hand went to her head wound. My bad.

Morelli took several steps back, away from the Jaguar.

Nora saw him. I heard her say, "Huh?"

He pointed to her dead partner. She looked at Jed, then
turned back to Morelli. "You scum-sucking wop pig!" she
screamed, changing the Brando insult from *One-Eyed Jacks*
just a bit to fit the situation.

Morelli waited for her to throw open the Jaguar's door
and take a step toward him, her hands poised like claws. He
shouted "Sparare!" And his men *sparared*, big time. Bullets
ripped into Nora, the beautiful car, the corpse of her dead
partner.

I'd thought they were noisy before. Now they were firing
off a hundred rounds or so in the dead of night, in the sleepy
little town of Laguna Niguel. Maybe they knew precisely how
long it would take the Orange County Sheriff's Department to
get somebody out there to investigate. More likely they simply
didn't give a shit who heard them. They wanted to call attention to the fact that it wasn't a good idea to fuck with them.

Morelli didn't strike me as the kind of man who'd just
forget about a cab driver who made the mistake of stopping

to pick up a good-looking blonde. There wasn't much I could do about that at the moment. Maybe if I'd had a simple old Springfield, the kind I grew up with, and enough ammo and time, I could have put the whole thing to bed that night. Though in all honesty I'd never tried to go six for six, even when I was at the top of my game.

So I just stood there and watched them pile into the Escalades and drive away.

I could hear sirens in the distance.

Time to run. But I took one last look at the bloody, bullet-ridden couple and said, not just to myself, "Faye Dunaway, Warren Beatty. *Bonnie and Clyde*."

PART III

LUSH LIFE

BLACK STAR CANYON

BY ROBERT WARD

Dana Point

I t had been a weird year for Johnny Mavis. First off, his pilot *Boys in Blue* had gotten picked up by TNT and aired to generally favorable reviews, and a good piece of the audience. By the second week, the show was ranked fifteenth and Johnny was a big shot. Because he had never written a pilot before, he wasn't actually the show runner—and that's where his problems began. The guy they brought in to actually run the show, Ray Danes, was an old-timer, and a killer at network politics. Within two months Johnny had gotten into serious jackpots with Danes over the show's "direction." Danes wanted a lighter tone, and saw "blue skies" and lots of pastels. Sort of old-school *Miami Vice*an, though not quite as edgy. But Johnny meant the show to have a nasty satirical edge, the Boys in Blue being dirty, bribe-taking hustlers who were grafting all they could, and wouldn't think twice about offing anyone who might indict them. The problem was, by the tenth week the show had started to lose steam because it was neither a laugh riot with blue skies nor as mean as, say, *The Shield*. The war between the two producer's "visions" for *The Boys* had to be settled by the network, and the network execs decided to go with the horse they knew best (and who had dirt on them all): old, conniving Ray Danes.

Johnny was given a nice payoff and fired from his own show. He could still make money as a consultant, about five grand a week, but consulting is one thing he would never do. He was persona non-asshole on the lot, as they saying goes. Bye-bye, Johnny; B. Goode.

For the next couple of weeks, Johnny moped around his Laurel Canyon home, watched daytime TV, and hated going down to shop at Bristol Farms because he'd invariably run into people from the show. (*Johnny, how you doing? Getting something else set up? Oh, not yet? Well, good luck, kid.*) What hurt even worse was now that Danes had control of the show, it was soaring to the top. Rated number three in the U.S.A. Critics loved it for being "a breath of fresh air after the fetid waters of its former incarnation." Probably win a few Emmys and everyone involved would be gold at the studios. Just what Johnny boy didn't need to hear.

So what the fuck would he do? Write another pilot? Try and break into features? That was a bitch, and they hardly made anything but dumb teenage movies anymore. What was he going to write about that hadn't been done. ET as a gay hand puppet who gave teenagers crack and blow jobs from another planet? Nah, too dark again. Black humor was out. The new fake earnestness and paens to lost innocence were back in. The lower the market fell, the more people wanted sunshine, kisses, and the deep bliss of special effects.

So not Johnny's thing.

He needed a break, a goddamned fresh start, a real honest-to-fucking-God epiphany.

And then, one fine sunny day (like all the other fine sunny days in L.A.), he got it.

An obese writer pal, Terry Dills, a semitalented guy he'd help break into the biz a few years ago, suggested that Johnny use his second home down at Dana Point.

"It's right on the ocean. You go down there, you surf a little, and you chill. I'll come down on the weekends and we'll meet some beach bunnies and party. You'll get the sour taste of the last gig out of your mouth. And bingo, you'll come up with something fresh."

Johnny started to say, "I don't know, man, Orange County?" but then he thought, *Fuck it, why not try something off-beat, new? Orange County, on the beach, beautiful girls, fun-loving surf guys. Frankie and Annette, and Harvey Lembeck as Eric Von Zipper, what could be bad?*

"It's great down there in the O.C.," Dills said. "You even got a great basketball court like three blocks down from my place. Right over the ocean."

"Really?" Johnny replied. He had always been a hoops guy; back in high school in Maryland he'd been all-state. But since getting into the TV hustle, he'd had little time to go balling.

"It's just the thing for you," Terry said. "Stay as long as you want. You're going to come back a new man. Trust me, pal."

Johnny smiled and shook his head. Most of his life he'd been lucky. Yeah, there had been ups and downs, but something had always come along. Taking a little break in the O.C. might be just the ticket.

He was out of Laurel Canyon the very next day.

Dana Point was fantastic. The view from the cliffs, the gorgeous waves splashing, hell, even the name of Dill's street, Golden Lantern . . . had a magical quality about it. He could even see it being the title of something . . . a mystery, a thriller, whatever. He had his payoff money and what was the hurry?

Terry hadn't bullshitted him about the house, either. Man, a '20s Craftsman, not one of the hideous architectural monsters he'd seen on the way down near Laguna . . . where every new architect tried to out-Gehry Frank G. No, this was his kind of place, old school, modest, with a cool front porch and even a '50s red metal glider. He could just sit out here, roll a joint, and listen to the waves—and what could be better than that?

And for the first week that's exactly what he did. Drove down to the beach, went body surfing with some local kids, sat on his NBC towel, and watched the birds dive for fish and crabs. Oh man, this was perfect. He shopped, cooked lobster, drank good wine, and communed with good old Johnny boy. He listened to his inner voices, and they told him he was on the right path, that he had become blown up, full of the nauseous gas of self-promotion, that he needed to reduce himself, slim down to human size. And for six days he did. He explored the old house, sat on the glider, got stoned, and listened to his old John Hiatt records, and Miles, and Eric Dolphy. He was there, he thought. The right place, the right time.

And this weekend Terry would come down and they'd check out the clubs near Dana Point, maybe find some blond-haired surfer girls. Oh yeah . . . this was going to be a fine vacation.

Except Terry Dills didn't make it down. He had a rewrite for a hot new writer/director named Jake Pyne. Pyne specialized in yuppie thrillers. This one was a story of not-so-nice yuppies being attacked by their own greed in the form of a satanic insurance salesman. Very upscale horror. Terry had a Thursday deadline and no time to party.

"But enjoy, Johnny. Everything's good, right?"

"Oh yeah, great, bro," Johnny said. "Love this place."

But in truth, he was feeling a little bit lonely. After all, he wasn't exactly freaking Siddhartha. A week or so was all he could take of examining his inner being. He had to face it, the inner guy wasn't all that well developed anyway.

Sitting alone for a few more days might make him go into another nosedive, one even worse than when they'd tossed him off his own show. Christ—what the hell was he gonna do?

Then he remembered something . . . the basketball court, only a few minutes away. Yeah, he could get down there, shoot some hoops, nothing like the camaraderie of the ball game. Maybe he'd even make a few new friends. People not in the freaking business.

He ran into the bedroom and changed into his Nikes. He had that feeling inside . . . the one he'd had as a kid. He couldn't wait, man. Let this old Baltimore East Coast boy show these O.C. guys how to jack it up.

A few minutes later he was running down the street, bouncing his ball. Just like a happy kid. Not a care in the world.

The court, which was only two blocks from the ocean, was just as cool as he'd imagined. The rims were new and they actually had fresh twine up there. When you played street ball back in N.Y.C. or Baltimore, you NEVER had a net up there. Well, that wasn't quite true. You had one for about five minutes until one of the players decided to take it down and put it up somewhere closer to his 'hood.

Man, these ballers from Dana Point were polite.

But they could play. There were some big white boys, two who wore UCLA letter jackets, and another one—a Czech named Toni—who had started at Pepperdine. They could run and shoot, but they played a West Coast finesse ball. More about speed than rebounds, muscle, or trash talk. All three of the guys were in their late twenties, and in law school. In be-tween plays and during water breaks they talked about making partner at Jones Gray as soon as possible. Turned out JG, as the blond guy Mark said, was paying, "$160,000 for first-year employees." The other two guys nodded and Toni added, "Why I love America." They all laughed at that.

All but the fourth guy, a big wide Italian guy named Eddie Ivarone. Eddie wore painter's pants—not retro painter's pants that you bought at Old Navy but real ones covered with real paint. This was because Eddie was a housepainter. He was working on a condo unit right nearby, he explained, down near the lighthouse. He didn't live that close, though.

"My pad is over in Mission Viejo," he said. "Drive over here to show these yuppies who is really the court king."

The three law students laughed a little, and one of them, Joel, another blond guy with a space between his front two teeth, patted Eddie on his wide shoulders. "He's a beast," he said in a slightly patronizing way.

Right away Johnny liked Ivarone. Even just shooting around, he knew Eddie was the kind of guy who would be a workhorse under the basket, dig out the rebounds and pass to Johnny to pump it back up. Eddie had a friend with him too, a short guy with a bald head named Stenz. Stenz didn't say much but Johnny recognized the type. Catholic kid who was fast and tough. Maybe the three of them could give the taller, sleeker lawyers a good game.

The first few games of three-on-three half-court ball didn't start that way. The three ex–college players had obviously played together for a while. Their passing and teamwork were excellent. They played without any noticeable emotion, just efficiently, and effectively. In no time at all the first two half-court games of 15 were over, and the scores weren't pretty. 15–5, 15–9, and 15–10.

Johnny, Eddie, and Stenz were improving, but not by that much. Then Johnny had an idea.

He called a time-out and brought his team over to the water fountain.

"We're guarding the wrong guys," he said. "Eddie should be on Toni. He's their scorer but you can muscle him outside. If he drives, I'll give you help. Stenz, you wait in the middle for the kick-out pass. When it comes, grab it."

The two housepainters looked at one another and shrugged.

"What the fuck?" Stenz said. "I'm up for it."

They went back on the court with their new defensive lineup, and the results were stunning. With Eddie's big body on him, Toni couldn't get underneath. He had to shoot outside, and just as Johnny had predicted he was mostly short with his shots. Without their driving attack the three lawyers started gunning from long range. They missed shot after shot, and lost 15–7.

Johnny felt good about the win, especially his part in figuring it out. But Eddie and Stenz were ecstatic. They trash talked the lawyers, who took it all with a grain of salt, or at least pretended to.

After gulping down some more water, the six guys played again. This time the three grad students worked harder, and came closer. But a beautiful pass from Eddie to Johnny under the bucket, threaded right through two other players, set up the winning score, and Johnny didn't miss.

Once again, Eddie and Stenz carried their celebration to the extreme, but Johnny got a kick out of it. The lawyers seemed like the passionless guys who would probably end up working in property law or corporate tax write-offs.

So he was happy to win, and even felt better for Eddie and

Stenz, working guys who probably spent most of their lives on the short end of the stick. It was nice to see them celebrating, even if Eddie was carrying it a bit over the top.

By the end of the long day, Johnny was happy he had come. It'd been a really good afternoon, and he felt fulfilled.

He started to say goodbye to everyone, when Eddie put his arm over his shoulder.

"Hey, man let's not break up the team yet."

Johnny was touched by the bigger man's obvious affection.

"Sorry, I haven't played for a while," he replied. "Gotta watch the knees."

"No, no, no," Eddie said. "I'm played out too, but we oughta get us some beers. There's a place not far away, off Harbor Drive. Called Minelli's. Great subs, pizza, pasta. Let me and Stenz buy you a cold one."

Johnny was going to say thanks but no thanks. As much as he'd enjoyed playing with these guys, he wasn't sure he wanted to spend the evening with them. Still, he didn't relish going back to Terry's house and staring at the moon again.

"Okay, I'll come down for a little while. Can't stay out too late, though. Got work tomorrow."

"Yeah, that's fine, bud," Eddie said. "A couple of brews and we're on our way home. Leave your car here. We'll get you back."

Johnny was going to say no to that too. He wasn't at all sure he wouldn't feel trapped by these people . . . but what the hell, he didn't want to be a snob. After all, they had been a great team.

"All right. Why not?'

"All fucking right!" Eddie said, scratching his five-o'clock shadow. "The team endures."

"*The Big Lebowski*," Johnny said. "You guys like that movie?"

"Like it?" Eddie Ivarone said. "We *are* it."

They all laughed at that one and then walked over to Eddie's primered 1971 Dodge Super Bee.

"Hop in the trusty chariot," Eddie said. "Cause this is the way we roll."

The pizza place was exactly as Johnny had imagined it, dark, wooden booths, pitchers of beer, and mediocre pizza. There was a pool table and a jukebox, and a small bar with five stools. In short, a dump, the kind of place Johnny had hung out in when he was a kid in Baltimore. The kind of a place he'd wanted to escape from. But today, saved from the agonies of solitude, Johnny decided to embrace Eddie and Stenz, and have a good old-fashioned drinking session, with pitchers of beer and discussions of old-time TV shows, and after a few rounds, a little singing along with the jukebox. It was all great fun, and soon Eddie's girl came by, an attractive, if slightly sluttish woman named Connie. She had short blond hair, and a long, sexy body which she poured into tight jeans and an Oakland Raiders T-shirt.

She was a waitress at a nearby Denny's, and when she smiled she showed a little too much gum, but she was fun, warm, and liked Johnny right away. He could tell because when he got around to mentioning what he did for a living, the two men were impressed: a TV producer.

"Whoa, Eddie, do you know what we have here? A real Hollywood celebrity. Man, are we lucky or what?" she teased.

Eddie and Stenz looked at Johnny to see how he would respond to her baiting, and when he laughed and wagged a finger at her, they were relieved, and began doing their little Hollywood routine too.

"Oh, I'll have the café con leche jamba juice with the cappuccino latte," Eddie said.

"Yeah, and I'll have the profiterole with a side of endive gooseberry . . . whatever," Stenz added, not quite able to pull off the joke.

"You got me," Johnny said. "Guilty as charged. Just the other day I ate a fig tart for breakfast."

"Gag me," Connie said.

"With a pomegranate smoothie chaser," Johnny said.

They all laughed again, and Johnny could see that they were pleased by his good sportsmanship.

"That must be great to be a producer on TV," Eddie said. "But what the heck does a producer do anyway?"

"He gets all the money together, silly," Connie said.

Johnny laughed but shook his head. "No, no, no. That's what a movie producer does. But in TV, the networks and the studios put up the money. In TV, the producer is really a writer. All those names you see at the end of the show, *Story Editor, Co-Producer, Co–Executive Producer,* and *Executive Producer,* all those guys are really the show's writers."

"Ohhh," Connie said. "So that's what you are? A writer?"

"Yep," Johnny replied, taking another sip of beer.

Connie nodded like she got it, but Eddie shook his head.

"Gee, I read in the paper that TV producers make a ton of money. But I never knew they were just writers."

There was a long silence after that.

Johnny, who had heard this before, and from people much better educated than his current crew, just smiled.

"All that for just knowing words," Stenz said.

"Yeah, that's kinda weird," Eddie said.

"For God's sake, you guys," Connie said, starting to feel embarrassed, "you are being so rude."

"No, it's fine," Johnny said. "I think the guys here don't quite understand. How do you think a script gets done?"

"Well, I never thought about it that much," Eddie answered. "But I guess like they set up a situation for the actors, who kind of make up the dialogue to fit, you know . . . that situation."

"Yeah, they improvise the dialogue," Stenz said. "Right?"

"Wrong," Johnny said. "Every word that is spoken on 99 percent of all TV shows is written in the script, and the actors have no freedom to improvise."

"Yeah, but I seen actors come on Leno and say they wrote their scenes," Eddie said.

"Yeah, they say it sometimes," Johnny said. "But that's not true. They say it because they want the audience to think they do everything. But trust me, most actors couldn't write a decent scene much less a whole script."

"Huh," Eddie said. "So the word guy is the boss, then?"

"Yep," Johnny said. "But we don't make a big deal out of it. The audience likes to think the whole thing is real, so we don't go running around telling them that we did it all."

"I'll be damned. And so all the stories and stuff, that's the writers too?"

"Yep, all that stuff."

"Hmmmm," Eddie said. He looked as though he was having a hard time believing it.

"Well, here's to the word man," Connie said, toasting Johnny.

Eddie and Stenz joined in but they didn't look all that happy about it.

Soon the talk drifted to other subjects, though, like who was the sexiest actress on TV, and they laughed and ate pizza and drank beer. By the end of the night Johnny was almost feeling like they could become friends. What the hell, it was only going to be for a week or so anyway.

During the next three days Johnny worked up a routine. First thing in the morning, a brisk walk on the beach, then get back and drink his second cup of coffee and work on his new idea . . . an idea he had gotten talking to Eddie and the rest for the past few days. It was called *Hometown*, and it was about a guy who comes back to his working-class hometown, after living in a flashy place like L.A., and once there finds himself getting involved with the kind of working-class people he thought he'd left behind. He even had the log line for it. *They say you can't go home again, but what if home is the only place left go to?*

Oh yeah, the networks would love that. It would be a hit . . . he could feel it. A show with heart, and a lot of the heart would be from Eddie and Stenz and Con. He'd owe them and he wouldn't forget them when the show made it either. He'd find a way to make them participants in the profits. Not a lot of money, obviously, but not a trifle either. He'd be a mensch and take care of them. Though he hadn't told them any of this yet. No use starting a feeding frenzy for something that might take awhile to happen.

But happen it would.

Even though he'd been kicked off of *Boys in Blue*, he'd still created the number three show in the nation. Yeah, he'd have clout for *Hometown*, and someday (maybe even sooner than later) he'd get it on the air.

Every day after working on his characters, and the pilot outline for the show, Johnny headed down to play ball with his new pals. Since the three of them had become hot as a team, new challengers began showing up at the park to take them on. There were three financial guys from Long Beach, whom they demolished 15-4, and there were three restaurateurs from Newport, rich ballplayers, whom Eddie destroyed almost singlehandedly.

After that game they headed out to Minelli's and had two or three extra pitchers of beer, and threw in a pretty decent lasagna with the pepperoni and garlic pizza.

It was a hell of a day, and a hell of a good time.

Right up to the moment it wasn't anymore.

Even after it happened, Johnny couldn't really remember how it had gone bad.

Maybe Eddie had downed a few too many beers, and maybe it was the Vicodin he had admitted he took just to give the booze a little extra kick. Or maybe it was just one of those days . . . but somewhere along the third hour of partying, Eddie got a little morose.

They were all still partying, and then Eddie said it, the thing that had been there all along in the back of his mind: "Here's to our Hollywood buddy. May he remember us when he heads back to la-la land and starts hanging with the big shots again."

That stopped everyone cold, and then Johnny realized all eyes were turned to him.

"Hey," he said, "I wouldn't do that. You guys are my buds. I mean, yeah, I gotta go back to work, but you guys will come up and we'll play some of the celebs who practice at the Hollywood Y."

Stenz made a fist and said, "Yeah, right!" but Eddie only looked over at Johnny with a cynical leer.

"Hey, Mr. Big Shot, you think we bought that bit you told us about coming down here to get a little R & R before you started working again? Well, you must think we're nuts. Cause we saw a bit on *Entertainment Tonight* about you, how you were kicked off your own show, and how you came down here to get away from the tabloid reporters."

"Jesus, Ed, why you gotta get all judgmental all of a sudden?" Connie said. "We don't care why Johnny came down here. He's still our friend."

Johnny managed a tortured smile at Connie, who reached over and patted his hand.

Johnny thought maybe the attack would be over then, but Eddie was just warming up: "Say what you want, Connie, but Johnny's down here slumming. You think we're ever gonna hear from this guy again once he gets back to Latte Land?"

Stenz stared down at his feet, and Connie just shook her head.

Johnny let out a long breath, and slid out from the booth.

"Okay," he said. "I better go. Seems like things are getting a little too unpleasant."

"No, Johnny," Connie said in a panicky voice. "Don't go. He doesn't know what he's saying."

Eddie turned his head and stared blankly across the room.

"No, I think he means it. I don't want to bum you guys out. So—take it easy."

He started to walk toward the front door, when Connie ran up behind him and grabbed his wrist. He turned to see tears on her face.

"This isn't really about you," she said. "He's really furious at me."

"Why?" Johnny asked.

"Cause I'm pregnant."

"Oh," he said. "And you want to keep the baby."

Connie nodded. "Yes, more than anything in the world."

Eddie came staggering up behind her, mean-drunk.

"Yes, more than anything in the world," he said in whiny mimicry. "Oh, I have to have a little baby with me at all times. So I can play kootchie-kootchie-koo with it. Fucking bitch. She put a hole in my rubber, man. This is like entrapment. Well, I'm not having it, see . . . I'm not. And you're not either, bitch."

He reached out and grabbed her arm and jerked her toward him. Johnny grabbed Connie's other arm and for a few seconds they battled one another in an absurd tug of war. Until Johnny let go, and Connie fell into Eddie. They were both off balance and went down , upsetting a table and a pitcher of Sam Adams.

The owner of the place, Dan Minelli, came running toward them, his hair a great frizzy mess, like Larry Fine's.

"You make a huge mess," he said, "you gotta pay. You all gotta pay for this."

Johnny waved a twenty at him and headed outside as quickly as he could. Thanking God he'd brought his own car, he trotted over to his BMW, opened the door, and hustled away.

Later that afternoon, he sat on the front porch smoking a joint.

This was better, way better. He'd been crazy to get involved with those people. It was all about his sentimental attachment to people from his old hometown. When he was dealing with the sharks in Hollywood, guys who would throw you off your own show, he sentimentalized working-class people, the kind of people he'd grown up with in row-house Baltimore. They were more lively, had the ability to appreciate simple things, would be your friends through thick and thin . . . all the best qualities of working-class existence.

But when you met them again—or people just like them—you started to realize that there was a reason you'd left your old hometown. The people were too coarse, too selfish, too rude, and mainly just too fucking dumb to make it in the larger world.

It wasn't that he didn't like them, no . . . because he did. It was just too much to deal with.

But what of his new idea, *Hometown*? Did his new hostile understanding nullify the whole project?

No, not at all. Instead, it made it all the more interesting. The guy who comes back home wants kindness and Hallmark card simplicity, but instead finds out life in the adult world of the working class is tough too.

Yeah, maybe that would make the story even richer.

So maybe he wasn't nuts to hang with these people after all.

No, the thing to do was keep hanging out with them but look at them as a scientist looks at his specimens. Eddie was dead-on right. He'd never actually be friends with this crew but just the same . . . he could learn a few things, and in the end he'd throw them a bone once the day of principle photography began. A nice little piece of change.

It was good to finally get the thing sorted out. He was a camera, and they were his subjects, and from now on he would be there, play ball, maybe even go for a beer, but no more buddy-buddy. That was over. Totally.

After a couple of glasses of red wine, Johnny went to bed. Everything was going to be fine. He had his priorities straight and he would soon head back to the Hollywood Wars refreshed and renewed by his time in the O.C.

He'd been in a restless sleep for about three hours when the doorbell rang. Half out of it, Johnny got up and made his way through the hallway to the front room.

"Who is it?" he said, without opening the door.

"It's me, bro," came a sad voice. "Eddie."

Johnny thought about telling Eddie to bag it and head home. Looking over at Terry's clock, he realized it was 3 a.m. Jesus, this was the last guy he wanted to deal with now. But what the hell, Eddie's voice sounded kind of high and pathetic. He unlocked the front door and let him in.

Eddie looked like he'd actually shrunk. His shoulders were all hunched up, and his eyes were cloudy. "I'm sorry to bother you," he said. "But I just need to talk to you, man. It can't wait."

"Why not? It's 3 a.m."

"I know, bro, but after that scene tonight, things got worse. Connie's gonna leave me, man. I can't make it without her."

"Well, where is she now?"

"Out at her sister's house. Out in Black Star Canyon. I gotta go there but I don't want to go alone cause I might lose it. Man, I know it's a huge thing to ask, but would you drive out there with me?"

"Black Star Canyon?" Johnny loved the name of the place! Jesus, this could be a whole episode, or better, a three-parter for the series. Maybe it was even the name of the series, cause it was like a ton better than *Hometown*.

"Okay," he said. "I'll do it, Ed, but you have to promise me that if I come you won't start anything. How do you know she's even awake?"

"I know. I just talked to her on the cell. She can't sleep either. Man, it's so great of you. You're a real bud."

"Let me get dressed," Johnny said. "I'll only be a minute."

They drove inland in silence through Cook's Corner, with its ugly little houses, greasy food joints, and a scummy-looking bar called JC's Place. There wasn't even a sign at this joint, just a gold star and the letters JC on the door. Johnny shuddered at the thought of the kind of men who hung out in there.

They stopped at a barren crossroads and he saw a falling-down house with a collapsed screen porch and a Naugahyde couch lying out front of the place. It was all just a little too real for him. The toughest place he'd been in the last three years was Barney's Beanery, the old Jim Morrison hangout. And all the "tough guys" who hung out there were actors playing Jimmy Dean.

Next they came to two-lane Santiago Canyon Road, and as they drove through steeper and steeper hills, and Johnny looked at the brush and chaparral, and thought of what might be coming toward them from the other lane. Terrible people with bad yellow teeth who had never even heard of sweeps week.

They drove faster and Eddie started talking about Connie and how she and her sister had always dissed him. "She laughs at me, bro. She thinks I'm nothing. She wants a guy . . . a guy like you. She said that to me, bro. It's funny man, cause what you do ain't even real."

"What do you mean?" Johnny replied. He felt a fury building in him. All his writing life he'd had to put up with morons who talked about his talent for "words" with that certain nasty little inflection, as though words were just a cover for cowardice.

"What do I mean?" Eddie said. "Well, you look at the big mansions in Newport Beach, I painted all of those places. When you see a house there and talk about how cool it is, it's because you see my paint on it. That's real, man. But words, what you do, making up little stories you put on TV. Even if you do make all the actors say the stuff, it's still not real. But look how much money you get for it. Look how many women would fuck you for it. You see, that ain't right, is it?"

Johnny had a desire to reach over and throttle Eddie. Take him by his throat—

"Depends on what you value," Johnny said. "Words are imagination. People have always valued imagination, Ed."

"No, well, I can see people liking a director or an actor, but a guy who uses words? I mean, be honest, how do you get those jobs, John? Aren't they all about who you know, or screwing some big suit's daughter or something?"

"No, not really, Eddie. You need to have talent. And if you think writing scripts is so easy, then try it sometime. What the hell, why aren't you doing it right now? Why do a tough job like house painting when you could easily be making millions using shitty little words?"

Eddie bit his lip and looked over at Johnny in a sorrowful way. "Hey, no offense. Just always thought people who could do something, you know, like did it. People who can't do nothing, they trick people with words. But maybe I'm wrong, bud. Maybe I'm wrong."

"Yeah, maybe you are," Johnny said.

They drove on through the night hills, and then turned down a road that seemed to stretch to the yellow moon.

"This is it. This is where she is," Eddie said. "Black Star Canyon. Just down the road."

He turned left down what looked a like a road made of dust. They made another turn and the back end skidded a little, and then they were suddenly pulling up in a dry gulch–ridden place, with no houses in sight.

"We're here, bro," Eddie said.

"Where's the house?" Johnny asked, looking out at the barren hills.

"The house? Her sister's place? Oh, it's back in Mission Viejo. Just a few doors down from ours."

Eddie reached into his door well and pulled out a snub-nosed .38.

"Get out, Johnny."

"What?"

"Get out. Now!"

Johnny felt like something was crushing his heart. He got out of the car, and stood in the whirling dust. Eddie did too.

"Now look in the trunk, bud," Eddie said. Reaching inside, he popped the trunk.

Johnny walked around to the back slowly, very slowly . . . already knowing what he would find.

And there she was, Connie, lying crumpled in the trunk, blood all over her face and dress.

"You see how it is, Johnny boy," Eddie said. "I don't want no baby. I'm just not cut out for managing the Little League. And maybe now you can understand how I don't have much patience with mere words. What you do—*let's pretend*—that don't quite make it. What's lying in there, that would be the real thing. If you know what I mean."

"You know you can't get away with this." When Johnny said it he almost laughed at himself. It was one of the lines all TV writers hated most. So corny, so hackneyed. So Barnaby Jones.

But given his messy situation, so appropriate.

"Oh yes I can," Eddie replied. "My girlfriend gets pregnant by a slick guy from Hollywood. She demands that he takes care of the baby, and when she refuses to have an abortion he brings her out here to kill her. But lo and behold, they fight and kill one another instead. Stenz is going to swear he heard you two fighting. Connie dumped him last year. Unlike you, asshole, he's a real pal."

Johnny felt the fury whipping through him again, but worse, he felt a cringe-inducing embarrassment. "Did you have this in mind all the time?" he asked. "From the first day?"

"That's right," Eddie answered. "From day one. See, Johnny boy, you ain't the only sharp guy in town. I betcha I could write those scripts with their twists and turns even better than you. Now you stand right over there." He pointed out into the night desert.

Moths fluttered through the moonbeams. They were really beautiful, Johnny thought. He started to walk out to the lonely patch of ground, to his own little doom, but instead found himself walking right for Ed.

"Not this way," Eddie said. "Out there. Back up."

But Johnny didn't back up. "No, I know what you want. You want to turn me into a thing that you shoot. But I'm not going to let you do it. You have to shoot me in the face." He felt a wild panic inside but also a kind of demented hilarity. He had seen this scene in a crime movie from the '40s a couple of years ago. He was pretty sure he had quoted the lines verbatim.

Eddie suddenly seemed less confident. "I will shoot you right in the fucking eye. I fucking will. Now get over there."

He gestured with the gun. But Johnny smiled and kept walking toward him.

"In the face, Ed. In the face or in the balls, but in the front. You got the cojones?"

"Back up," Eddie said. "You don't get it."

He started to say something else, but Johnny leaped on him, and put his hands around his throat. Eddie screamed and fell back, and Johnny choked him down, tightening his grip.

"What's the matter, Ed, you think I just deal in words? Motherfucker!"

The whole thing was over in about thirty seconds. Eddie lay in the sand with his tongue hanging out. His face was purple under the moon. The gun was now in Johnny's hand.

He started back to the car.

When suddenly an apparition stood in front of him.

Blood-spackled Connie was up out of the trunk, like a zombie from the B's.

Johnny made a funny shrieking sound, and aimed the gun at her. But she ran by him and threw herself on Eddie's body.

"Ed, oh Christ," she said. "Oh, Ed." She turned, bloodied and manic. "It was a joke," she said. "He wanted to show you he was a good idea man. I tried to talk him out of it. But he wanted to show you . . . So when you went back up to Hollywood you wouldn't forget him."

"Very funny," Johnny said. He walked back to the trunk of the car and saw the oilskin with the car jack and tire iron in it.

She got up and followed him there. He looked at her dumb mouth and blood-splattered cheeks. And felt a tremendous disdain.

"What are you doing?" she said. "We've got to go in to the police and report what you've done."

"I knew you were going to say that. So you're not even pregnant?"

ROBERT WARD // 225

"No, of course not."

"Too bad," Johnny said.

He held the iron over his head and looked down at her with real sorrow in his eyes.

"Johnny, you can't do this. You're not a murderer. You're a writer."

Johnny smiled.

"No," he said. "Up to now I've always been a wordsmith. But I think maybe Ed was right. The real thing. It's a lot more exciting than fucking words."

He brought the tire iron down on her head, crushing her face with one mighty blow. Under the pig's blood, human blood began to flow. He hit her a few more times, and felt even more refreshed than he had on the front porch. Power slammed through him like two thousand volts.

Connie fell behind the car.

Johnny looked inside the well-stocked trunk and found a small shovel. It would be a lot of work, but with all the adrenaline coursing through him, he was up to it. Besides, it was great being out here in nature, digging like a real man, under the lunatic moon.

He strode out into the desert like some kind of Karloffian monster, and started to dig.

Then he remembered Stenz.

A week later, Johnny was back in Hollywood and sold *Hometown* to NBC. He'd learned his lessons well from *Boys in Blue*. *Hometown* was full of sentimental types: the good buddy with a drinking problem; the old girlfriend who had been a hooker but had a serious heart of gold; Mr. Mooby, the kindly janitor who was secretly a Nazi. Problems that the hero, Dave, could solve, because Dave, unlike his creator, was smart, and good.

It was shot in a sunny, blue-sky way and sold to Hallmark in a flash.

CBS gave him an overall deal at two million a year.

The bodies of Eddie and Connie were never found.

Johnny only went back to the O.C. one more time. To hire his new assistant at a salary of two hundred thousand a year. Stenz was delighted with his new digs in Hollywood, and turned out to be the most loyal employee Johnny ever had.

The following season Johnny had three new series on the air. Leonardo Stenz was Co–Executive Producer on all three.

And whenever interviewed, Johnny still maintains that none of his good fortune would have ever happened if he hadn't taken his two weeks to renew himself down in the laid-back and beautiful O.C.

THE PERFORMER

BY GARY PHILLIPS

Los Alamitos

A very Randolph finished the stretched-out riff of Billy Joel's "Just the Way You Are," hoping his playing covered the flat notes coming out of his mouth. He'd meant to take his voice up in pitch during the last chorus, not down. The throat was the second thing to go. There was polite applause from the Seaside Lounge crowd, and Randolph nodded slowly while noodling the keys.

An aging couple, both in bright attire, their matching sterling-gray hair arranged just so, walked by the piano, hand in hand. The woman, peach-colored lipstick gothically enticing in the bar's subdued lighting, dropped a five into the large brandy snifter for tips. She smiled. Randolph smiled. The man gave a quick wave to a short-haired woman at a table near the window, and the two headed for the door. The man let his hand glide down to briefly and tenderly flutter against the woman's backside.

"This is for Emily," Randolph announced, and began a leisurely intro into "Straighten Up and Fly Right." He channeled Nat "King" Cole's artful syncopation, letting it build while several patrons bobbed their heads and tapped their feat to the rhythm.

"Cool down, papa, don't you blow . . . your . . . toppppp," he finished in the key he meant to, and this time the applause was more heartfelt. He stood and bowed and blew a kiss to

Emily, the woman the guy had waved to, sitting at her usual spot next to the window overlooking the medical center down below. For sixty-three, Randolph reflected, she looked good, handsome in her dark blue dress and diamond brooch, an ever-present martini glass near her steady blood-nailed hand. She lifted her drink and toasted him with a sip and a toothy grin.

Randolph finished his set with an instrumental rendition of Fats Waller's "Ain't Misbehavin'," adding, "Don't forget the sand dab special, folks, Rene swears they are to die for." That got a few chuckles and he offered a wave en route to the bar. Sitting at one end of it was a National Guard trooper in his camouflage, a combat service badge dully gleaming over his flapped breast pocket. He was drinking a beer from a pint glass and was having an animated conversation on his cell phone. He turned his body away and hunched over some as Randolph approached the opposite end of the bar.

Carlson, the head bartender, came over with his Jack and Coke. "You tinkled them good tonight," he commented, setting the squat glass on a napkin with the establishment's name on it.

"Thanks, man." Randolph watched the logo become distorted by the wet bottom of the glass, then took it to his lips.

"I guess you have to go easy on that stuff, don't you? Or does it help your playing?"

Randolph looked over at the woman who'd just sat down beside him. She was young—that is, younger than him. In her late twenties, he figured, jeans and some kind of loose faux-suede top. Not too much makeup, Rite Aid earrings. Pretty, but not overwhelmingly so. He sized her up as the wife or girl-friend of some soldier or marine over in Iraq or Afghanistan. Lonely. Bored. There was a lot of that in Los Alamitos.

"Everything in moderation," he replied to her. He didn't

offer to buy her a drink, making sure he kept his eyes on her face and not down on that alert swell beneath the shirt's fabric. The bare arms, though, impressively toned.

"I used to play guitar in high school," she said. "Even had us an all-girl band for a while. But you know how it goes." She elevated a shoulder.

"Not the next Bangles, huh?"

She frowned.

"Before your time," Carlson piped in. A not so subtle reminder that Randolph was probably a decade and a half older than the woman. Randolph resisted a remark. Goddamn Carlson was older than he was but worked out on the weights, and had bragged about getting pectoral implants. *So I can pick up pussy more easily*, he'd cracked to Randolph and Rene Suarez, the chef.

"Can I have a gin and tonic?" the woman asked, looking from Carlson back to Randolph.

"Yours to command," the bartender said, and went to prepare her drink.

"What do you do now?" What the hell, no sense making it easy for Carlson. Besides, Randolph was just making chitchat, no more, no less.

"Work at the PX on the base. Original around here, right?"

Carlson returned with her drink. "Me lady."

"Shit fire," the soldier down the bar snapped, then threw his cell across the bar top. It landed in another customer's glass, the drink's owner glaring at him.

"Aw, hell, here we go. Another old lady done told her hero boy bye-bye." Carlson, himself a vet, double-timed to cool out the service man.

"Your husband on his second or third tour?" Randolph

asked the woman. They both watched Carlson putting an arm around the shouldiers of the soldier, who dropped his head, mumbling words of self-pity.

"He was killed, about half a year ago. Roadside bomb hit their convoy coming into Paktika Province." She drank some. "Jeff was Army then. After he rotated out, he wanted to do something about what he'd seen over there. Something different." She shook her head. "Jeff's a . . . sweetheart. He worked for CARE International delivering food and relief." She put the gin down quietly.

"Damn. Sure sorry to hear that."

"Lori. My name's Lori." She offered her hand and he shook it, smiling crookedly at her.

He told her his name and for several minutes they sat side by side in a shared silence. Carlson returned after escorting the soldier outside.

"Sorry, folks, I'm back," he announced, and moved behind the bar to fulfill his enabling duties.

"Hey, look," Randolph said, "let me get your second G and T, okay? I'm not, you know, trying anything funny."

"Thanks but no thanks, Avery." She'd swiveled her body toward him slightly and was touching his arm. "I better get going. Inventory tomorrow, so I've got to be in early."

The young widow got off the stool and strolled out of the landlocked Seaside Lounge.

"You get her number?" Carlson asked when he came back over to Randolph.

"Kind of," the piano player answered, looking off, then readying the order of songs in his head for the next set.

A week later, Randolph was finishing off a loud and fairly incoherent sing-along version of "Volare" when Lori returned to the bar. She was wearing a modest skirt, a shirt and sweater top combo, and earrings that sparkled in the low artificial light. Randolph banged the keys with his heel à la Little Richard for the climax, everyone clapping and laughing. He stood, breathing heavy, pumping both fists in the air to more acclaim. A patron shouted, "Right on, baby," above the din.

"Glad you came back," he said to her. She lingered at the side of the piano, her purse atop the instrument. Normally he'd say something about that but he didn't want to break the mood—his at least. People came by and gave him pats on the back and shoulders. The brandy snifter was brimming with bills tonight.

"Want to go somewhere, have a sandwich or something? I'm hungry."

She leaned in closer to him. "Hungry for what?" Her smoke-colored eyes remained steady on him.

"There's a little hole-in-the-wall place over on Cerritos," he answered neutrally, but not breaking his gaze from hers. "They have great vegetarian burritos with fire-roasted peppers. Magnifico."

"But I like meat."

They grinned at each other like overheated teenagers as Randolph collected his tip money. Over in the corner at her customary table, Emily Bravera sipped her martini carefully as if testing the stuff for poison, watching the couple above the rim of her glass.

Randolph and the woman descended the outside stairs of the Seaside Lounge, which was lodged on the second floor of an aging '80s strip mall. Down on the parking lot asphalt he became aware of a familiar odor and glanced up to see Carlson the bartender taking one of his Camel breaks. He leaned on the railing, the unfiltered cigarette smoldering in his blunt fingers. Lazily he looked at them. The two men then nodded briefly at each other. Randolph walked the woman to her eight-year-old bronze Camry that had a dark blue driver's door. He gave her the directions to where they were going, standing near her and pointing off into the distance.

"See you there." She gave him a peck on his cheek, her fingers holding onto his upper arm. Her hair was freshly washed and smelled of blueberries and mint.

At Agamotto's Late-Nite Eatery and Coffee Emporium, they ate and talked. Lori McLaughlin was originally from Buffalo. She'd met her late husband Jeff, a local boy from Long Beach, when she'd come out to Southern California four years earlier, winding up with a job at a dog food manufacturer.

"That's a trip," Randolph remarked. "Like big vats where the meat and whatnot is all mixed together?"

"This place, Emerald Valley, is like the Escalade of dog food makers," she said, biting into her barbequed meatloaf sandwich. She then pointed at her food. "Good cuts of meat like this, natural ingredients, grains—they make a high-end product for trendy pet stores in West L.A. and further down south here in Orange County like Newport Beach and Lake Forest."

"But not for us peasants here in Los Al." They both chuckled. "You have family back in Buffalo?" Randolph asked.

She sipped some of her beer and dabbed a napkin to her mouth. "Let's just say there's a reason I came out here, putting as much distance as I could between me and that so-called family." Still holding the napkin, she squeezed his hand. "Okay?"

"Okay."

A lanky youngster in a stained apron behind the counter gave the couple a grunt as they departed. He returned his attention to a news item on the small TV he watched, an image of Long Beach cops leaving a burglarized condo in Belmont Shores earlier that day.

Back in Randolph's car, after she had him pull behind a closed liquor store, they made out. There was a bare bulb streaked with an oily substance over the metal back door of the establishment, and slivered fractions of the light filtered into the car's interior and over their grasping forms. Randolph had his hand over her sweater, cupping one of her breasts as they kissed. He moved his thumb across her hardening nipple. She placed one of her hands on his zipper and rubbed.

"That feels good," he murmured.

"This'll feel even better." She tongued his ear and unzipped him. Involuntarily, he sucked in his stomach. "I didn't catch any hairs did I, Avery?"

"No. Lightheaded is all."

"Mmmm." She worked his shaft and then bent down. Randolph leaned back, eyes fluttering, noting that he needed to clean his headliner. Try as he might to fixate on prosaic matters to prolong the sensation, he soon wheezed, "Hey, careful, I'm . . . I'm about to come."

She gave him a lingering lick along his penis, returning to the tip. "Uh-huh." And then she let him climax in her mouth.

"Sweet mother of mercy!" Randolph exclaimed, grinning like a goon.

From her purse Lori McLaughlin produced a half pint of Jack Daniel's, broke the seal, took a swig, and handed it across.

"Remember your motto," she said as he had a taste. "Everything in moderation."

"Most assuredly," he retorted.

She took something else from her purse and presented it to him. "Because you're not through, piano man. You have encores tonight."

He took the offered orange tablet of Cialis. "I'm not that old, you know."

"I know, darling." McLaughlin had pulled up her skirt and, using her middle finger, was touching herself. He stared and said nothing. She continued this for several moments, then slipped off her light blue panties and pressed them to his face. He breathed in deep and popped the Cialis in his mouth, not bothering to wash it down with the booze.

Two hours later, at her three-and-a-half-room apartment not far from the joint-forces base, Randolph pulled on his cigar-smoking Woody Woodpecker boxers and went into the kitch-enette in search of juice or cold water. He spotted a past-due notice from SoCal Edison on the counter.

On a book ledge crowded with knickknacks, he noticed a picture of a square-jawed, handsome lance corporal he took to be the late husband. He picked up the photo to see it better by the moonlight. The confident look of the soldier reminded him of his father, a decorated combat captain who died in Vietnam. A man he never met and only knew from Polaroids and letters his mother kept. He sighed inwardly, set the picture down, and traipsed to the refrigerator.

Inside he found an open can of Diet Pepsi. One hand on the door, the light from inside the refrigerator casting its glow about the compact kitchenette, Randolph glanced at a print of a leafy country lane hanging on the wall. It wasn't anything special, more like the kind of mass-produced image demon-strating the virtues of the frame.

Guzzling the soda, looking sideways at the lane, cold air blowing against his lower legs, he suddenly felt a massive, pulsing erection.

"Magnifico," he said, proudly stalking back into the bedroom, moving his hips to let his member swing from side to side. He hummed "Rocket Man" and sent up a prayer of thanks to the horny bastard who'd cooked up the orange tablet wonder.

In the morning Randolph stretched, scratched his side, and rubbed his whiskered face. In the other room he could hear Lori McLaughlin talking on the phone.

". . . No, you listen to me, Karen, that's not going to happen, you understand? I won't stand still why you try that kind of shit with me."

He got up and used the bathroom. When he stepped out, McLaughlin was sitting on the edge of the bed in her cloth robe, hunched forward, arms across her upper thighs like a player waiting to get called back into the game. He sat next her her, putting an arm around her shoulders.

"Can I help with anything?"

She made a sound in her throat. "I could lie to you and tell you it's nothing," she began, "but you might as well know now." She regarded him for a moment. "I was talking to my wonderful ex–mother-in-law. A woman who would make Big Bird slap the shit out of her." She chuckled scornfully.

"This involve a child?" he asked, having also noticed last night an assortment of toys in a cardboard box in a corner of the living room.

"Yes. My daughter Farley."

"Farley?"

"Jeff had a good buddy who lost his legs over there. She's

just two and a half and, well, you can see I'm not exactly living the O.C. lifestyle."

"Who *is* around here?" He gave her a squeeze.

She jutted her chin in a westerly direction. "Over in Rossmoor they are. Them and their wall."

"Screw 'em," Randolph said. "They think they shit gold."

She snuggled closer to him, putting a hand on his thigh. "Jeff's mother, Karen, has recently stepped up her alleged concern about how tough it is for me to feed and raise Farley on my own. How she can provide for her and all that. Her third husband, not Jeff's father, owned a firm that supplied some kind of guidance system for missiles. Anyway, he dropped dead of a stroke and left her sitting pretty in a mortgage-free McMansion in Irvine. That's where Farley is now." She rubbed his thigh and, eyeing him, continued, "I didn't plan on seducing you, Avery. But Karen suddenly showed up yesterday when I went to pick up Farley from the sitter after work. And, well, she demanded time with her granddaughter. She lords it over me, what with her paying for the child care and other things for Farley."

She scooted over to her pressboard nightstand, opened a drawer, and took out a digital print. She handed it across to Randolph, who smiled at the photo of a bright-eyed toddler held aloft by her beaming mother. She took it back, lingered on it, then returned it to the drawer.

"So I was just a way for you to blow off steam? A revenge schtupp aimed at your mother-in-law?"

She shoved him playfully and clambered on top of him as he lay on his back, wrapping her in his arms. "How observant of you, Dr. Phil." They kissed eagerly as he undid her robe.

On a Thursday evening several days later, they lay in bed

in Randolph's apartment near the racetrack. Intermingled yells of delight and disappointment could be heard through a cracked sliding window over the bed as the last race finished.

Randolph dialed the radio from the news on the rock station Lori had put on to the jazz station from the college campus in Long Beach. "Suddenly," a McCoy Tyner number, was in midplay. Randolph let his mind drift as the pianist-composer did his thing.

"You bet much?" she asked, laying partially on top of him. His finger gently followed Tyner stroke for stoke on her shapely butt.

"Now and then I go over there, but I play the ponies like I know poker, not too damn good." He began kneading her flesh, getting aroused.

She nuzzled his neck. "What if you could make about thirty thousand on a sure thing?"

"You know a horse doppler?"

"I know where to get sixty, maybe seventy thousand tax-free dollars. Half for you and half for me, Avery. Between your couple of nights a week at the Seaside and substitute music teaching, you're not exactly living la vida loca either."

He stopped rubbing and focused. "What are you talking about, Lori?"

"Remember I told you about Emerald Valley?"

"The dog food company."

"The owner, Brice, he's an old hippie, still smokes marijuana, gives his money to saving the rain forest and all that crap."

"Okay. But I'm not comprehending."

"He has a safe in his office. He's still down with the people, don't trust the system, so he's always kept cash around, different places, you see? One of them is his office cause he's always got some burned-out acid head or old surfing bro fall-ing by for a touch." She paused, placing her hand firmly on his chest. "Even gives it up to an ex-employee or two. I had to go see him for a loan and he's always had a thing for me. Gave me a handful of those Cialis pills, saying to leave a trail of them through the forest and he'd find his way to me. Laughing and having a good time." Her tone had frosted.

"This about keeping Karen at bay?"

"She told me she's going to initiate, her words, *legal action*. If I just show her I can afford a lawyer, she'll back down. I know how her wormy mind works. She's cheap in so many ways."

"Why not ask Brice for a loan? Sounds to me like he'd do it for you and not sweat when you could pay him back. The good fight and all that."

She pulled slowly on his limp penis. "Because he'd want something in return, Avery. Brice is a freak, get it? He's been in trouble in the past for beating off in his office in front of females. He'd want me to do kinky things to him regularly for repayment. Do you want me to do that?" She started to stroke him slowly. His breath got short as he grew hard. "I might be willing to be a thief, but I'm no ho."

She continued with her handjob. "Unless you're going to bitch up. Turn your head when I have to shove a studded dildo up his ass and hear him scream 'Mommy.' Make like I'm not your woman." She took his balls in her hand.

"Not likely," he groaned, as he put his fingers to her throat and applied pressure. She gasped and he leveraged her under him.

"Fuck me rough, baby," she demanded—and he did.

The plan wasn't elaborate. It was straightforward and textbook efficient. Emerald Valley Premium Dog Foods was in a 17,000-square-foot, one-story landscaped building in a cul-de-sac off an industrial park not far from a 605 Freeway off-ramp. Lori McLaughlin had made a Sunday after-hours rendezvous to get the money from a thrilled Brice Hovis. McLaughlin told Randolph he'd insisted that she think of the loan as a long-term investment in her and her daughter's futures, and to come by the office to finalize the deal.

She knew the layout of the factory, and once she got Hovis wound up, she'd explained with a sneer, she'd leave a side door to the parking lot, used by employees when they had to work overtime, unlatched.

Dressed in overalls obtained that day from a thrift store and wearing rubber dishwashing gloves, Avery Randolph gained access to the facility at the appointed time. Inside, he quickly spotted the thin strip of light coming from the office door at the far end the plant. He eased forward on tennis shoes also purchased at the thrift store. His outfit would be burned afterward.

Randolph passed belt feeders, tall stainless steel devices with large conical vats atop them, automated packaging stations, and heavy machinery bolted to the concrete floor with drive shafts that led to partially encased circular rotors he assumed were used to chop and grind the meat Emerald Valley turned into dog food. Stilled circulation fans were set at various strategic locations in the ceiling.

McLaughlin had explained to him that the business, like a lot of pet food manufacturers, bought rendered meat from elsewhere that was shipped to them, along with grains and cereals from other suppliers. Randolph was pleasantly surprised that the air smelled like cheeseburgers.

Coming to the end of a large boxlike machine on stout

legs—a dryer, he could tell from its stamped label—he approached the office. He halted, shutting out all distractions, getting it together for his performance. *It's all about the in-between, man*, a jazz guitarist reminded him at a recent studio gig.

He heard Hovis moaning between whaps. The tang of marijuana cut through the burger aroma.

"Goddamnit, yes, oh yes, doctor."

Randolph stepped into the light to see Hovis leaning over his desk in a stripper/nurse costume, short skirt up over a thong, with high heels and a red wig lopsided on his bald head. McLaughlin, in her underwear beneath an open lab coat, was holding a dog hairbrush, the kind with short wire bristles. She'd been using it on the man's tenderized rear end. There was a strap-on dildo and a plastic enema bottle filled with clear liquid occupying the paper-laden desk.

Hovis straightened up and stammered, "Who . . . What is this?" There was a good-sized alligator clamp dangling from his penis over the thong.

By then Randolph, trying not to giggle too much, had covered the distance between them and squirted liberal amounts of pepper spray into the man's eyes.

"This is not safe," the dog-food man blurted, hands grabbing at his face while he did a run-in-place dance of pain in his night nurse uniform.

McLaughlin slugged him over the head with a smoking bong, shattering it. Hovis ran and crashed into a tall filing cabinet, knocking it and himself over.

"Don't either one of you fuckin move," Randolph blared. He quickly tied a handkerchief around the downed man's tearing eyes and McLaughlin made sounds like she was being manhandled. Randolph tied Hovis up with cord he'd brought along and fixed a ball gag around his mouth. The man writhed and whimpered on his side, then lay still.

"Where is it, bitch?" Randolph growled, giving it his best Steven Seagal guttural rasp.

"I don't know what you're talking about." She slapped her thigh for effect and grunted.

"We'll see about that. Come here, let me show you what me and that dildo are gonna do to you." He marched her out and returned after a suitable period to begin tearing up the office. He knew where Hovis kept the money, but had to sell the search.

He kicked over a surfboard leaning in a corner. Above that, in a compartment Hovis had installed, the cash was hidden in the ceiling. "Well, what do we have here?" He walked over to Hovis and kicked him, eliciting a stifled yell. "Clever cocksucker, aren't you? Your girlfriend held out, but it's a good thing for both of you I got eyes." He slid a chair over, stood on it, and pushed up on the acoustic tile, revealing a large fishing tackle box. He pulled it down, assessed the contents, and exited the office.

Hovis wasn't aware that McLaughlin knew where he kept the money. She'd spied on him once when she was working there. Though naturally he'd suspect her, she would aim his suspicions toward a fired employee. Or so she'd told Randolph.

On the darkened factory floor, he removed his disguise of a bushy Afro wig, false goatee, and a Halloween rubber nose. McLaughlin, in her bra and panties, stilettos off so as not to make noise, came over and gave him a passionate kiss. He rubbed his hand between her legs.

"Better get going. I'll meet you back at my place, Avery."

"I like it when you say my name," he whispered back.

"I know."

He punched her hard, twice, in the face, while she held onto him for balance. Like a boxer clearing her vision, she shook her head, and then she broke off one of her heels. She put the shoes on and wobbled into the office while Randolph turned back toward the way he had come in.

"Brice, Brice, are you all right?" she screamed, running into the office. McLaughlin's face rearranged itself from feigned concern to icy resolve. "Briiice," she drew out, hand beside her mouth but barely saying his name. "Briiiice, my demented shithead, can you get up?" She guffawed and removed a sharp letter opener from a pen caddy on the desk. She sauntered over, cut Brice Hovis's legs loose, and removed the ball gag and handkerchief. His hands remained bound.

"Oh my God, are you all right, Steph?" His eyes were red and wet. He looked from her to the open ceiling and back.

Her fingers trilled the tip of the letter opener. "I'm fine, Brice. Real fuckin good." She flicked the blade and nicked his thigh. Crimson ran behind the black mesh stocking material.

"Hey," he gasped, backing up, "this is no time for that. Untie me, would you?"

Swaying her body she stepped closer, waving the letter opener around like a drunk musketeer. "And what if I don't, Brice? What if I go too far this time?" She took another nick out of him, this time from his chest.

Brice looked about, panicked, while backpeddling in his heels and skirt. "Quit fucking around, Stephanie."

"I'm serious as a fever, Bricey. Come on, beg for your life." She placed her hand on her mound. "It makes me wet." She lunged forward and tackled Hovis, then straddled him.

Down on the floor, he squirmed and bucked but ceased when she put the tip to his throat, letting it sink in a centimeter.

"Why?" he pleaded. "Why are you doing this?"

"Because I can, cunt." She made another cut and Hovis's eyes went wide.

"Yo, *Steph*—is that your real name?"

The woman looked up to see Randolph, his disguise back on, standing in the doorway. She chortled. "Yeah, so? What're you gonna do about it, homeboy?"

"This," he said calmly, shooting her in the mouth as she laughed at him.

The woman's body tumbled off of Hovis, her heelless shoe landing across his leg. Randolph tied up the terrified, bleeding exec again and walked out of the office.

"There's something like ninety thousand in here," a woman's voice said behind him. He turned to Emily Bravera, who was dressed in slacks and a striped shirt. She was hunched on one knee, having counted the contents of the tackle box. She relatched the lid.

"Not bad," Randolph said. "Plus, Hovis can't squawk to the law since he was hiding it from the IRS."

"Well, he does have some explaining to do in that get-up of his and two bodies sprawled out." Her arm in the crook of his, he holding the strong box, the two strolled out to the parking lot.

Laying dead under dim lighting on the uneven asphalt was the bartender, Alfonso Carlson. He'd been in wait for Randolph, to ambush and kill him. But Bravera, a one-time investigating officer with the Criminal Investigation Command of the U.S. Army, had done the bushwhacking. Inside was the bartender's daughter, Stephanie Carlson. The Command's motto was: *Do what has to be done.*

Before they departed, Bravera put her face close to Randolph's, squeezing his cheeks in her blood-nailed fingers. Her tan was prominent against his burnished-copper skin. "You liked fucking her, didn't you?"

"Only doing my job, cap'n."

"Just remember, Thelonious, I know how to use a rifle with a scope."

"I keep that information uppermost in my mind."

"See that you do." She kissed him deep and long.

At the Seaside Lounge, Avery Randolph began a mournful rendition of "On Green Dolphin Street." At her table by the window, Emily Bravera sat and drank sparingly, appreciating his handling of the tune. The two had been working this area for more than a month now, pulling off several lucrative burglaries in Long Beach and south along the Orange County coast. Jewelry, a few spicy homemade DVDs, cash, and even gold bars horded against the next meltdown. For it wasn't only old hippies like Brice Hovis who failed to report all their income.

The front they'd constructed involved Bravera posing as a general's widow living in Rossmoor. Real estate being what it was these days, the realtor was happy to rent to the widow on a month-to-month basis. She was personable, knowledgable on a variety of subjects, worked out at the local gym, and managed to get herself invited to this or that soiree or club event—thus being able to scope out various domiciles.

Bravera had knowledge of security systems and Randolph knew a thing or two about safes. For him, tumblers and electronic lock sequencing were merely different sets of notes to master. Tomorrow they were going to take down the beach house of the matching-hair couple. Yes, they agreed, the two of them had one sweet hustle going.

When the alleged Lori McLaughlin had come on to him,

the possessive Bravera did some checking and turned up that she was Carlson's daughter. Randolph and Bravera didn't know what the pitch was, but figured the two were setting him up for an Oswald—be the fall guy. The piano player had hinted to the bartender that he'd beaten a dope charge in Baltimore. That was a lie, just part of the dodge, like his funky apartment near the track. But the Carlsons must have figured a footloose brother hiding out in Orange County, wanted on a criminal charge elsewhere, was a good fit for a robbery-murder here in town.

Randolph and his older lover and partner, not wishing to pass up an opportunity for enrichment, had let the scheme unfold. In another month or so, not so foolish to push their luck, they'd move on.

"Like Duke explained, man, you gotta play with intent to do something," the pianist said sotto voce, then hummed and teased the keys, ending his extended version of "On Green Dolphin Street." There was sustained clapping and several patrons rose and dropped large bills into the snifter. Before the tune, Randolph had announced he was taking up a collection to bury father and daughter. Bravera put in a fifty, smiling at him. He lifted the glass with both hands, bowing slightly to the gathered from his piano seat.

THE HAPPIEST PLACE

BY GORDON MCALPINE

Anaheim

The happiest place on the entire planet, my ass . . .
Derek called me into the office, his voice an out-of-tune reed instrument in my earpiece, just as I was herding a dozen sunburned tourists and their jabbering children off the teacup ride, which had broken down for the third time in a week. "Carl, we need to see you immediately," Derek said. "Headquarters, now." He acted as if being a security day-shift lead made him Batman, or at least Commissioner Gordon. Sure, he had military and a little police experience on his resume, and since 9/11 that was all anybody valued in security. The downing of the Twin Towers changed everything at the park—not because terrorists have ever shown up on Huck Finn's Island or among the mannequin pirates on the splash-splash boat ride, but because the new security hires all thought they were better than the rest of us, especially me. My twenty-three years of experience counted for nothing to them. All that mattered was that I'd been hired during a "kinder, gentler" period of American history, sans military or police experience, when former school teachers like me were considered adequate for the job of herding tourists off broken-down attractions, managing crowd-control during the fireworks display, or busting preteens for smoking cigarettes on the sky ride. I knew the new breed thought of me as a middle-aged, hefty embarrassment, particularly after I became literally the

last of the "old guard." I knew how much they wanted to put rat ears on my head, shove a tail up my ass, and send me out the main gate forever. But I always did my job and there was nothing they could do to get rid of me—at least, not until the day Derek called me away from the teacups.

When I got to the security office, Derek wasn't even involved in the inquiry.

It was Jeffrey, the department head, former FBI, who asked me to take a seat in the conference room, which I'd visited only once before, in '98, to help plan a birthday party for one of the secretaries. The room hadn't changed. Dozens of large, framed photographs of the park's long-dead founder lined the walls. Two grim Anaheim city policemen entered, their handcuffs jangling on their polyester pants and their boots echoing across the linoleum floor. They sat at the long table, accompanied by a lawyer from corporate, a stenographer, two interns, and a video technician. Excepting the cops, everyone wore standard employee name tags—first names only. *Bob, Tom, Steve* . . . Friendly, huh? But how else would you expect employee relations to be at the world's happiest place? The video technician made final adjustments to a small camera pointed in my direction, then indicated we could begin.

"We're videotaping for legal purposes," Jeffrey said, his smooth delivery more like that of a weatherman than a top-cop. He was weatherman handsome too. All he needed was a name like Dallas Raines or Johnny Mountain and his toothy grin would have been on TV screens instead of here in my face.

"What's this all about?" I asked.

"We've had a complaint," Jeffrey said, indicating a manila folder on the desk. "A female guest in her teens filed a report that says you followed her around the park, leering at her."

"What?" I recalled no particular young lady. How could

I? Every hour of every day I saw thousands of girls in their teens walking around the park (just as I saw thousands of sour-faced, divorced fathers scrambling to keep up with their children, thousands of overwrought mothers toting handy-wipes and pushing strollers, thousands of obese tourists reeking of sweat and tanning lotion, thousands of school-age boys and girls who moved like flocks of birds from one "land" to the next, thousands of retirees in souvenir T-shirts and sun visors, thousands of foreigners in baseball caps, thousands of chattering children in pirate hats, thousands and thousands and thousands of everything . . .). "One paranoid guest files a complaint and you call me in for this inquisition?"

Jeffrey smiled. His manner remained friendly but cold-blooded, doubtless a technique learned at Quantico. He turned his chair to face me directly. "Need I remind you that here at the park we do not tolerate dissatisfaction in any form from any of our guests."

"Sure, but one report—"

He interrupted: "Are you suggesting that following *only* one young woman around the park, bothering her with unwanted and aggressive sexual attentions, is acceptable?" He straightened in his chair, his expression growing stern.

"Aggressive sexual attentions?" This was outrageous. The others at the table averted their eyes. At first, I assumed they were embarrassed to be part of this kangaroo court. But after a moment I realized they were embarrassed for me, as if I'd actually done something wrong. "Look, I don't even talk to guests, male or female, unless they talk to me first. So even if I happened to be following an attractive young woman, it would only have been out of boredom, nothing more."

"Is following an attractive young woman 'out of boredom' a part of your job description?" Jeffrey asked.

"I was speaking hypothetically."

"But if one actually did such a thing?" he pressed.

"Well, no. Obviously, it's not part of my job description, *if* I did such a thing."

He nodded, smug, and turned to the video technician across the table. "Run the video, please."

Every square foot of the park is covered by cameras, primarily for the legal department's use in defending lawsuits (as opposed to the stated purpose of busting criminals or terrorists or nine-year-old boys pocketing souvenir pencils from the gift shops). The particular time-stamped surveillance footage compiled for our viewing showed me walking directly behind a nubile park guest who wore a revealing halter top and very short shorts. From the angle of the camera it appeared that I may indeed have been staring at her ass. But one angle proved nothing. Unfortunately, they had more than one angle—the video cut to another camera that picked up where the first left off, capturing the two of us moving in single file through the Land of Clichéd Yesteryear to the Land of Harmless Adventures and on to the Land of Saccharine Fantasy, the footage from all the cameras edited together to form a single, incriminating sequence. I didn't remember the girl, though for a few minutes of a particular day she had undeniably engaged my attention. It was not pleasant to observe—the security guard uniform made me look heavier than I actually am (and everyone knows video adds ten to twenty pounds to anyone's appearance); additionally, I was old enough to be the girl's father and my attentions toward her, isolated and edited in this manner, were humiliating.

Jeffrey turned to the stenographer. "Will you please read back to us what Carl said after I asked him if following young women 'out of boredom' was part of his job description?"

"There's no need for that," I interjected.

The stenographer looked from me to Jeffrey, awaiting direction.

At last Jeffrey indicated to the stenographer to remain silent.

I'd had enough. "Okay, fine. I won't follow any women around the park, ever again. Okay?"

Jeffrey was not satisfied. "Why don't you tell us why you left teaching?"

"That's irrelevant . . . it was in the late '80s, for God's sake."

Jeffrey pulled a paper from a file. "On your application here you indicated that you resigned from your teaching position."

"I did."

"We dug a little deeper, contacting the school district, and discovered that you were pressured to go. Why don't you explain?"

"Look, I never touched anybody."

"No one said you did. Please answer the question."

"One of the girls needed a little watching over. She was just a freshman, a lonely kid. My concern was only for her safety. Would I be in this uniform if I didn't take an interest in the welfare of others?"

"You 'maintained surveillance' on this girl after school hours?"

"Well, that's generally when the bad things happen . . ."

He nodded. "Bad things, indeed."

"Look, I'm not some kind of stalker, if that's what you're suggesting."

Jeffrey shrugged. "It's not me who suggests it. It's you, Carl. It's your behavior."

The silence and averted eyes among those gathered around the table suggested they concurred.

In this manner, the security department had its way with me.

Over the next half hour we arrived at a settlement that reduced my retirement benefits by 50 percent. The lawyer had all the paperwork ready. He was very friendly. I merely had to sign at the places he'd marked with colorful, sticky arrows. A child could have done it.

"Why now?" I asked as the inquisition came to its inglorious end. "After all these years?"

Jeffrey nodded. "You're right, it's our oversight. We should never have hired you. But at least we identified the problem before any serious harm was done."

Harm? I never touched anybody—not in all these years.

Happiest place on the planet, my ass . . .

So you can imagine my surprise when five weeks later I got a call at home from none other than supercop Jeffrey.

"How've you been?" he asked, exuding his weatherman charm.

"Fine," I said, though I'd actually not been so good. It's funny, but that overpriced, overcrowded, oversanitized amusement park, known the world over for its fairy-tale castle, which is actually made of plaster so thin that on that last day, as my former colleagues marched me across the park on my way out forever, I was almost able to punch my fist right through it . . . well, despite all that, the place gets into your blood. The truth is, I missed the park as one misses a lover. Hell, more than one misses a lover. It's been three years now since Mandy went back to her old job in Bangkok, where I'd met her on a humid night, paid her bar fee, and then won her heart with my tales of foiling the amorous antics, petty thievery, and juvenile pranks of park guests (everybody the world over has heard of the park, and being in its employ is almost like being a celebrity). The first gift I ever gave Mandy, the first acknowledgment of my deeper-than-mere-business feelings for her, was my spare name tag from the park, which I'd brought along on vacation in hopes I might indeed meet a young woman worthy of wearing it. So, sure, I suffered sleepless nights after Mandy left me. We'd had a good eighteen months and I really thought she loved her new country and our little apartment. Nobody likes losing a lover or wife or whatever. But losing the park proved harder yet, almost enough to make me start drinking again. There's no place like it, unless you count its iterations in Florida and overseas.

"I want you to know I didn't enjoy doing what I had to do, Carl," Jeffrey said over the phone.

What did he want from me, sympathy?

"It's the bitch end of the job, let me tell you," he continued.

I'd be damned if I'd let him know how bad I'd been feeling. "Well, I've been great, Jeffrey. How're things at the park?"

He laughed. "As if you care anymore, right?"

I pretended to laugh too. "Right you are, Jeffrey."

It didn't make matters easier for me that my garden apartment, which I'd only recently cleared of the last signs that Mandy had ever inhabited it with me, was barely a mile from the park's front gate. Every night at 9:30, when the fireworks display started, the sounds of explosions would jerk me away from whatever TV show I'd been employing as distraction. *Boom, boom, boom!* I felt every sonic reverberation in the deepest part of my chest. I've always loved fireworks. Most nights I'd still walk onto my tiny patio to watch them—gunpowder flowers blossoming over the park, red, white, and blue. *Boom, boom, boom!* When that became too painful, I'd close my eyes.

But even then I couldn't help picturing the thousands of guests lined along the park's main avenue or along the banks of its circular river, their eyes turned heavenward, a scene I helped supervise for years. Afterward, the quiet on my patio was even more painful than the display itself—silence and the drifting away of the smoke clouds into the night sky. Who wouldn't miss a place like the park, a place that offers to all (except me, now) a simulation of life designed to surpass the real thing. Losing it had made me almost angry enough to want to hurt somebody. But I'd be damned if I'd let Jeffrey know how I felt about these things.

"Carl, can you meet me tomorrow morning for breakfast?"

The head of park security, former FBI, wanted to eat with me?

"Carl, are you still there?"

"Yeah, sure."

"Yeah you're still there, or yeah you'll meet me?" he asked.

"Why do you want to have breakfast with me, Jeffrey?"

"Look, I know you were good at your job, Carl."

I did my job but I don't know that I was actually good at it. I only know that I showed up every day.

"Have you found employment yet?" Jeffrey asked.

"I've got a lot of irons in the fire," I said, a lie.

"I may have a job for you, Carl."

"Me? Why?"

After a moment of silence: "Maybe I feel a little guilty about the way it went down with you, Carl."

Maybe he did, maybe he didn't.

What the hell did I have to lose?

We met the next morning at a Carl's Jr. across the street from the main library on Harbor Boulevard and Broadway, three miles north and a world away from the park. He chose the place. Fast food didn't seem like much of a gesture toward reconciliation. Was the Carl's Jr. a play on my name? There were plenty of tourist joints around the park that served better breakfasts. And there were restaurants near the stadium and diners and cafés farther east in Orange or Tustin where park employees often went to escape the crowds and to enjoy food that was less generic than tourist fare. I asked myself what Sherlock Holmes would have made of Jeffrey's wanting to meet here and I arrived at this: the Carl's Jr. at Harbor and Broadway was a place we'd likely not be seen by anybody who knew either of us (most of the patrons and some of the employees didn't even speak English). Only three miles from the park, we were virtually guaranteed of being strangers to anyone we might meet.

In this, I was right.

But it was the last time I'd be right for a long while.

I parked my Camry next to Jeffrey's SUV.

He sat at an inside booth, nursing a coffee and browsing the morning paper. He grinned when he saw me and extended his hand to shake without sliding out of the booth to stand. "Morning, Carl." He was dressed "resort casual," khakis, loafers, monogrammed golf shirt. The face of his expensive wristwatch was black and of a width and diameter about half that of a hockey puck. I'd come in my suit and tie, which felt ridiculous in a Carl's Jr. But this was a job interview, wasn't it? And my Aunt Janice always said that one can never be overdressed, either for church or for a business meeting.

I slid into the booth across from Jeffrey. "So what's this all about?"

"Maybe you want to get yourself a coffee and a roll before we get started," he said, folding away his newspaper.

I was hungry (after all, this was supposed to be breakfast) so I did as he suggested.

"Well, that ought to fill you up," Jeffrey said when I returned with my tray.

A coffee, orange juice, jumbo breakfast burrito, and side of hash browns . . . Why not? This wasn't a Weight Watchers meeting! But Jeffrey looked at my tray like it was piled with fresh, steaming shit. He couldn't resist putting on superior airs. I'd seen it in my days at the park. Fine, he was Ivy League. Then Quantico. Good for him. But what kind of former undercover agent is constitutionally unable to conceal his smugness at least some of the time?

"I'd like to engage your assistance," he said.

"What?"

"It's about my wife."

I put down my breakfast burrito.

Jeffrey leaned toward me over the Formica tabletop. He smelled of expensive cologne, which mixed strangely with the greasy odors from the breakfast foods. He pushed my tray toward the napkin dispenser against the wall and tapped his fist on my forearm, a "man's man" gesture of intimacy. I fought the impulse to pull away.

"You're a good man, Carl," he said. "I knew it even when I was letting you go, but I had no choice."

"Yeah?"

"Look, I know damn well that corporate policy and fear of litigation should never trump a man's twenty years of good service," he continued. "But you'll have to trust me that I had no choice. Do you trust me, Carl?"

It was actually twenty-three years, but I didn't correct him. "Would I be here otherwise, Jeffrey?"

"Good." He leaned back into his side of the booth.

I picked up the breakfast burrito and took a bite, unsure of what else to do.

"I want to employ you as a private detective," he said.

Once again I put the burrito down. "Me?"

He nodded.

"Why?" I asked.

"I need you to shadow my wife."

"Oh? I see. But still . . . why me?"

"It's a delicate job, Carl." He lowered his voice. "Look, I'm well known in law-enforcement circles. You understand that. Every city in this county has its own little chief of police, but just as there's only one park, one citadel, there's only one me. So I can't go to a regular agency. You know that the park expects only the most respectable behavior from its top employees. And also from their wives . . ." He looked to me for some kind of response.

"Oh, right."

"I need to know the truth about her. But I can't allow anything unsavory to *ever* get out. Understand, Carl?"

"Sure."

He looked around the Carl's Jr. When he was sure nobody was paying us any attention, he removed from his front trousers pocket a roll of cash held together with two rubber bands. He set it on the tabletop and then slid it across like a shuffleboard disc into my lap. "It's two grand, all in twenties," he said. "It'll get you started on the job."

I hadn't held so much cash in my hand at one time since my vacation in Bangkok (where cash passes *out* of your hand instead of into it).

"I need your help, Carl," he said, his expression suddenly strained.

They sure as hell didn't teach this at Quantico, I thought.

It turns out the bastard was as pathetic a human being as the rest of us. (Or so I believed at the time.) Anyway, I admit I enjoyed his muted anguish. But I was clever enough not to show it. "Okay, Jeffrey. I'll help you."

He removed a reporter's notebook from his back pocket and gave it to me. "You got a pen?"

I patted my shirt pocket. No pen.

He gave me a Bic.

"You might want to note down what I'm about to tell you," he said.

"Right." I flipped the pad open. Just like that I was a private eye.

Jeffrey's wife Melinda was thirteen years his junior. They had no children together, though on weekends Jeffrey's four young daughters from two previous marriages occasionally visited their home, which was located near the golf course on a quiet cul-de-sac in Anaheim Hills. It was a million-and-a-half-dollar property. Melinda held no job, but kept busy with volunteer work at the children's hospital in Orange. She worked out on Mondays, Wednesdays, and Fridays at a Pilates studio on Imperial Highway and on Tuesdays and Thursdays with a private trainer (female) at the twenty-four-hour fitness club. Her body was well toned. She drove a two-year-old, leased Mercedes E-class and her blond hair was just the right shade for her skin color, just the right length for her bone structure. She got her manicures, pedicures, and facials at a salon on Lakeview that was run by a Vietnamese woman named Tran, and she shopped for groceries at the Vons Pavilions in the Target shopping center on Weir Canyon Road. She rarely ventured off the hill to the flats of Anaheim, which were generally too seedy for one of her refined sensibilities. In conversation at the tennis club she poked fun at the park and all it stood for, assuming a position of cultural superiority, even though it was the park that provided her husband with the means to keep her in luxury. She seemed a predictable third wife for a man like Jeffrey. No surprise there. What's funny is that you might not suspect a woman like her would also appeal to a man like me, but after shadowing her for just a day or two, I found myself becoming very fond of her, despite her superficialities, her arrogance, and the fact that, quite literally, she didn't know I existed.

"She's seeing another man," Jeffrey had told me at Carl's Jr. that first morning.

But I discovered nothing that suggested infidelity. Not in the first week, nor in the second, nor the third. I faithfully kept at it, every day and every night. Melinda took conversational French classes at Fullerton College on Tuesday and Thursday nights from 7 to 10 and enjoyed a few happy hour margaritas every Wednesday with her girlfriends, some of whom were actually as well groomed and physically fit as she was.

Otherwise, she was rarely out of the house after dark. Further, I can say with certainty—because I'd snuck into the backyard to peek through a window—that there was nothing illicit about the two consecutive afternoon visits from the plumber; also, the Latino gardeners and the Polynesian pool boy merely did their jobs, unlike the stereotypical shirtless lotharios you find filling their professions in porno films. Melinda wasn't seeing anybody and nobody was seeing her (except me, of course). Even Jeffrey saw little of her, working long days that often stretched past midnight. I thought Melinda must be the loneliest woman in the world, poor thing. But I kept my notes and my increasing faith in her goodness to myself. Jeffrey had instructed me never to contact him, which was just as well as I'd lost my cell phone a few days before he hired me as a PI and hadn't had time to replace it since I'd started shadowing his wife.

Actually, I was glad to be rid of my cell phone.

It felt good to be cut off from everyone in the world—except Melinda.

Of course, I did speak in person to some of those in her life. For example, I used one of the hours when Melinda was in the Pilates studio to visit her dry cleaner, who occupied the same strip mall. I initiated conversation with him by pretending to be one of her neighbors. He agreed with me that she was always very friendly. Unfortunately, I couldn't get details from him about the particulars of her cleaning and laundering needs (such as whether he'd ever been asked to work out unusual or incriminating stains on either her outer- or underwear). Believe me, I took the job seriously. I was thorough. Melinda's French teacher at Fullerton College, a sixtyish woman called Madame Juliette, who I'm not sure believed that I was a visiting professor from Cypress College, told me only that Melinda had exceptional pronunciation and above-average vocabulary skills. When I met Melinda's supervisor at the children's hospital in Orange, a small man in a wheelchair, I claimed to be a reporter for the O.C. *Weekly* who wrote the "Volunteers Among Us" column. He told me Melinda had a wonderful way with children and lamented the fact that she and Jeffrey were childless. The receptionist at the Anaheim Hills Tennis Club told me, after I'd slipped her a series of twenty-dollar bills, that half of their married members cheated on their spouses, often hooking up with their mixed-doubles partners, but that Melinda was in the faithful 50 percent, a paragon of marital constancy.

The woman was an angel.

Why would I ever want to murder her?

But wait, I'm getting a little ahead of myself.

Approximately three and a half weeks into my surveillance, Jeffrey called me at my apartment at 2:30 in the morning. The lateness of the hour was not as distressing as it might seem; after all, I was only ever home between midnight and 5 a.m., otherwise always shadowing Melinda, and so the middle of the night was the only time I was available for communication.

"You're a hard man to reach, Carl."

This was the first I'd spoken to Jeffrey since Carl's Jr. Now, in the background of his call, I could make out the sound of light traffic, as if he were phoning from the side of a freeway. "I've been on the job, Jeffrey." My answering machine was empty so he obviously hadn't tried that hard to reach me.

"Good man," he said.

I liked being called that. "I've compiled copious notes about your wife's every move these past few weeks," I said. "That notebook you gave me is just about full. And I'm pleased to report that, to date, my observations indicate—"

"That's fine, Carl," he interrupted. "We'll discuss your observations later. Now, I want you to just listen to me."

"Oh, okay."

"Tomorrow I want you to take the day off. Get a haircut, go to a movie, wash your car, whatever. Just stay away from Melinda. It's critical that she not suspect she's being watched."

"Oh, I've been very careful about that, Jeffrey." Or had I left more of a footprint that I thought? Maybe talking to a few of her neighbors the day before hadn't been such a good idea.

Jeffrey continued: "Now get this part right, Carl. At 11 o'clock tomorrow night, not a moment later, not a moment sooner, I want you to park your car in front of my house. Bring your camera. I'll see that the front door is unlocked and the silent alarm turned off. Just quietly walk in."

"Now wait a minute," I said. "I'm not so sure about breaking and entering and—"

Again, he cut me off. "It's *my* goddamn house, Carl. You won't be 'breaking and entering' because I'm inviting you to enter, understand?"

"Oh, right. But why?"

"Because tomorrow night the other man will be there, in bed with my wife."

What other man? I thought. "How do you know, Jeffrey?"

"Trust me, I know."

"Well, what do you want me to do about it?"

"Take a picture of them together. That's all. Then get out. The master bedroom is at the back of the house."

This was an ugly business. But it was a little exciting too. And while I still privately doubted that the Melinda I'd observed these past weeks was actually having an affair, the prospect of seeing her naked and in flagrante delicto (and photographing it!) held an undeniable appeal. I didn't know if I wanted to be right or wrong about her. I'm sure you understand.

"Any questions, Carl?"

"Where will you be during all this, Jeffrey?"

"Don't worry about me, buddy. I'll be all right."

I hadn't been worried about him.

"I'll call you at this same time tomorrow," he said.

I slept little that night and the following day passed at a snail's pace despite the fact that I followed Jeffrey's advice by getting a haircut, washing my car, and seeing a matinee. After eating a hamburger for dinner at the Carl's Jr. where Jeffrey and I had breakfasted (call me sentimental), I returned to my apartment to watch *Jeopardy*, *Wheel of Fortune*, and three CBS sitcoms. I left my apartment only after the fireworks ended at the park. I cruised up and down Harbor Boulevard for forty minutes, casually observing the tourists on the sidewalks outside the motels. They were all shapes and sizes, though I'd guess they tended a little more toward fat than the national average. At 10:30 I turned off Harbor and headed east on Katella Avenue past the Angels' stadium to the 57 freeway, then I took the 91 to Imperial Highway and headed up Anaheim Hills Road almost as far as the golf club. I parked in front of the darkened house at 10:56 p.m. (I know the exact time because I jotted it on the last page of my reporter's notebook.)

At 11 p.m. I pushed open the front door, which was ajar, and went inside.

Darkness. Silence.

There seems little point in my describing the interior of the house except to say it was what you'd expect in such a neighborhood—stylish and neat. I didn't take it in much beyond that. Interior decorating is not my thing. Besides, my mind was elsewhere. I flipped on my flashlight. The hallway that led to the back of the house was lined with framed photographs of Melinda and Jeffrey smiling together in various locations, such as Japan, France, Florida. I turned a corner and saw the closed double doors that led to the master bedroom. Still, no sound from within. Surely, no sex. Melinda was likely just sleeping inside, alone. *That'a girl*, I thought, only half-disappointed by what I was not going to get to see.

Of course, I still had to open the bedroom door and look inside just to be sure. It was my job.

I wish I hadn't done it.

By the light of a reading lamp burning beside the king-size

bed, I saw Melinda sprawled on the rumpled bedspread, her vacant eyes open and askew. Most of her clothes had been ripped off her body. I knew right away she was dead. Poor Melinda. There were red marks at her throat and blood on one of her swollen lips. She'd been knocked around and then strangled and then, you know . . . It was ugly. Even twenty-three years of working security at the park doesn't prepare you for something like this. At first, I didn't know what to do. Had Jeffrey been right about a lover in the house, a lover turned murderer? Had I arrived only a few minutes too late to save poor Melinda? Or might the killer still be hiding in the house? I turned and looked around the room.

But I was alone.

At least, I was alone until the police arrived just three or four minutes after I'd entered Melinda's bedroom.

Jeffrey hadn't shut off the silent alarm, the bastard.

"Officers, officers!" I shouted as they burst into the bedroom. "I was just about to call you!"

They pressed around me, their automatic weapons pointed at my face, and shouted for me to show my hands and to lay spread-eagled on the floor, which I did. My training in security prepared me for such treatment; they were only taking proper precautions.

Still, I tried to explain: "The killer may still be in the house!" I shouted. One of them wrenched my arm behind my back to apply the cuffs. They weren't interested in what I had to say, though one of them recited my Miranda rights. "Look, you've got it all wrong, guys! I work for Jeffrey, I'm private security!"

Somebody hit me hard with his elbow in the back of my head. My face hit the floor and I tasted blood.

Then he hit me again.

The next thing I knew I was in the back of a patrol car.

"Just shut up!" the driver said every time I tried to explain.

It was not until an hour later in the police interrogation room that I realized how completely I'd been set up. Should I have seen it coming? Maybe, but I possess a trusting nature. And Jeffrey is a formidable enemy, particularly when you don't know he's your enemy. The interrogator told me that "poor, distraught" Jeffrey had managed to communicate through his tears that he'd had no contact with me whatsoever since the day he fired me from the park. No phone calls, no meeting at Carl's Jr., no private investigation.

He'd lined it all up: The videotaped testimony from my hearing at the park suggested I had a history of "stalking"; my subsequent firing suggested I had motive to get revenge on Jeffrey (by taking away the love of his life, just as he'd taken away the park from me); my reporter's notebook, confiscated at the time of my arrest, indicated I'd been following Melinda for weeks, noting her every move; my interviews with some of her neighbors and so forth reinforced the idea that my attentions had been "obsessive"; my being in the house at roughly the time of her murder, and the broken lock on the front door . . . well, that seemed to speak for itself. Not good, any of it.

Obviously, Jeffrey killed her. Surely, you can see that. My part, as patsy, just made it a "perfect crime."

But nobody wanted to hear that.

The staff at the Carl's Jr. did not recall Jeffrey and me ever having eaten there, but why would they as it had been almost a month previous? The calls from Jeffrey to my home phone, the most recent of which had occurred the night before the murder, proved to have been placed from my own lost cell phone, which Jeffrey must have stolen from my apartment before initiating his plan.

My attorney advised me to cop a plea.

I told him to go to hell.

When the DA started rooting around in my past, things got no better. I still don't know how they thought they'd ever locate Mandy in Bangkok. She doesn't exactly work a desk in an office—besides, she's probably going by another name these days. That's how it works there. Just because immigration has no record of her ever exiting the U.S.A. doesn't mean she didn't go back, for God's sake. There are a million ways for girls to get around bureaucrats! I'd never have hurt Mandy, however much she hurt me. And who'd have guessed that the student I took such an interest in during my last year of teaching was shortly thereafter murdered? My sixth sense alerted me to her need for special protection. I was right! Do I get no credit for that? If the school district hadn't gotten in my way all those years ago, she might be alive today. Any inference now of my having killed her is ridiculous. Look, whose past wouldn't reveal unseemly coincidences if put under a microscope? Yours? I doubt it.

Maybe I'll cop a plea after all.

But let me ask you this: after all my years working in park security (which is a branch of law enforcement, after all), do you think I'm fool enough to commit a murder and leave every clue pointing to me? Of course not! Any true detective of the Sherlock Holmes ilk would understand that the vast number of details that seem to incriminate me, actually exonerate me! Besides, if I did kill poor Melinda, then much of this report is a pure fiction. Talk about fantasy-land! And knowing what you know about me, do you honestly believe I'm capable of making something like this up?

DARK MATTER

BY MARTIN J. SMITH

Balboa Island

I should have left the minute I gave it to him, should have just tossed the eviction notice across the doorstep and onto the cracked tiles of the old mansion's foyer. A smarter man would have hoofed right back to the Sentra and caught the car ferry off Balboa Island. Me? I stood there like the wide-eyed fan I once was, rooted to the front steps of his formerly grand palace at the island's southern tip. I'd specifically asked for this delivery, just for the chance to meet somebody I once idolized. Now I was staring into the face of a faded nobody with the saddest eyes I'd ever seen. When he answered my knock, he looked like someone peering up from the bottom of a well.

"Been 'specting you," he said, slurring a bit.

"Wheels of justice don't turn so fast, but now you've got the paperwork. Court order came down yesterday."

I resisted the urge to apologize. I'd read everything ever written about him, including the entire bankruptcy file. He could only blame himself for this latest bit of unpleasantness. He'd never stopped living like the star he once was, even if the money ran out years ago. It showed. The fenders on the Porsche out front were rusted through and the canvas top was ripped in three places. The house was the choicest piece of real estate on this tony Newport Harbor refuge, but pretty run-down. His ex, the third, owned it now. The judge gave him twenty-four hours to vacate.

I looked at my watch. "Anyway, the sheriff'll be here this time tomorrow morning."

"Splendid."

He cinched the belt of his robe, raised his highball glass, swirled the ice, and took a sip of something thick and amber—something completely wrong for 9:40 in the morning. His bony chest was unnaturally tan, almost orange, the hair on it white.

"Question for you, sir," he said. "Know anythin 'bout dark matter?"

I'd seen my share of people in denial. I serve eviction notices for the Superior Court of Orange County, California. I am a $15.50-an-hour destroyer of worlds, the death messenger of the American Dream. Nothing surprises me—guys with guns, screeching women, unleashed dogs. It's why I carry pepper spray in a little holster on my belt. But this, this was the worst of it. I'd just delivered a final curb stomp to somebody who'd once meant a lot to me, somebody who'd obviously given up. What was I thinking when I asked to handle this one?

"Dark. Mat-ter," he repeated, working hard to enunciate.

I knew all about his eccentricities. Guy was one of the kings of cock-rock when he was, like, nineteen. So big even a teen dork like me played his first album to death. He was white-hot after that first record, the swaggering lead singer of *the* '70s band. Life was good. Spent millions on anything that moved—cars, horses, women. For years he kept exotic animals as house pets, and claimed some mystical connection to them—right up until Animal Control took them away after his panther killed a neighbor's dog.

Nothing lasts. The second album rose briefly, then sank to oblivion. The third? It was over. The band broke up. That was more than thirty-five years ago, half a lifetime of autograph shows, *Behind the Music* cameos, and the occasional Japanese royalty check. The passing harbor tour boats used to point out his house, but that stopped years ago. No one even called him for session work anymore, because of the drinking. I have this friend who works at *TMZ*, the celebrity scandal show. She said that during his latest divorce, his ex was shopping a videotape that showed him butt-naked on a lawn chair, pasty and late-life saggy, getting blown by a Goth-looking high-school sophomore. Its release actually might have *helped* his career. But my friend told me the show had passed on the tape.

The executive producer didn't even recognize his name.

What do you do when you peak at nineteen? You move to Balboa Island, that's what. You fall down a well.

"Dark matter?" I said.

He stood up straight and squared his shoulders. "Astrophysics. Cosmology. C'mon, *you* know."

He swayed and bumped against the doorframe and motioned me closer, like he was about to share a secret. I stood my ground, but leaned in a little, near enough to smell the booze but far enough to cut and run if he was as drunk and nuts as he seemed. I also caught a whiff of something that made me think of a dirty litter box.

"Can't see dark matter," he said, "'s invisible. But it's *there*."

"Where?"

"All 'round us. Most of th' mass in th' observ-a-ble universe?" He grinned. "Dark matter."

"I'll be damned. And you can't even see it?"

That brought a somber shake of his head, still crowned by that goofy hair-metal cut, improbably black. "But y'see what dark matter *does*."

I took a small step backward. His breath was toxic. "Which is?"

He lit up. Perfect rows of bright white teeth split the weathered skin of his face. "Changes things. Affects things. See, mass has weight, and weight creates grrra-vi-ty." Took his time pronouncing each syllable of the word. "And grrra-vi-ty doesn't lie, man. Doesn't lie." Another wink. "C'mere. I'll show you."

With that he turned from the open door and scuffed down the hall, the soft soles of his UGG boots making a *schik-schik-schik* as he moved away. For some reason, don't ask me why, I followed. Say what you will about celebrity, but there's definitely something magnetic about it. Seductive. Dangerous. No one's immune. Maybe that's what he was talking about? Anyway, as soon as I stepped across his threshold I was thinking, *Dude, you really gotta ask for that raise.*

More than eighty rehab facilities dot the Balboa Peninsula within a mile of this exclusive island; Southern California's celebrities like to dry out in tidy, well-appointed luxury, and by the beach. I'd never been inside one of those, but this place struck me as probably the exact opposite. Piles of stuff everywhere—books, clothes, newspapers. One side of the hall was just drywall, installed but never plastered or painted. The other side was '70s-era flocked wallpaper hung by an amateur. A classic Fender Strat with a snapped neck lay at the base of a stairway leading to a second story, its looping strings holding the pieces together like thin steel ligaments.

"Mind your way right here," he called back over his shoulder, sidestepping something. It looked like a mound of shit the size of a football.

When I got closer, I realized it *was* a pile of shit.

"Whoa," I said, and stopped.

"Cheers," he said, lifting the glass again as he moved off down the hall. "Best to let it air-dry a bit."

He waved me on, turning left toward a sun-filled room facing the harbor's main channel. "Right in here."

My father taught me caution in all things. He lived life by the Law of Worst Possible Consequences and communicated it to us daily. An unbuckled seat belt would lead directly to death. So would a carelessly placed skateboard, improperly inflated tires, or an incautious remark to the wrong cop. To be honest, it's probably why I gravitated to a career wreaking legal vengeance on people who live too close to the edge. Still, something irresistible was pulling me around the corner into the unknown, into a room filled with cast-off dorm furniture.

The space itself was a realtor's wet dream. Vast windows overlooked the main channel of Newport Harbor. Electric Duffy boats slid past, and the mast and mainsail of an enormous passing yacht briefly dominated the view. Here was a daily parade of all that the Good Life could offer, no longer within reach from this ringside seat.

No matter how ramshackle this castle, the thought of losing it must be torturing the king.

"Sweet," I said, crossing between a battered couch and a shredded La-Z-Boy recliner, which lay on its side in the middle of the room. It looked like a toy tossed aside by a giant child.

I joined him at one of the windows. "You've lived here a long time, right?"

He drained his drink before answering. "Three albums. Three marriages."

He turned away from the view and headed for the bar across the room. That's when I noticed her.

She was stretched out in a claw-footed tub, gray and glassy-eyed and naked except for a pair of strappy red-stiletto heels. Maybe early forties, with the look of a tired old groupie. She had stringy, damp blond hair on her head. The dark roots were the same color as the fluffy patch between her legs. He'd half-filled the tub with party ice he must have bought last night or early this morning at the 7-Eleven on the peninsula. A dozen crumpled plastic ice bags were piled at one end. Best guess: she hadn't been there long; for an ongoing obsession, he'd be using dry ice.

I tamped down my clutching fear. I'd never seen a dead body before.

"Sh-she may need help," I managed.

Absurd, I know. My other option was to just crap myself and run.

"Who?" he said, his back to me, pouring himself another drink.

I pointed to the tub even though he wasn't watching. "Her."

When he turned around, he was stirring his drink with the index finger of one hand. He did that for a long time without saying a word, without even looking at the chilling body in the middle of the room. Suddenly, he seemed to notice her.

"Hoo boy," he said, cheerful, as if he'd simply neglected to introduce her. "Dam'nest thing, that."

"She definitely doesn't look okay."

"Oh no. She's definitely not." He took a sip. "No par-medics necessary, 'm afraid."

Time to go. I sidestepped toward the hallway.

"Wait," he said. "Her . . . this . . . tha's not what I wanted to show you."

"Dude," I said, "this is seriously fucked up."

"I *know*!" he said. "She comes by th' house to party, then overdoses. Self-control's sush a problem with some people."

She didn't look like she'd been killed. No blood. No bullet wounds or knife holes. No bruises at her throat. Just the waxy gray corpse of a woman who'd stopped by to party.

On ice.

"When, um . . ."

"Lass night. She found my coke and jus' . . . overdid!"

"Jesus," I said. "I'm sorry."

"Me too! Terrific talent, that one." He winked. "Not a kid anymore, but she sure knew how to work it."

I struggled for words. "Sorry for your loss."

"But now y'see what I mean 'bout dark matter?"

I sidestepped again toward the hallway, quietly unsnapping the plastic holster of my pepper spray as I did. "Not really."

He reached into the pocket of his robe. When he pulled it out, I saw something black in his hand and swallowed hard. Who carries a gun in their bathrobe? Nobody sane. He seemed as surprised as I was to see it. He slid it back in and fished into the robe's other pocket. Whatever he pulled out of that he pointed across the room toward me. The widescreen beside me blinked to life.

A TV remote.

"DVD," he said, "'s a Science Channel thing on the cosmos or some such, 'bout dark matter. Been watching it all mornin', tryin' to sort this out. All this shit slidin' toward th' center, t'ward me. I mean, where do I go from here? M'whole comeback thing?" He nodded to the dead woman. "This'll complicate plans a bit."

A bit?

"You said it was an accident. I can't imagine they'd—"

He waved my words away like gnats. "So I'm listenin' to this show, about how dark matter's invisible, but y'know it's there cause it has gravity, 'cause it pulls things into its orbit. All sortsa things. And I'm thinking, see, how *I'm* sort of like dark matter."

I said nothing. He sensed my confusion.

"Shit happens, you know? To *me*. All the time. I always seem to land right in the middle of it. And I had this . . ." He paused to enunciate. ". . . epi-phany. I just wanted t'show somebody."

I looked at my watch again. Made a point of doing so. "Really gotta get back."

"Won' take long. Wanna drink?"

"Can't."

"I told you to stay."

Those final words were hard and sharp enough to cut glass, scary, the dopey-drunk voice completely gone. I stared at him until something flashed in the corner of my eye. My first glance to the left registered nothing. The second registered something that didn't compute at all. Why would a full-grown Siberian tiger be standing in the doorway, right between me and the only way out of the room?

Things started to add up. The giant shit pile in the hall. The suffocating litter-box smell. Even the shredded La-Z-Boy, which I suddenly realized was just an overworked scratching post.

"Really need to get going," I said.

"Pussy, sit!" he called out.

The tiger didn't move, just kept its intense yellow eyes fixed on me. It filled the door frame.

"Sit!" he commanded.

I sat back on the window ledge, just in case he was talking to me. Slowly, the tiger sat. Head level. Ears back. Gaze steady.

"That's Pussy!" he said. "Raised 'er right here. Took 'er in as an orphaned cub, had 'er a year." He wandered across the room and scratched the tiger between the ears. "Harmless old bird now. Mostly. No sudd'n moves, though. Big cats never lose those instincts. Don't want 'er thinkin yer a threat. Y'sure don' want her thinkin' yer wounded."

My body was flushed with primal juices. Every nerve was on fire. "It lives here?"

He shook his head. "Refuge. Up in Ventura. Snuck 'er out yesterday and drove 'er down in my panel van, brought 'er in after dark." He gestured grandly around the room. "We lived here together once. Happy days, y'know, and I jus' wanted her to see the place again, b'fore . . . well, you know."

"I see."

"Figured we'd spend a li'l time together before the big move." He held an index finger up to his pursed lips. "Don' tell the neighbors."

"Not a word."

"Nice people, but they'd go apeshit. Always do." He tipped his glass toward the bathtub. "Course, now there's this situation."

"Complicated, like you said."

"I *still* generate a lot of grav'ty, even if I'm invisible."

"I'm sure you do." I don't know why, but I added: "I played *AniMosity* to death when I was a kid. Great album."

"Thanks."

I'd kicked into some weird survival mode, desperate to say anything that might get me out of this. He hadn't threatened me. I didn't think he was capable of violence. On the other hand, I was in a room with a dead groupie, a live tiger, and a desperate armed man who was drinking heavily before 10 a.m. Things were beyond weird already.

"I even liked the second album."

I instantly regretted my phrasing, but he smiled.

"*Beastiary*?" he said. "More mature, don' you think? Record company hated it. After that, they just bailed on the third record. No support a'tall."

"Bastards," I said. "For what it's worth, though, I bought *Zoology* too. Got all three."

"Appreciate that."

"You guys ever think about a fourth studio album? Reunion tour, maybe?"

"Never been that desp'rate."

"I'd love to see that. Lot of people would."

He drained the rest of his drink during the awkward silence, dumped the ice into the tub, and set the glass gently on the dead woman's pubic mound. When he turned back toward me, the look he gave me had the same edge I'd noticed in his voice.

"So I guess we have a l'il situation, then?" he said.

"Meaning?"

"You barged into m'house like some stalker-fan. You and this woman."

"You invited me . . . Wait. Me and this woman?"

The wheels were coming off this bus pretty fast. Could he hear how loud I swallowed?

"'s a big house," he said, picking up the empty glass again. "What were you two doin' upstairs all night, anyway?"

An alibi wouldn't be a problem. I was at dinner with five friends until midnight. Which was completely beside the point. Nothing mattered now except the moment. And with this guy's loose grip on reality, I was in no position to argue.

"My lips are sealed," I lied. "You can handle this any way you want."

"You're in *my* house."

"Yessir, I am."

"You followed me in."

"You told me to."

"The *hell* I did."

"I'll just go then."

I'd taken about three tentative steps toward the door where the tiger sat when the highball glass exploded against the window frame just beside me. Heavy crystal ricocheted off the back of my head. When I touched the spot, my fingers came away bloody.

Straight ahead, Pussy leaned ever so slightly forward.

Which would be a more pathetic end to my life? Death at the hands of my teen idol—now an aging, drunk rocker—or death by tiger attack in the rocker's Balboa Island rumpus room? Either way, I imagined snickering at my funeral.

"You're pretty upset, I can tell," I said. "It's a bad time . . ."

He walked halfway across the room, his chest heaving. Either he was working himself into a rage, or he was out of breath from throwing his glass.

"Don't patronize, you little prick."

"Never."

"You have *no* idea what this is like for me."

"I can't—"

"To lose a home? To see everythin' taken away? What tha' does to a man?"

I knew. "This won't help, but doing what I do, I know there are a lot of people out there going through exactly what—"

"Christ!" He swept an arm across a scene littered by the debris of his reckless life. "You think I'm a credit whore, doncha? You think tha's what this's about? I *earned* all this."

"Of course you did. You *rocked*."

He took a deep breath. "Don't mind me sayin', but it takes some big-ass cojones to come into my house, tell me I'm just like all those assistan' credit managers and den'al hygienists and Roto-Rooters who couldn't pay the mortgage on some—" He spat the next word. "—*tract* house. You thin' they have a clue whaddit means to lose somethin' like this?"

A home is a home. Square footage and harbor views can't measure pride or pain. I wanted to tell him about the family in Santa Ana I'd evicted just last week, immigrants who'd worked two decades to buy a teeny two-bedroom. They raised six kids there and kept it immaculate right up until the father was deported during an INS sweep at the taquería where he worked. This guy needed to hear that story. I wasn't about to tell him.

"I have to go," I said, eyeing Pussy.

"Shit storm's comin'," he slurred.

"Please don't blame the messenger."

That's when he started clenching and unclenching his fists. He dropped his eyes to the floor, looking for some last chance to snatch his fantasy life from the swirl as it all circled the drain. He spoke quietly. "Don' go. I'm just . . . need a few hours t'get m'head together. All this dark matter. You c'n do that for me. Ya *gotta* do that for me."

I tapped my watch. "If I don't check in soon, the office'll come looking for me. It's policy."

"Tha's bullshit."

"It's really not."

"I said i's *bullshit*."

"I know you did. Doesn't change policy, though. They keep a pretty close eye on us."

He thought about that for an uncomfortably long time. "So you're saying I'm fucked."

"I'm not saying—"

"This's really happenin'?"

He was losing his tenuous grip. My situation wasn't exactly

improving, either. I edged another step closer to the door. I'd watched him scratch Pussy between the ears. That was good enough for me. I'd take my chances with the tiger.

"Instincts!" he reminded, his voice rising.

When I hesitated, he stepped around the upended La-Z-Boy, and in three quick steps was halfway across the room, coming directly at me. His groped into his pocket and the robe fell open, exposing his chest, his remarkably flat stomach, and the withered manjunk of a still-breathing fossil.

"Meaning?"

"They crush th' windpipe, but it takes *minutes* to die. No sudd'n moves, now."

He pulled the gun out almost casually. There was a tremor in his hand that I hadn't noticed before. He stopped about twenty feet away, swaying. Even so, the barrel looked awfully steady, pointed right at my head. "I ask't you a favor, tha's all. One little favor." He stepped slowly forward.

"You're trying to make it look like I had something to do with this," I said. "I can't let you do that."

"You two broke into m'house, you and partygirl there. Y'got into my thin's. I saw all that."

"You know that's not true. The cops will know it too."

He was maybe ten feet away, but still coming. I retreated until my back hit the corner where the window met the wall. Nowhere else to go. I went for my belt.

"See this?" I said, holding up a tiny canister.

He wobbled, trying to make sense of the sudden change in my voice. He came two steps closer, but it wasn't a hostile advance. He lowered the gun and squinted at my hand like a man who wished he'd brought his reading glasses. That's when I hit him with a jet of forced-cone pepper spray. Nailed him right in the eyes.

The gun fell to the floor as both hands shot to his face.

"Christ!" he screamed. "Y'prick!"

He staggered, shrieking as he backpedaled. Behind him, Pussy rose into a crouch. Her ears lay back against a head the size of a medicine ball. She twitched her whiskers, missing nothing.

"I was *kidding*!" he screamed. "Christ Jesus, it *burns*!"

The La-Z-Boy was right behind him, and he hit it in full backward stride. The impact sent his feet straight into the air and he came down hard on his back, robe fully open. He tried to leverage his momentum into a backward somersault, but tipped to one side and fell hard against the edge of the couch. It knocked him back to the floor, where his head thumped the hardwood. His hands never left his chem-scorched eyes even as one of his flailing legs caught Pussy square on the jaw. The big cat snarled, hackles up.

"Gaaaaaaa!" he screamed.

Pussy was on her blinded prey in a single bound. The roar that announced her attack was brief and deep, all business, the sound of heavy equipment at full throttle.

"Pussy! No!"

The animal didn't stop. She batted him with her powerful right paw, almost playful, and the blow sent him reeling. He regained his balance, but her claws had opened wide gashes along his left shoulder. His orange skin hung in ribbons as he groped blindly with one hand for the source of the pain. Desperate to orient himself, he tried to open eyes that were all but welded shut.

I edged closer to the hallway door.

Pussy's shoulders rose, her head dropped. When he fell to his knees, she lunged.

"Yaa—" was the only sound he made before she clamped

down on his throat. She held him to the floor with giant fore-paws as his skinny legs thrashed.

By then I was racing for the front door. Behind me, the same sound of savagery I'd heard on all those National Geographic specials. They never ended well. My heart was pounding as I jerked open the heavy front door and stepped back into the cramped serenity of Balboa Island. I pulled the door shut, muffling Pussy's roar.

I prayed my thanks there on his doorstep, waiting for my breathing to slow. Before I moved toward my car, I looked around. The cottages and mansions of Balboa Island were bathed in brilliant midmorning sun. The sails of passing yachts bobbed along the harbor's main channel. Nothing was changed. Life went on. But behind me I felt a real and unmistakable force, like the gravitational pull of something dark and invisible.

ON THE NIGHT IN QUESTION

BY PATRICIA MCFALL

Garden Grove

When the first letter arrived, Fred Mackie was standing just inside his front door. He didn't know or care if the mail carrier saw him through the curtains as the envelope slipped through the slot, bounced off his right shoe, and glided across the floor tile until it stopped. He'd had a feeling today would be the day, and he savored being right. Like with a lot of items he'd order from unreliable dot-coms, Fred was never sure whether or not anything would arrive. But this wasn't some *item* he'd ordered. It was a connection that he hoped would transform his life. Way too shy to approach a pretty woman, he was well past thirty without every having a real being-in-love relationship.

He'd made a New Year's resolution that he wouldn't be alone after this year.

In California, people doing time weren't allowed to have e-mail. But there were websites like InmatePlaymate.com that exchanged people's snail-mail addresses for a reasonable fee. Playmate number 403, with her long blond hair, sparkling blue eyes, and mysterious smile, had taken him on.

He picked up the pale-yellow envelope and turned it over. The flap illustration showed three kittens in a wicker basket, playing with a ball of pink yarn. *California Frontier Institute for Women* was stamped diagonally across the image. Turning the envelope back over, he observed the old *LOVE* stamp and some one-centers to update the postage. The postmark was February 14—Valentine's Day. She'd written his address in childish handwriting, the "i" in Mackie dotted with a little heart. Smiling and shaking his head, Fred went to the kitchen to get a steak knife, and slit through the paper flap with precision. There was a single sheet inside. He sniffed, but it wasn't scented.

> *Hi Fred,*
>
> *I recieved your message after you saw me on the website. I am writting this letter to thank you for being my "penn pal" lol. I am "403" but please call me Angel. The address to write to is on the envellope. From now on write here. Did the website tell you the rules about how mail gets read by other's both ways?*
>
> *Take care,*
> *Kiss kiss Angel*

Fred liked that last part—so affectionate. He was careful wording his reply, wanting his first letter to be eloquent. He hammered at the keyboard, glancing every few minutes at the color image of Angel's website profile lying beside his desktop. He'd Photoshopped the image to put himself there, behind her, grinning like a mega-lotto winner, hands resting on her shoulders—actually, pretty close to the swell of her chest. He wrote how glad he was to hear from her, how much he'd already thought about her.

He didn't mention anything about her being in prison. That could wait. In a way, it was beside the point. He wanted to help her think about the future and forget her troubles. Instead, he asked if she had a boyfriend. *I bet you have a boyfriend*, he wrote, *but if not, consider me a candidate!* He added a smiley-face icon, something he thought he would never do, but here it just seemed right. Fred told her about his life and where he lived in West Garden Grove in a *remodeled home, well maintained but in need of a woman's touch.* He hoped that wasn't too forward. He didn't want to scare her away; that was why he left out his picture. He wrapped up by asking her to please write back ASAP.

Going over his letter, he polished it up. He took out the part calling himself a shy geek, also the mention of how many cops lived in his neighborhood. He got rid of his horrible childhood, how he escaped his hateful parents by moving from the upper Midwest to California and hadn't seen them in years, what he secretly called his "witness self-protection program." He called himself single instead of never married. Why be negative?

Fred printed it, signed it, sealed it in an envelope, and drove to the post office. He used the automated machine to send it express. He didn't need some snotty clerk snickering at Angel's prison address. They might even throw it in the trash—after they ripped it open and read it, the creeps. Someone should go postal and rip *them* open.

After the first exchanges, things moved pretty fast even if the mail didn't. Then Angel wrote that even though he couldn't call her, she could call him collect. Fred did a solitary endzone dance and demanded in his reply, *Why didn't you mention it before? Call me any old time!* He gave his home number, but not the cell or office. Too distracting.

Fred worked at a nationwide income-tax preparation company. After ten years, the job was routine enough for him to sneak online and daydream—that's how he'd found InmatePlaymates.com. In his free time, he'd toss back a few Coronas with his cop buddy and across-the-street neighbor Manny Delgado, maybe go to a Ducks game, whatever.

These days Fred was interested in working off a beer belly, not drinking it. Since Angel had soon asked pointedly about a picture, he dug one out taken at a workmate's wedding a few years earlier. Fred was quite a bit thinner back then—but he knew he'd be at least down to that weight by the time he could go on a visit. If he laid off the energy bars and bottled Frappuccino and used the stairs at work, he'd be back into his old clothes in no time flat. Old clothes, nothing—he'd buy the new ones he'd budgeted for. During tax season, he couldn't get away. He'd be working long hours including weekends, so he and Angel would have to wait awhile. Besides, they hadn't even discussed a visit yet.

In the picture, he'd taken off his glasses and held them behind his back. He wore dark slacks, a white shirt, and a narrow black tie. Now he smiled, realizing that to her he might look like a slightly plump Mormon on bike patrol. He could have altered it electronically to include sunglasses so he'd look more like John Belushi as a Blues Brother, but changing an image for his own entertainment and deceiving her were two different things.

He wanted Angel to see how he was and think he was still okay, so her next letter was a huge relief. She even said something that gave him a hot shiver of anticipation:

Hi Fred.

Your picture was a pleasant suprise. I always thought men who can wear plus sizes are more attractive, they are fun to cuddle. At certain times you just need something to grab on to and who wants a hand full of skinny ribs and no butt? Your so cute I feel more lonelier now!

Kisses and big bare hugs,
Angel

Bare or bear, either was fine with him.

That next week was a blur of work: run home and see if there was a letter, eat something "healthy" from the microwave, take a quick walk, go to sleep, and get up to do it over again. Fred had explained to Angel about tax season but began to take work home so he'd be there in case she called. Soon the letters were pouring through the door slot. Twice they passed in the mail because they had so much to say. He was getting pretty good at flirting and double meanings, if he did say so himself. In fact, he'd never felt better, like on a high, full of energy, smiling. He was rocketing through the tax forms. He told Angel to call him, and soon. Her next letter said, *Thanks for the offer, I will call you March 1st Friday so, dont go on a date just kidding lol!*

Did she really think he'd do that to her? With everything she'd told him about the abuse and terror her parents and ex-boyfriend had made her endure, all he wanted to do was protect and care for her. He didn't expect more than gratitude, at first, but he knew she would want to show it, someday, when she had the chance.

Friday arrived. Because he didn't want to get stuck in evening rush-hour traffic, Fred left work early and undetected. He kept his cool on the freeway. There was the usual nasty honking and flipping off, but he drove just under the speed of traffic and in the slow lane, thwarting any thug who tried to use it to pass on the right. Pretty soon, he was almost to the intersection he secretly called White Trash Corners at the southern edge of his neighborhood. Twice every workday,

Fred's freeway shortcut took him through the four-way stop.

Uh—glee! The first house had gray paint, gray trim, a never-watered grayish tan lawn, and a gray fence that looked like it was put together without nails in a wind tunnel, leaning this way and that. Not to code. The old guy who lived there with a mousy little wife often put up handwritten screeds in his window about politics or the Bible. Fred didn't bother reading them.

The second house had peeling, dirty white paint and trim. The residents were a guy and his two grown sons. It seemed all they did was watch over their beer cans as the original asphalt driveway cracked, separated, and disappeared under the thatchy so-called lawn, where a truck and two cars were parked. The truck never moved.

The third house took a woman's touch to be bad. In front, right on the corner, were three stumps of what had probably been palm trees. The lady there decorated those stumps for every holiday, small and large, and usually left them up until it was time for the next holiday. Just so you wouldn't forget her fat ass, she had a country-style garden decoration, really just some painted plywood, that showed the back view of some damn woman bent over, probably picking up dogshit decorations.

The last house was the kind that even solicitors would pass by. The cinder-block wall running along the street was disintegrating a brick at a time, especially since the kids in the area started helping them. All covered with ivy up and over the roof. Big security-alarm posting by the front door. Never a sign of life; someone could be dead in there for all anybody knew.

It was like the four houses were in a worst-yard contest, like the opposite of those shows that told you how to make your place look good. Fred decided he'd push back. He picked up some business cards at a home-improvement store and went around the corners late one night—tree trimming, painting, driveway repair, landscape, masonry—even an auto-shop card under the truck's windshield wiper and a therapist's card for the religion nut jammed behind one of his window screens.

Whenever he left that place, Fred felt glad he lived in West Garden Grove, which was totally safe. He liked coming up his street, with its parkway trees controlled by regular severe pruning. Of four models in the tract, his was the Alpine, which he kept nice with maintenance and inventory schedules for everything from A/C filters to Ziploc bags.

His neighbor Manny Delgado, who had just made sergeant at the GGPD, liked to joke about all the old farts working the west end just before they retired—because nothing ever happened there.

Kind of true. It was a strange city, like somebody said about Oakland, no *there* there. Only a mile or so north to south but stretched out west to east, Garden Grove was sandwiched between other cities like a slice of cheese. He wouldn't want to live in midtown, which might as well be Westminster and its Little Saigon, where teenage Asian gangs roamed. The east end, same thing, but with Latino gangs. He'd been meaning to ask Manny what it took to qualify for the police, be part of the solution to crime. He felt ready for a change, and he was getting in shape. Of course, Angel might not like it, but he'd talk to her.

Fred hurried home, unlocked the front door, and looked for a letter, finding instead the visit application Angel had sent. Man, he could feel it now. It was really happening. No phone messages except for a gym manager returning his call. Parking the cordless phone on the toilet tank, he took a quick shower and changed into loose-knit pants and a comfy old Angels baseball shirt. He switched on the TV, grabbed a diet cherry soda from the fridge, and opened a cabinet to get some microwave popcorn—but then he heard the weird twangy intro music for *Cold Case Files* and hurried in to see if he could outguess the detectives.

Somewhere, his cordless phone was ringing.

Fred stared for a split second at the remote in the palm of his hand. He shook it and put it to his ear before he grasped the problem. Running down the hall to get it before it went to message, he snatched up the phone atop the toilet tank and, trying not to sound breathless, gasped, "Angel?"

There was a pause, then a click. A mechanical voice said, *This is the California State Department of Corrections with a collect call from*—pause, and another voice saying, *Angela May Winkler*, then the machine again, *Please choose from the following options . . .*

The first option was to take the call and accept charges, so he waited no longer and pressed that number.

Another pause. Then a real voice silky as butter dripping and slithering down between kernels of fresh popcorn: "Hey, Fred, this is Angel. Are you there?"

He took a breath. "Oh, yeah, I'm really here. How's Daddy's little Angel girl?"

Some weeks later, Angel sent Fred his approved visitor's permit. Even though the phone calls had given him a sense of what Angel would be like, he wanted to be face-to-face, touch her, feel her touching him.

Mother's Day Sunday, Fred got up at dawn because he couldn't sleep. The prison had a whole load of restrictions on visitors, and he'd skimmed the booklet—but they were guidelines, not ironclad laws, right? Most sounded like they made sense—no medicine, even over-the-counter. No hats. No tobacco or alcohol. No food; you had to buy it from their vending machines. No chewing gum? That one made him wonder. You couldn't go in there dressed like an inmate, like in a movie he saw where two guys switched places. He laughed out loud at the rule that said women who set off the metal detectors with an underwire bra had to go in without it.

Fred showered and weighed himself, proud to be ten pounds and one belt-notch smaller than before, and put on his new khakis, loose Hawaiian shirt, and Brand X huaraches—the finest sandals made in Mexico, according to Manny.

Glad he started early, he joined the slow-moving line of cars leading into the prison, showed his pass at the gate, parked in the visitor area, and followed the obvious path—they weren't taking any chances on somebody wandering away. Everything was drab, institutional, painted government green, but the lawn and flower borders were surprisingly well tended, the windows spotless.

The path ended in a slow-mo line of people and a sign that read:

Inmate Visiting
Friday, Saturday, Sunday
8:00 a.m.—2:00 p.m.
Reception

Fred got in behind a granny with two little girls maybe four and six, who ran around on the cracked, dusty asphalt and ignored her yelling their names every few minutes. She finally gave up, peering down at what looked like birth certificates. Maybe she was embarrassed how they disobeyed her.

He'd have suggested she pop them good once in a while instead of calling them, but he didn't know any Spanish. Amazing how often people could miss the obvious solution to their problem.

Right behind him, someone did that *ahem* kind of throat-clearing, so he turned around to see a grim-looking, scrawny, straight-lipped redneck nodding at the candy-shop bag Fred was carrying.

"You must be a first-timer," the man announced. "They don't let anybody take in gifts like candy. Afraid of contraband."

"I know," said Fred, trying not to sound defensive. "I read the guidelines, and it isn't candy. Thought maybe I'd take in a few women's magazines—*Mother's Day* and all."

The man smiled, and his lined face—more sandblasted than chiseled—seemed surprisingly kind. "Mama's contraband is still contraband. If I was you, I'd go back to your car and send 'em through channels, because those guards will just toss 'em." Know-it-all was still sort of smiling.

"Well, maybe they will and maybe they won't," Fred muttered and turned away. Guy was probably right, but Fred wasn't about to lose his place in line.

He was closer to the front now, everybody getting out their IDs, women carrying see-through plastic pouches instead of purses, watching what they said but trying to act friendly. Visitors with kids produced birth certificates. A few teen girls buttoned up their blouses, smoothed down their skirts, and covered their stomachs. Not because they respected good old Mom; it was the rules. He remembered Angel saying that whenever a guard didn't like what girls had on, they got to cover up in old baggy thrift store clothes, or leave. "This place, all they want to do is control everything you do. *Everything.* Even when it makes no sense—hell, 'specially then—just to show you how they can. Shit." He wished she wouldn't swear, but those words came straight from the heart.

She'd added that having so few choices was why it was important to keep money in her canteen account since they couldn't have cash. "Thanks, sweetie," she'd said after he sent a couple-hundred transfer to her with the usual bureaucratic hurdles. "With a little canteen account, now I can get myself shampoo, deodorant, makeup—girly things. I'm so lucky to have you."

Poor kid, so alone. His eyes had watered a little then. He knew what it was like to be lonesome. After numerous humiliating ordeals called "dates," Fred took his sex life private, getting along with toys and DVDs. Cheaper and safer.

Fred went through a metal detector like at an airport, then finished the check-in routine at the desk, where a guard counted his money, stamped his wrist, looked closely at the pass and his ID, and confiscated the bag, saying, "Nothing from outside comes inside, nothing inside goes out."

Inmate visiting was in a big boxy room with picnic tables, walls punctuated by vending machines behind heavy yellow stripes on the floor. Prisoners weren't allowed to handle money, he remembered. He sat, twisted sideways on the assigned bench, since his seat faced the back wall and he wanted to watch Angel come out. A guard unlocked a door and brought out a group of women, but none of them could be Angel, so he calmed down and waited.

About fifteen minutes later, another group came out and he spotted her. She looked like her picture—a little shorter, maybe. She was dressed like a nurse, scrubs the same color as the tired green buildings, some painfully white new running shoes. He stood and watched as she approached. Angel didn't wait, just said, "Aloha, FRED!" threw her hands around his neck and kissed his cheek hard, saying in his ear, "Sorry I can't give you a lei." He didn't hesitate and kissed her on the mouth, carried away to another place, blissed out, breathless and trembling and ready to keep right on going where it led, and to hell with everyone else.

Angel pulled back, whispering, "Guards don't like you to overdo it, even if *I* do. No matter how much we want to, we can't hug or kiss again until you leave." She looked up, beaming into his face. "Well, what did you bring me?"

"Uh—well, I tried to bring something but they, I mean the guards, wouldn't let—" He gestured back the way he'd come.

"I know that. Just a little joke. We have to sit across from each other. It's okay to hold hands on top of the table."

They sat playing together with their hands; she smiled at him and he smiled back, but from time to time her eyes flicked to the side as someone came or went. Not paranoid, but vigilant.

Fred thought it made her seem vulnerable, a good person stuck in a bad place. Finally he managed, "I knew you'd be just as beautiful and sexy as your picture."

"Thank you—sure don't feel like it in these clothes."

"Don't worry. I can get past your clothes."

"I wish you could."

He tried to picture her naked. He could tell she had a good body. Not perfect, nobody was perfect—but she was so pretty, even better than he'd hoped.

The room had filled with visitors, the majority women with kids. Mothers, sisters, friends? Their own kids or the inmates'? Almost all of them looked poor. So what if the atmosphere wasn't romantic? This was a little bit of paradise with only two people in it. And the most intoxicating thing was that he could tell from everything Angel said and did that she felt exactly the same way. He couldn't get enough of that way she looked at him, like he was a big fat birthday present.

He wanted to talk and said the first thing that came to mind. "Why don't they let you bring in chewing gum?"

"I dunno. So you can't use it to stick things together and make a weapon?"

"Amazing what people will think up, huh."

She smiled indulgently. "What the fuck else they got to do with their time, squeezy bear?"

Fred didn't want to talk yet about her cleaning up her mouth, so he asked if she wanted anything from the vending machines. "I don't want to ask for a Slim Jim. You might think I was ba-a-a-d," she said, tucking a bit of hair behind her ear. "Maybe some beef jerky. Surprise me."

He stepped over the yellow line and bought the jerky, which came in a cellophane sleeve and looked about five-to-twenty-five years past its pull date, and some peanut M&Ms. He wasn't hungry himself, so he got a cup of sour-smelling machine coffee and a bottle of water.

Fred returned and tossed her the jerky lightly.

She pointed at his other hand. "What else you got there, squeezy bear?"

"Squeezy bear, huh? I kind of like that name."

"I thought you might. That's how I always think about you, just a big ol' huggy squeezy bear."

"I won't deny it. I don't need any other name for you, though, cause Angel fits just right. I got this for you too." As he held up the bag of chocolate candies, he couldn't help grinning.

"Ooh, I'll take dessert first!"

"Okay, but I get to feed 'em to you."

"Uh-uh. We can't touch."

"See, we won't be," he said like a spy setting up a meeting. "I'll give 'em to you one by one. I'll hold this side of the candy and you get the other side with your teeth."

"Can't—a guard can terminate the visit for that kind of shit, and they do."

He sighed. "Another rule. Okay." So much for the fantasy of watching her lick chocolate off his fingers.

She ripped the bag open, tilted it to get a mouthful of candy, and wolfed it. Then she started on the jerky, chewing more thoughtfully, still glancing around. She looked like a sweet little puppy learning to guard her dish.

He tried to ignore the helpless gesturing of the people around them, their crying diluted by quiet attempts to laugh, sing sweetly, or pray with confidence. Everyone tried desperately to have a private visit in an exposed public place. One table over, an inmate asked, "Don't you think I know what's going on?" The visitor said, "You don't know what it's like," and muttered about how hard he had it. When she whispered into his ear, he shot up out of his seat and said, not quite shouting, "You too, bitch!" He raised a hand swiftly, but it was to signal a guard.

The whole room went silent, waiting, all the guards intent as one of them took the inmate away and another led the guy out. A few seconds later came several tentative whispers, shifting on benches, footsteps, the clinking of coins in machines.

Fred looked across at Angel, softened inside when he saw how relieved she was, and swore he could hear his happily beating heart. Love lifted him to a different plane from other people.

She smiled and said, "All it takes is one asshole to stop everyone's visit, but not this time."

They chatted about Fred's job and his house and his plans to buy a new car, when a crackling loudspeaker announced that Inmate Visiting had filled to capacity and that the first-in, first-out policy would apply. Several pass numbers were called, none of them Fred's, and the guard broadcast, "Say goodbye to your inmate."

Angel looked stricken.

"Hey, it's okay," Fred said. "I don't have to go right now, do I? I was at least ten people from the front."

"Not that—I wanted to tell you some good news. My counselor gave me a release date—"

"When?"

"June 1. Time off and early release to relieve overcrowding."

"Great! You're saying—"

"I'll be free. I go live my life again, report to my parole officer, and don't reoffend." Angel rolled her eyes. "As if I would."

Fred stroked the palm of her hand. "Look, I've been wanting to ask how you got to be here . . ."

She answered in a whisper, leaning in. "Sure. I got nothing to hide. These two so-called friends—" she spat the word "—asked me to drive 'em someplace. Then they tell me to wait in this strip mall and they go in a jewelry store? So I wait, but then a few minutes later I hear like a lot of sirens, and I'm freaking, I'm panicked, I start the car and go."

"You poor kid. And the cops?"

"Busted 'em. These guys, Mitch and Dan, tried to say I left them there on purpose and even that I set up the whole job. I didn't do *anything*, but you know the way things work . . ." She paused to wave at the surroundings. "I had to take a plea and testify against them. At least they're going to be down for a long time, and I only have two more weeks. Can't wait!"

"Angel, honey," he said with concern. "*Can* you wait? Do you think you can handle it until you get out?"

She laughed. "After a year and a half, I can do two weeks standing on my head."

He squeezed her hand. "What then? Do you have family—"

"My folks don't want me, squeezy bear. They pretty much disowned me. My brother Gordie would help if he could, but they've already got a full house. Anyway, don't worry about my problems. I'll be fine. At least I'll be free."

That called for a definitive move. Fred sprinted to the edge of what could be a cliff and jumped off, saying, "You can stay with me, Angel. We can be together."

He heard the loudspeaker again—his pass number with some others, then, "Say goodbye to your inmate."

"I'll come back next weekend and—"

"No, don't. Another rule, you know. We can go over all the details the next time we talk. Oh, I can't stand to let you go!" She stood up, popped the last of the beef jerky into her mouth, and then, laughing, spit it back into the wrapper it came in. "I know that's gross, honey, but there's just no damned way you can chew it but slow. Now come over here and say goodbye."

It was a great kiss, even if it tasted bad.

On the day of her release, Angel didn't want Fred to pick her up and said she'd stay with her brother Gordie Bacon's family until the weekend, and then she'd move over to Fred's for a while, if that was okay with him. Sure, he said.

On Saturday morning, Gordie backed a small rental van into the driveway with the "few things" Angel mentioned. He jumped out of the driver's seat and opened the back. As Fred went outside, he looked at Gordie. Buff, but not too.

Outdoor tan. The kind of guy who always looked like he needed a shave, which some women unaccountably found attractive.

They shook, Fred saying, "Hey, good to meet you, man. Give you a hand?"

"No need, but I tell you what. Angel's *dying* to show you her new hair," he warned, gesturing with his head.

Fred trotted around to the passenger side, and out stepped the new Angel, with jet-black, straight, chin-length hair and a black-and-brown checked sundress. She flew straight into his arms. "Squeezy bear, I sure hope you like—"

"There's nothing about you I don't like," he murmured into her new hair, which smelled like flowers, and confidently began their long and satisfying first real kiss. He heard the front screen door slam behind her brother. Fred, who had managed to lose another 2.7 pounds, was feeling pretty wonderful with Angel right there in his arms. He wasn't really into making out in public, but when he heard a mower switched off, by instinct he opened one eye, amused to see his cop pal Manny had stopped cutting his lawn across the street to openly gawk, grin, and give him a thumbs-up, which Fred stealthily returned behind Angel's back. One arm around her shoulders, he steered her into her new home.

Gordie had helped himself to a beer—at 9 a.m. He had one of the ESPN channels on. He could have asked or apologized, but instead said, "Either of you want one?" like he was the host and they were the strangers.

When the beer ran out hours later, Fred did end up helping with the few boxes, which Angel said to leave in the garage because she couldn't deal with them yet. One was light like clothes, another clinky like dishes. There was also a rusty stationary bike and a hibachi with cobwebs on the grill. She'd brought a traveling bag with her for the first few days, she said.

Gordie, with an exaggerated leer, wished the lovebirds goodnight.

That night, Fred offered Angel the guest bedroom, not wanting to push too hard, but she let out a musical giggle and started to undress him. They made love, and it was amazing how she enjoyed it and came so much and had so many ways to keep him going. The next morning she insisted on preparing scrambled eggs and toast for him. She was bright and perky, but he was pleasantly spent, wanting to go back to bed, rest up, and start again. He knew she wanted that too.

Over breakfast, he swallowed a big bite of eggs, wiped his mouth with the paper towel she'd put by his plate, and said, "Mind if I ask you a personal question?"

"Oh, baby, I don't have any secrets from you. I'm fallin' in love with you. That's my secret, and now you know."

Fred forgot what he'd meant to ask and sat frozen, amazed, the paper towel hanging from his hand.

Fred took ten days off that first month, and nobody at work bothered him with calls or e-mail. He'd never felt better.

Things were still good with Angel, even if it was tough sometimes to train her where to put things away, do cleaning in the correct order, or understand that energy-conscious people turned out lights when they left rooms and set their thermostats at seventy-eight degrees. Though the summer sun beat down and the nights were warm, Angel didn't like going outside, day or night. Backyard barbecue was fine, but no walks or errands. At first he thought great sex had turned her into a homebody, but one evening when they were watching TV, a car backed into the driveway to turn around, and instantly she was very still, like she'd been on Mother's Day. A morning or two later, she'd gone into the bedroom when the UPS guy came.

"What's the matter, my angel? Is something—"

"Nothing, I'm just weird. Not used to being free yet, I guess. Just ignore it."

But the way she said it, Fred knew she was frightened. He needed to talk to her about it soon.

The next weekend, Angel came in while Fred was on the Internet and caught him looking at engagement rings. She just bent over and kissed him, getting into it, and drew him away to bed. He didn't even have time to pop the question. She wanted to get married soon, and to take his name.

"Speaking of names," he sighed contentedly, remembering the flaw in his happy life, "you've never been married before, right?"

"Not me. I was waiting for the right one."

"So how come you're Winkler and he's Bacon?"

She paused. "That's because he's my stepbrother. We have different fathers."

"You mean half-brother?"

"Yeah, that's what I meant."

"Now that explains why you don't look anything alike, huh."

If they were getting married, he had to lay down the law about Gordie, their constant guest since his wife Fiona started working nights. Fred hadn't even met her, after a month! Gordie, being drunk most of the time and lazy all of the time, ended up on the couch—a lot—and left in the mornings after Fred went to work. He was a conceited asshole, but worse, a cheapskate who never once brought anything to share until

Fred cut back on the Bud supply and ran out of beer twice in a row. Even though Gordie had to walk to the supermarket and pay for more himself, he kept missing the point. Angel and Fred hardly had a minute alone. Gordie was a nuisance.

On Monday, Fred went to downtown Santa Ana to pick up the form for a marriage license. While he was there, he decided to look up the transcript of those guys' trials. He remembered their first names, Mitch—probably Mitchell—and Dan/Daniel, and he had Angel's full name and inmate number. He gave this information to a nice middle-aged woman with a motherly need to help him, bless her. She ticked away at her keyboard for a while, found the last names, and looked them up.

"Looks like they pled out after the preliminary hearing."

"But Miss Winkler told me she testified against these guys."

"She must have meant the prelim, hon, and that's a good thing. Every prelim has a transcript. Would you like me to get you the file?"

As he sat and read the transcript, Fred understood why Angel was so frightened, why she changed her looks, why she wanted his name. She'd even hinted about buying a new house, and that fit too. It was her witness self-protection. But why hadn't she told him?

On the night in question, according to her testimony, Mitchell Hoffman and Danforth Green asked her for a ride but gave no indication that they planned to rob a jewelry store. "At the strip mall," she said, "I saw both of them leave the car carrying guns. I overheard them agree they wouldn't hesitate to shoot—including me, if I got out of line." She'd been terrified, and when she heard shots from inside the store and saw them running out with their guns, she fled for her life. No, she said, "I didn't know an old man was in there that got shot and he would have made it except for the heart attack it gave him."

No, she didn't know what became of the guns when the men ran from the store and when they were apprehended hiding five blocks east thirty minutes later. Yes, she understood that both claimed—immediately after being taken into custody, in separate interviews where they could not collaborate—that the whole thing was her idea, that she'd put them up to it and given them the guns, and that she'd driven away and left them high and dry. Well, the only explanation she could think of was that those interviews must have come from "them cooking up some story ahead of time to pin it on me if it all went sideways."

After the prelim, Fred learned, the two men had taken pleas rather than face trial, each getting twenty years for the death of the jeweler, including enhancements for their previous criminal records and for the guns used in commission of a crime.

Fred let out a low whistle. Sometimes the safest place to be was in prison. Those guys could have friends and family outside settle the score. Even though Angel told the truth, had knowingly done nothing criminal, and had to serve time, she'd made mortal enemies.

But maybe they didn't know about her early release yet, and there was still time.

Fred went straight to a sporting goods store to buy ammunition and a cleaning kit for his dad's old revolver.

As soon as he got home, he told Angel that he had found out what she was scared of.

She looked at him blankly, guarded and waiting.

"First, sweetheart, Gordie coming over here all the time is dangerous. He's making a perfect beeline to you. All anyone has to do is follow him. Gordie has to start hanging out at his *own* place. We need to list the house, and as soon as we're married I need to get some life insurance, that's for damn sure, because I may have to defend you."

"I can't believe how brave you are." Angel's smile was hard to read.

Fred went to a shooting range. He hadn't been in a long time. The manager didn't give a shit, just showed him how the targets worked, gave him the earphones, and left him alone.

Fred started with a bull's-eye target and practiced, aiming carefully before each shot. The first two went wide, one not even hitting the target surface, the other making a neat hole in the upper right corner. Some internal pressure shot up, a kind of embarrassment where he didn't feel like a man should feel when he was learning how to protect his home and wife-to-be. He took a deep breath and started over, adjusting his stance, checking to see if the desk guy was watching, but he was looking at his computer screen.

Fred shot again, and hit the outermost circle. He shot again without moving, and hit just above the previous shot. He liked the heavy feel of the handgun now. He was learning.

The manager changed the target to a graphic, a large line drawing like a poster that depicted a bad guy using a terrified, busty hostage as a shield, holding a big butcher knife to her throat.

Now this was the real deal. Defend and protect. He adjusted and readjusted his aim, finally squeezed one off—and hit the girl's shoulder. Just a graze, but still, what a dumb shot.

Fred's knees quivered a little when he got ready again, but something stopped his hand. The week before, he'd been explaining to Angel that the salad/dessert forks and the dinner forks were to be neatly stacked with tines facing the back, in the two adjacent sections of the wooden silverware tray in the drawer by the dishwasher. He pointed out that if she would only load them into the dishwasher in the correct baskets, the rest of the job would be foolproof.

She'd given him a sharp watchful stare much like he'd seen on Mother's Day, but back then he'd thought it was cute. This time it was anything but—hard, he'd have to call it—like she was thinking, *Foolproof? Who are you calling a fool, fool?*

She'd said, "Maybe I know a way that's even better than yours. Maybe you can learn something from me." He'd let that go, just pointing at the drawer again and then leaving for work without kissing her.

He stood there with the gun in his hand. What about the prelim transcript, when the two guys' stories matched completely? Fred watched those crime shows all the time, and he knew that cops said—Manny had agreed with this view—that it was always easier to tell the truth because you just said what happened. When you lied, you had to make stuff up as you went along, and then you'd forget what you'd put into one version and screw it up the next time. Each version would be different. The truth was always the same.

He needed to ask her directly why the guys' stories didn't vary, how that could have happened, just to stop this nagging feeling. At last Fred aimed and squeezed, and the bullet flew just over the villain's head, so he immediately lowered the aim a fraction and shot again. He gasped.

He'd shot her through the heart.

This terrible *doubt* was interfering with his concentration.

He needed to get home where he could talk it out with her, be sure she wasn't lying about *anything*, and if she was, find out why, get her to share her fears and let him help.

As he pulled up, Fred muttered *Son of a bitch* when he saw Gordie's truck parked in his driveway. He couldn't even get to his own garage.

What was that asshole doing here in the late afternoon, anyway? Fred had made it clear to Angel that it was dangerous—and here the truck was, like a big neon sign pointing right at her for anybody with a grudge. In fact, who knew what else might be in there? He could be walking into a firefight. He parked at the curb, got out, retrieved the gun, and stuck it into the back waistband of his khakis. He was supposed to take out the unused rounds but he had been so anxious to get home that he forgot. Or so he told himself.

Fred turned his house key silently, glad that his maintenance schedule included quarterly lubrication of door hardware and locks. The afternoon sun came from the side of the house, so at least there would be no silhouette or illumination through the glass. He turned the knob and slowly opened the door. The living room and the kitchen—what he could see of them—were empty.

Then he heard Angel whimper. God, was it possible that Gordie was one of the bad guys? Or that they'd both been taken hostage? Why would Angel let them in? He had to do something. The sound was coming from the end of the hall, where the home office and master bedroom were. He tiptoed soundlessly on the soft carpet. The next thing he heard came from the master, the unmistakable rhythmic thumps, the squeaky bedspring syncopation.

She spoke tensely. "Did you hear something?"

"No," said Gordie. "Don't take forever, darlin', or I'll pretend I'm Fat Fuck Freddie again."

Fred didn't move or breathe, though his pulse beat in his ears. The squeaky noises started up again. He crept to the edge of the open door—they hadn't even thought to close it!—and slowly moved far enough over to see. Gordie was on top, and she was kicking her feet and snorting like an animal. On the floor not far from Gordie's reach was a handgun.

Fred backed up several steps, his legs trembling. What could he do? He reached around to get the weapon. His shaking hand jerked, loosening the waistband, and the revolver fell down his pants leg, making a dull thud on the carpet. Not loud. Almost silent.

That's when she started to scream.

Gordie didn't get it, saying, "What *is* this? I thought you liked this— Hey, what are you—? That *hurt*, bitch."

"Help," she shouted, "he's raping me!" And kept screaming as Fred picked up his gun and returned to stand in the doorway.

Her stricken face peered over Gordie's shoulder. "Oh, thank God! Fred—help me, he's hurting me—"

Something changed as Fred recognized the first honest emotion he'd ever seen on her face: sheer terror. She'd just noticed the gun in his hand. She dropped flat in a split second, out of the line of fire.

Gordie started to get off her, but Fred took two quick steps and fired at his naked back. Flipping over, face red from exertion, Gordie stared at the gushing red coming from his well-developed right pectoral. He winced as the pain came and said something, although the shot had made Fred temporarily deaf. Then he heard Gordie babble:

"Don't do it, man. Please. Just don't do it. Ain't what it looks like here—we're just—it don't mean nothing. And this," he clutched his left hand over the blood on his chest, "why, this is just a flesh— Aw, shit!"

It must hurt pretty bad. Maybe the man had learned his lesson. Fred glanced over where Angel was still hiding under the covers—just like her to do something that immature, like if she closed her eyes, nobody could see her instead of the other way around.

Except for the noise Gordie was making about his wound, saying "Oh, shit" over and over, it was quiet. The man wasn't even thinking enough to reach for the handgun only inches from his drooping hand—maybe his muscles weren't working right.

Thank God the situation was contained. Fred grabbed Gordie's gun and put it out of his reach on the dresser.

Then he followed Gordie's gaze to where Angel lay.

Fred walked over and pulled back the bedclothes. The bullet must have gone through Gordie and straight into her heart. Almost no blood. She looked scared and beautiful. It couldn't be. Fred couldn't have done this. Not to *her*.

Gordie's feverish voice cut in: "Fred? It was an accident, right? Everything will be okay—"

Everything okay?

Fred turned and shot him twice in the chest. Gordie hit the headboard and remained sitting until his head slumped onto his hairy chest and he fell to one side.

For a long time, Fred stood there in a world gone blank. Finally, he felt the gun in his hand. He set it down and walked out of the room, down the hall, out the front door, and across the street. What was he going to tell Manny?

ABOUT THE CONTRIBUTORS

Judy Alexander

BARBARA DEMARCO-BARRETT'S first book, *Pen on Fire: A Busy Woman's Guide to Igniting the Writer Within*, was a *Los Angeles Times* best seller and won a 2005 ASJA Outstanding Book Award. Her articles and essays have appeared in many publications, including *Orange Coast Magazine*, the *Los Angeles Times*, *Westways*, and *Poets & Writers*. She has taught creative writing at UC, Irvine Extension, since 2000, and also produces and hosts a radio show, *Writers on Writing*, on KUCI-FM.

Ralph Palumbo

MARY CASTILLO, a former reporter for *Los Angeles Times Community News*, is the author of three novels and two novellas.

Lang Photography

DAN DULING is an award-winning playwright, best known for *Stranglehold*, which won the Oregon Playwrights Award. He is also a former journalist, having written for publications such as the *L.A. Weekly*, the *Los Angeles Times*, and the *Los Angeles Herald-Examiner*. The feature film *Last Lives*, based on his screenplay, originally premiered on the Sci-Fi Channel and is now available on DVD. Behind the Orange Curtain, Duling is the scriptwriter for the Pageant of the Masters in Laguna Beach.

Sandra Levinson

ROBERT S. LEVINSON is the author of the novels *The Traitor in Us All*, *In the Key of Death*, *Where the Lies Begin*, and *Ask a Dead Man*, as well as the Neil Gulliver and Stevie Marriner series of mystery-thrillers, which to date consist of *The Elvis and Marilyn Affair*, *The James Dean Affair*, *The John Lennon Affair*, and *Hot Paint: The Andy Warhol Affair*. The Derringer Award–winner's short stories appear often in the *Ellery Queen* and *Alfred Hitchcock* mystery magazines.

J. Bryson

DICK LOCHTE is the author of ten popular crime novels, including, most recently, *Croaked!* His novel *Sleeping Dog* won a Nero Wolfe Award, was nominated for Edgar, Shamus, and Anthony awards, and was named one of the "100 Favorite Mysteries of the Century" by the Independent Booksellers Association. Lochte, who lives in Southern California with his wife and son, is also an award-winning drama critic and has written screenplays for such actors as Jodie Foster, Martin Sheen, and Roger Moore.

LAWRENCE MADDOX works as a film and television editor, and has written a number of independent features. He lives with his wife in northeast Los Angeles, less than an hour's drive from the badlands beyond the Orange Curtain.

GORDON MCALPINE is the author of three novels, *Joy in Mudville, The Persistence of Memory*, and *Mystery Box*. His short fiction and book reviews have been featured in magazines and journals both in the U.S. and abroad. He lives in Orange County with his wife and three children.

PATRICIA MCFALL is a freelance writer and editor. She also teaches fiction and coaches writers privately. She has published one suspense novel, a half-dozen short stories, and many newspaper features. Her work has appeared in *Ellery Queen Mystery Magazine, Orange Coast Magazine*, and *Writer's Digest*.

T. JEFFERSON PARKER was born in Los Angeles and has lived in Southern California his whole life. He has published seventeen novels, numerous articles and short stories, and is a three-time Edgar Award winner. His most recent novel is *Iron River*.

GARY PHILLIPS writes stories of chicanery and misadventure in various formats, including novels and short stories. He has contributed stories to several volumes in the Akashic Noir Series, including *Los Angeles Noir, Dublin Noir*, and *Phoenix Noir*. He recently published *Freedom's Fight*, a novel set in World War II.

Patty Lin

ROB ROBERGE is the author of the story collection *Working Backwards from the Worst Moment in My Life* and the novels *More Than They Could Chew*, and *Drive*. His stories have been featured in *ZYZZYVA, Chelsea, Other Voices, Alaska Quarterly Review*, and the *Literary Review*. His work has also been anthologized in *Another City, It's All Good*, and *SANTI: Lives of the Modern Saints*. Roberge plays guitar and sings with the L.A.-area bands the Violet Rays, the Danbury Shakes, and the Urinals.

Michael Kboury

MARTIN J. SMITH is currently editor-in-chief of *Orange Coast Magazine* and formerly senior editor of the *Los Angeles Times Magazine*. He is also the author of three crime novels, *Time Release, Shadow Image*, and the Edgar Award–nominated *Straw Men*, and is coauthor of two nonfiction pop culture histories, *Poplorica* and *Oops*.

Dan Chavkin

SUSAN STRAIGHT is a native of Riverside, California, just over the Orange County border. She has published six novels, including *Highwire Moon*, which was a finalist for the National Book Award, and *A Million Nightingales*, which was a finalist for the *Los Angeles Times* Book Prize. Her new novel, *One Candle*, will be published in 2010. Her short story "The Golden Gopher," from *Los Angeles Noir*, won an Edgar Award in 2008.

NATHAN WALPOW is the author of the Joe Portugal mystery series. His short story "Push Comes to Shove" was reprinted in the *Best American Mystery Stories* series. He is a past president of the Southern California chapter of Mystery Writers of America.

Cynthia Perry

ROBERT WARD'S 2006 novel *Four Kinds of Rain* was nominated for a Hammett Prize. He is a former writer-producer on TV shows *New York Undercover, Hill Street Blues,* and *Miami Vice*. His latest novel, *Total Immunity*, was published in 2009 by Harcourt.